ALSO BY GERBRAND BAKKER

The Twin
The Detour

GERBRAND BAKKER

June

TRANSLATED FROM THE DUTCH BY
David Colmer

1 3 5 7 9 10 8 6 4 2

Vintage
20 Vauxhall Bridge Road,
London SW1V 2SA

Vintage is part of the Penguin Random House group of companies whose
addresses can be found at global.penguinrandomhouse.com

Penguin
Random House
UK

First published in Vintage in 2016
First published in trade paperback by Harvill Secker in 2015

First published with the title *Juni* in 2009
by Uitgeverij Cossee, Amsterdam

penguin.co.uk/vintage

A CIP catalogue record for this book is available
from the British Library

ISBN 9780099563686

Lyrics from "Sugar Baby Love" written by Wayne Bickerton & Tony Waddington

Published by Bucks Music Group Limited, on behalf of The Bicycle Music
Company, and Warner Chappell North America

Reproduced by kind permission of Bucks/Warner Chappell

This book was published with the support of the Dutch Foundation for Literature

N ederlands
l letterenfonds
**dutch foundation
for literature**

Printed and bound in Great Britain by Clays Ltd, St Ives plc

Penguin Random House is committed to a sustainable future
for our business, our readers and our planet. This book is made
from Forest Stewardship Council® certified paper.

MIX
Paper from
responsible sources
FSC
www.fsc.org FSC® C018179

JUNE

Headline Material

'We're almost in Slootdorp,' the driver says. 'That's where the next mayor takes over.'

She looks out. Fields stretching away in broad bands on either side. Squat farmhouses with red-tiled roofs. Thank goodness it's not raining. Her view to the right is partly blocked by C. E. B. Röell, who is reading papers presumably related to their next destination. She takes off her gloves, lays them on her lap and flicks open the ashtray. Röell starts to huff. Ignore it. They're not even halfway yet, but it already feels like they've been on the road for most of the day. Once she's lit her cigarette and is drawing on it deeply, she sees the driver's eyes shining in the rear-view mirror. She knows that he would love to light up too, and if Röell weren't in the car, he would.

After a fairly early start in Soestdijk, the morning had been dedicated to the former island of Wieringen, where they made the unforgivable misjudgement of starting her itinerary by presenting her with a table covered with shrimp. At half past ten in the morning. Although the inappropriateness had actually begun even earlier, when the mayor had his own daughters present the flowers while his wife pretended she couldn't see the little children standing on the dyke around the harbour. After that, more schoolchildren and old-age pensioners – the inevitable schoolchildren and old-age pensioners. Still, it's just a Tuesday, a normal working day. In the town hall, a special council meeting was held in her honour. Most of the mayor's speech passed her by, thinking ahead as she was to this evening and the *Piet Hein*, and when she took a distracted sip of her coffee it tasted more or less like the mayor's words. The woman who had been commissioned to make a bronze bust of her was there too.

'What was that nun's name again?' she asks.

'Jezuolda Kwanten. Not a nun, a sister.' Röell doesn't look up, sticking doggedly to her reading. A brief summary will follow shortly.

Jezuolda Kwanten – of Tilburg – who had stared at her keenly for almost half an hour, occasionally sketching some-thing on a large sheet of yellowish paper, thus making it even more difficult to follow the mayor's lecture. She's in the car behind hers, with Beelaerts van Blokland and Van der Hoeven. Couldn't they have arranged that differently? she wonders. Röell in the second car and Van der Hoeven in hers? He's a fellow smoker. Jezuolda Kwanten is going to be present at all of the festivities, the whole day long: looking at her, measuring her up, sketching her. Not just today, but tomorrow too. When even being photographed is something she detests. And all for the sake of 'art', which will turn her into a 'bust'.

They drive into a village that is made up entirely of new houses. There are remarkably few people out on the streets and virtually no flags being waved.

'Slootdorp,' the driver says.

'What's his name?' she asks.

'Omta,' says Röell.

A group of people are standing in front of a hotel called the Lely. A very small group. No schoolchildren and pensioners here, no flowers, pennants or shrimp. She gets out of the car and the man wearing the chain of office holds out his hand. 'Welcome to Wieringermeer,' he says.

'Good morning, Mr Omta,' she says.

'You're not stopping here at all,' he says.

'What a shame,' she says.

'I'll drive ahead of you to the district boundary. This, by the way, is my wife.'

She shakes the mayoress's hand and climbs back into the car. Now, that's her kind of man. No moaning, no dawdling, no look in the eyes as if to say, 'Why aren't you spending hours here with us?' Did he actually call her 'Your Majesty'? Or even 'Ma'am'? The mayoress hadn't wasted any words either, she'd simply curtseyed. In any case, from what she's seen of Wieringermeer so far, she's glad she won't have to spend hours here. If that's even possible. Omta has climbed into a blue car and driven off slowly in front of her, leaving his wife behind, looking somewhat lost outside the hotel. The gusty June wind plays havoc with her hair while a flag flutters overhead.

'. . . sixteen ten,' Röell reads aloud. 'The Polder House, where we have our lunch appointment, dates from sixteen twelve. Cattle breeding in particular is highly developed here. Pedigree cattle. Mention should be made of the well-known herd of Miss A. G. Groneman, whose late uncle – it said father, but that's been crossed out and replaced with uncle – was made a Knight of the Order of Orange-Nassau for his many contributions in this field.'

'Will she be at the lunch?'

Röell picks up another document and mumbles quietly. A wisp of grey hair peeks out from under her yellow pillbox hat. 'Yes,' she says, after a while.

'That's sure to be entertaining. Miss. Never married, in other words.'

Röell gives her a short sharp look.

'Have a glass yourself sometime,' she says. 'Instead of looking at me like that.' Outside there are still long bands of fields and squat farmhouses, each identical to the next. The sun is shining, it must be about twenty-two degrees. Perfect weather for getting in and out of cars without a coat. Not too hot, not too cold. 'Besides,' she adds, 'I'm a great cow-lover.'

It will look like this here for months to come. Of course, the crops will grow and be harvested, but still. Early spring was and remains the most beautiful of the seasons. With different kinds of flowers coming up one after another in the palace gardens. Snowdrops around the beech trees, narcissus along the drive, snake's head in the small round border near the goods entrance. And a little later, of course, the first sweet peas in the greenhouse. The moment the leaves appear on the trees it starts to get rather boring, especially now the girls aren't running around on the lawn any more. Once the Parade has been and gone there isn't much to it. Unmitigated tedium until the first shades of autumn. 'Anything else of note?'

'This almost entirely agricultural district has entered a difficult phase recently, especially economically.'

'And why is that?'

'Not only because of the poor climatic conditions of recent years, but also due to the fact that prices and wages have increased, while the yield from their produce has not risen proportionally.'

'Oh, yes: prices, wages and yields. But everyone round here will still be out in their Sunday best when we arrive.'

'It also says that approximately ninety per cent of local businessmen have renovated or modernised their premises. The population has come to realise that to mark time is to fall behind and that progress is essential. And it goes without saying that forward thinking is the key to good government.'

'Absolutely. But they still said it.'

'Ah . . . council officials.'

'What do you mean by that?'

'Nothing.'

'I'm quite curious as to what they will be serving for lunch.'

'Yes.'

No, she thinks, I definitely don't want to suffer this again. This time I'll say something. The Government Information Service doesn't need to be present in the vehicle in the form of Röell. What on earth made them think I would prefer to travel in the same car as Röell rather than with Van der Hoeven? And perhaps Pappie would like to join me on a work trip again sometime soon.

Omta's blue car slows down and pulls over to stop behind a car parked on the roadside. The mayors get out simultaneously and shake hands. As the new mayor – 'Hartman,' Röell whispers – walks up to her car, the driver opens her door.

'Good afternoon, Your Majesty. Welcome to our district. Which, by the way, starts there.' He gestures at a bridge with white railings further down the road.

'Good afternoon, Mayor Hartman,' she says, doing her best to sound cheerful. 'I am delighted to be here for this – regrettably brief – visit.'

'Shall I lead the way?'

'Please.' As she gets back into the car, not forgetting to look at the driver, who invariably turns it into some kind of amateur theatrical performance, she notices her leather gloves lying on the back seat. She's already shaken two mayors' hands with hers bare. High time for a cigarette. Röell can scowl all she likes.

Balancing on the bridge railing are two boys in swimming trunks. One a redhead, the other brown-haired, both with their arms spread wide, fat drops of water falling from their elbows onto the freshly painted rail. When the car drives over the bridge, they jump, as if they've been waiting for that very moment. Grins on their faces. Apparently a royal visit doesn't interest them. Even if they did both look at the car before making the leap.

'Stone of help.'

'What?'

'Stone of help.'

'You've lost me.'

'That farm there. Eben-Ezer.'

The atmosphere here is very different. The countryside's older. The farms are more varied, the gardens more mature, the trees taller, the ditches full of water. Fewer crops, more cows. Ah, there's a shiny new van with the words *Blom's Breadery* on the side. The van is parked at an angle in front of a gleaming shop window bearing the same name. Apparently the baker is one of the ninety per cent of businessmen who have renovated and modernised. 'Breadery' is amusing. Modern too. She searches for shops that fall into the other ten per cent, but can't see any. Then she hears cheering and sees the crowd. She takes a deep breath and pulls on her gloves. Until lunch she won't shake a single hand with hers bare.

The driver opens the door. 'Your destination,' he says.

'Without any accidents,' she answers. She never addresses him by his Christian name.

Then everyone surrounds her again. Röell, of course, who has got out of the car unaided as the driver can't be everywhere at once. Van der Hoeven, Beelaerts van Blokland, Commissioner Kranenburg. Where's that nun got to? Is she still in the car? They won't lead her to tables full of shrimp or fish here; it's not a fishing village. Here, they're going to dance. She passes her handbag to Röell; she'll need to keep her hands free. The Polder House is a large farmhouse: whitewashed, with espaliered lindens out the front. She certainly can't get lost, there's only one possible route, right through a double line of children and mothers. Ah, there are two little ones with a bunch of flowers. The mayor tells her their names and she catches something about the butcher and the baker. These must be their children.

'Oh, thank you very much,' she says. 'What beautiful flowers, and so cleverly arranged. Did you do that yourselves?'

They stare at her as though she's speaking German.

'Of course not,' she says to make up for it. 'The florist put it together, didn't he?'

The girl nods bashfully, and she touches her gently on the cheek with a leather finger. The boy doesn't look at her and the relieved children slip back into the crowd.

Aren't these the very same children who were standing on the dyke this morning? The same heads of blond hair, the same bare knees and knitted cardigans. The very same children? An icy silence is hanging over them, as if they've all been struck dumb by pure awe. Awe or nerves. After introducing the children, the mayor hasn't said another word. She shakes her head. Röell takes her by the elbow. She pulls her arm free without looking at her private secretary and walks on slowly.

And what about that, what kind of peevish face is that boy pulling? Red hair and freckles, his head hanging. He's looking down at his feet, which are in new sandals. What does he have to look so indignant about? She almost takes a step towards him to ask what's bothering him. Why his red, white and blue flag is down at his knees. And while she's at it, she can ask the other boy, the bigger one – who has taken him by the hand and definitely isn't his brother, because his hair is raven – why he's looking at the little boy and not at her. It even makes her feel a little sad herself, that tummy thrust forward in anger and the transparently new Norwegian cardigan with its brass buttons, almost certainly knitted by his grandmother. Everything in the past few weeks building up to this one day, the kind of day that's over before you know it, and then being cross into the bargain, so that almost everything goes by in a blur. All around her, photographs are being taken, she hears the cameras clicking and there are even flashes, although that's hardly necessary in weather like this. She slows down a little, as if she can't go on until the boy has looked up at her, but the mayor has already walked ahead and she can feel the rest of the company jostling at her back.

She directs her gaze at a group of men and women in traditional costume a bit further along where there's a little more space. The children are holding little flags, but none are waving them. If not for the breeze, the flags would be hanging limply in the air. She hopes they'll have sherry in the Polder House. The skirts swish, the clogs of the black-suited men stamp on the asphalt. The bunch of flowers is annoyingly heavy. She wants her bag, she wants her cigarettes, she wants to sit down.

'This way please, Your Majesty. Luncheon is ready inside,' says the mayor.

Just say ma'am, she thinks. Ma'am and lunch.

In front of her, Jezuolda Kwanten slips inside, pencils and sketchbook at the ready.

'You can withdraw here for a moment if you would like to,' a woman says. 'With your lady-in-waiting. There's a toilet you can use if you so require.' She doesn't correct her.

Röell and Jezuolda Kwanten are sitting in the mayor's office, which, like this room, smells of fresh paint and wallpaper glue. All these lavatories, she thinks. All these lavatories everywhere, just for me. She has removed her gloves and raps a strangely shaped wall with a knuckle. It sounds hollow. Temporary, she concludes, and wonders where the men in the company have to go now the urinal's been walled off. She thinks of the lavatory at Amsterdam Central station: the motionless air, the unventilated rooms, the dusty curtains, the lavishly upholstered chairs that are almost never used. She feels the toilet paper: Edet, two-ply. A virginal bar of soap on the washbasin. I am sixty years old, she thinks. For more than twenty years I have been sitting in my official capacity on lavatories like this. How long can anyone bear it? She rises, washes her hands and flushes to keep up the pretence.

Bottles of apple and orange juice are arranged on the enormous French-polished table in the mayor's office. And one bottle of sherry. Röell is drinking orange juice, the artist doesn't have a drink. She pours two glasses of sherry and holds one out to Jezuolda Kwanten.

'No, thank you. I don't drink alcohol at all.'

'But you're an artist.'

The sister smiles, sits down on the most spacious seat and opens her large sketchbook.

The Queen smiles too. The glasses need emptying. It would be strange to leave the mayor's office while there is still a full glass on the table. The bunch of cigarettes sticking up from a vase needs to be thinned out a little too, at the very least. Lucky Strikes. Röell screws up her eyes but offers her a light all the same. She strolls around the spacious room and ends up in front of a large mirror. She studies her reflection, toasts herself and blows smoke in her own face.

'Miss Kwanten, could you perhaps clarify the actual distinction between a nun and a sister for me?' she asks.

'A nun takes solemn vows,' says Kwanten.

'And you haven't?'

'No. I am a member of the Order of the Sisters of Charity.'

Her glass is empty. She gestures at the full glass on the table. 'If you're not going to drink that, I will,' she says.

'I wouldn't mind a drop of sherry after all,' says Röell.

She looks askance at her secretary but has no choice other than to pass her the second glass. 'Who commissioned you to make the bust?'

'The city of Tilburg.'

'That's where you live as well?'

'Yes, ma'am.'

'How do you find the countryside around here?'

'Empty. Empty and cold.'

'Cold?' The Queen smiles. 'You're having a hard time of it today, then. Have you ever been to the island of Texel?'

'No, ma'am.'

'Tomorrow will be more to your taste.'

'Oh, I already think it's tremendous. I have the privilege of accompanying you for two days.' The sister's pencil scratches over the page.

The Queen pats her hair into place. 'Are you sure you won't take a small glass of sherry?'

'No, thank you, ma'am, really not.'

'Then I'll have another half a glass for you.'

Röell sighs and sips her sherry with a sour expression.

During lunch she is next to Van der Hoeven. The unmarried pedigree-cattle breeder has been seated diagonally opposite. Otherwise, the usual guests are sitting at the long, impeccably set table. The chairwomen of the country-women's association and the women's branch of the employers' federation, polder-board members, dyke reeves, councillors. But not the GP and not the notary. Kwanten isn't here either, she'll be having lunch somewhere else in the Polder House, probably in the company of the driver, amongst others. She's pleased to see that someone has thought of putting out sweet peas in a number of small vases. The inevitable oxtail soup – presumably the reasoning is that if one eats a certain soup at Christmas it must be appropriate on other festive occasions as well – is spicy. Milk and buttermilk are the drinks at the table. Or would Your Majesty prefer a dry white wine with her soup? She would, after a brief hesitation. Van der Hoeven and the mayoress join her and, on the other side of the table, the pedigree-cattle breeder has also accepted a glass. Her second private secretary's warm young voice is a calm counterweight to the nervous, somewhat high-pitched voice of the mayor.

She herself doesn't say much. She eats and drinks. The bread is fresh, the cheeses and sliced meats various and abundant. That Blom fellow bakes delicious bread, she thinks. Bright light enters the room through the tall windows and only now does she hear excited voices outside, even though the children seem to have gone. The cattle breeder is sitting just a little too far away for her to strike up a conversation. She nods almost imperceptibly at the handsome woman and raises her wine glass slightly. The woman nods and raises hers in reply, as if she's understood that the Queen would love to talk to her about the whys and wherefores of stud bulls, the weather, or anything else that might come up, if only they were that little bit closer. Then one of the women in the company stands up and is introduced by the mayoress as Mrs Backer-Breed, elocutionist.

During the performance, which is delivered partly in the local dialect, her thoughts drift again. She thinks about Pappie. Wondering if he'll be on the *Piet Hein* this evening. The man is impossible, of course, but he feels at home on the yacht. In just under a fortnight it will be his birthday and now, approaching sixty, he surely won't get up to any more foolishness. She sips a second glass of wine, evidently chosen by someone who knows what he's doing. When the company begins to applaud, she joins in. Then large dishes of fresh strawberries are brought out to the table with bowls of whipped cream. The coffee that concludes the lunch is strong. There's a soft crunching underfoot. They've scattered sand on the wooden floor of the council chamber.

She was right: the schoolchildren have disappeared. But there are still plenty of people about. Several newspaper photographers are hanging around too. The visit has already been officially concluded inside, now it's just a question of walking to the car and driving to the next village. The village that was named after her great-grandmother. Will the people who live there realise how strange that is? In contrast to the two previous mayors, this mayor will not lead the way. Röell has taken her bag off her hands again; she herself is walking towards the road with the flowers. The coffee has tempered the effect of the sherry and the white wine, but she still has a pleasantly light-headed feeling. Van der

Hoeven is walking beside her, bumping gently against her arm every now and then.

Out of the thinned and now disordered line of people, a large man in immaculate overalls steps forward onto the path. Lengths of cord in both hands and on the cords are two little goats. 'Ma'am,' he says.

'Yes?' she asks.

'I would like to offer you these two pygmy goats.'

'Oh,' she says. 'On behalf of whom?'

'On behalf of myself.'

'And you are?'

'Blauwboer.'

One of the goats starts to nibble at a bunch of Sweet William a woman is holding a little too close by. She hands Van der Hoeven her flowers and kneels down. The other goat sniffs at her leather glove with its soft nose. The animals are brown with a black blaze. And so small she could easily pick them up. She does just that and feels their tight round bellies against the palms of her hands. The farmer pays out a little cord.

'I have three grandsons,' she says.

'I know that, ma'am.'

'They'll be very pleased with this gift.' She feels the goats' little hearts racing in their chests.

'That was my idea,' the farmer says.

Photographers push forward, a policeman steps between them. *Queen ignores protocol to play with pygmy goats.* She can see tomorrow's headline already. When she bends to put the goats back down on the ground, she is overcome by a slight dizziness. Van der Hoeven takes hold of her elbow as she rises. One of the goats starts to bleat loudly.

'We can't take them with us now,' says her second private secretary.

'I realise that,' the farmer says.

She thanks the man warmly and walks on, leaving Van der Hoeven behind to arrange things. She has her hands free again. No handbag, no bouquet, no goats. Wiry brown hairs are stuck to her gloves. A goat for Willem-Alexander and a goat for Maurits. Someone from the stables will come to pick up the animals in the next few days. And they'll think of something else for Johan Friso.

The driver is standing beside the open door.

'How are we for time?' Röell asks.

'Nicely on schedule,' he replies. 'Nothing to worry about.'

Before getting into the car, she looks around. Flags are flying on almost all of the houses, and on the other side of the waterway that divides the village in two she sees the gleaming van again. Only now does she ask herself why the baker isn't out doing his rounds. Or is the area he covers so small that he can get it all done in the morning? People are walking away from the Polder House, still turning to look back, but not crowding around the car. They're returning to the order of the day, the children might be back in the classrooms already. No, they'll have the afternoon off, it's a holiday. Perhaps there's a village swimming pool they can go to. Then she sees a young woman coming towards her against the flow of the dissipating crowd, holding a child on her hip and trying to wheel a bicycle with her other hand. Someone running late and hurrying to catch a glimpse of the Queen. She gestures to the driver and walks towards the woman, seeing Röell start off after her out of the corner of her eye.

'What are you doing?' her private secretary asks.

Without replying, she waits for the woman to reach her.

'The time,' Röell says. 'We have to watch the time.'

Then the woman is standing opposite her, a little short of breath from hurrying.

'Were you too late leaving home?' she asks.

'Yes, I . . .'

'What an adorable little girl you have. What's your name?'

The child, two at most, looks at her with big blue eyes.

'Will you tell me? What your name is?'

'An-ne,' the child whispers.

'Hanne,' her mother says.

She pulls off her right glove to stroke the child's cheek. 'The "h" isn't easy.' The girl shrinks away, pressing her face against her mother's neck. 'And you are?'

'Anna Kaan, ma'am.'

Ah, this woman knows how things should be done. 'Did the time run away with you this morning?'

The woman looks at her, her startled expression making way for a smile. She doesn't answer. The bicycle, leaning against the woman's hip, slowly slides down and clatters onto the asphalt.

The Queen instinctively reaches out with both hands.

'It's fine,' the woman says.

'We have to go,' says Röell, standing somewhere behind her.

It's turned into a photo session after all. She doesn't see it, she hears it. Annoyingly close by. *Queen takes impromptu stroll.* A second potential headline for tomorrow's newspaper. 'There you have it,' she tells the woman. 'We have to go. Bye, Hanne.'

'Goodbye, ma'am,' says the woman. 'Thank you very much.'

'What for?'

'Taking the trouble to . . .'

'It's nothing,' she says. When she turns, it's not Röell but Jezuolda Kwanten standing behind her. Right behind her. She feels her warm breath on her face. It's as if she's trying to soak up every pore and imperfection in her model's skin so that she can make her bronze bust as lifelike as possible. The sister from the Order of the Sisters of Charity takes a step aside and follows her to the cars, one pace behind.

She gives one last wave in the direction of the Polder House gates, where the mayor and his wife are waiting politely. Then all the car doors bang shut. Even before they drive off, Röell has gathered up all kinds of documents and started to ruffle through them. The Queen lights a cigarette. The car turns and drives through the village extremely slowly. When she looks to the right she sees a graveyard, just behind the Polder House. Something she neither noticed nor heard mentioned before. They pass a water tower and a pumping station. At the very edge of the village, at the foot of a dyke, there is a windmill.

'Those goats,' Röell says.

'What about them?'

'That's really not done.'

'Why not?'

'With all due respect . . . goats!'

'So?'

'Who's going to take them to Soestdijk?'

'Van der Hoeven has arranged all that.'

'And that woman with that child.'

'She was late. That could happen to anyone.'

'You can just leave things like that to run their course.'

'I don't *want* things like that to run their course. It's just nice. For her and for that little girl. They'll remember it for the rest of their lives, this beautiful sunny day in June.' She draws on her cigarette. 'Not to say that's why I do it, of course.'

Röell purses her lips and looks through her papers.

'Try to put yourself in those people's shoes for once. What difference does a couple of minutes make?'

Röell doesn't respond. 'Eighteen forty-six,' she says. 'The polder is named after the consort of King Willem II.'

'You don't need to read that to me. What's this one called?'

'Warners.'

'What's on the programme?'

'A waterskiing demonstration. At two thirty in the afternoon on the Oude Veer.'

'Really?'

'The fourth event is barefoot waterskiing.'

The Queen stubs out her cigarette, pulls her right glove back on and goes back to staring out the window. This area is again slightly different from the previous district. Different roads and farmhouses, less grass. If only that waterskiing was already over. They'll have old-age pensioners there as well. If only Den Helder was over too. She's looking forward to the *Piet Hein*, it's been months since she was on the yacht. The polished pear wood, the green upholstered Rietveld armchairs, the bunks. Pappie, possibly, in the top bunk. And otherwise a quiet conversation – the drinks cabinet open – with Van der Hoeven. Tomorrow morning she might take the helm for a while, or at least stand at the captain's shoulder. Two months from now she'll be spending another few days on board for the naval review during the Harlingen fishing festival. 'Barefoot skiing,' she says. 'What *will* they think of next?'

Straw

I'll never celebrate anything again. Ever. What for? Celebrating your fiftieth wedding anniversary with only sons to show for it, what was I thinking? Never again. Straw's nowhere near as hard as you'd think. If you want to sit or lie down on straw you have to know how. You have to rub against it like a cow or a sheep and keep rubbing until all the sharp stiff bits have turned away. I'm an expert: three-quarters of a lifetime's experience with straw. It's not just a couple of bales, there are hundreds of them. What's all this straw still doing here anyway? What's it for?

She's lying on her back and staring up at the spot where a few roof tiles have slid down. It would have been different with a daughter. She wouldn't have just sat there drinking and stuffing her face. She wouldn't have made any snide remarks about the zoo where they spent the afternoon. She would have made a scrapbook with photos and stories; she would have written a song 'to the tune of', a funny song that rhymed and would have been sung by a lot more grandchildren than just that one, who made things even worse by sulking and answering back. A daughter would have squatted down next to her, next to her chair, to ask quietly if she was enjoying herself. Those horrible boys just drank and roared with laughter even though there was nothing to laugh about and all Zeeger did was join in, even if he didn't drink. Zeeger never drank.

Through the hole above her, a ray of dusty sunlight shines into the barn at an angle. An angle that tells her that it must be late in the afternoon. Friday afternoon.

Earlier in the day, just before climbing up the ladder, she'd turned on the light. It's still light now, but tonight it will get dark. She anticipated that. She pulled the rickety ladder up behind her, leant it against the straw to climb further, then pulled the ladder up behind her again. Lying on a pricklier bale of straw next to her are a water bottle, a packet of Viennese biscuits, a bottle of advocaat and the parade sword that normally hangs from the bottom bookshelf. The rickety ladder is a little further away.

Even though the side doors and large rear doors are all open, the air in the barn is motionless, not the slightest hint of a breeze. She sits up and grabs the water bottle, one and a half litres. While drinking, she looks at the junk in the milking parlour attic diagonally opposite the straw loft. A washing basket, bulb trays, a rusty boiler, roof tiles, an old coat (light blue), zinc washtubs, a pedal car, a crate with sacks of wool. The three round windows with the wrought-iron frames – one up near the roof ridge, the other two a good bit lower down, above the doors at either end of the long corridor that runs the whole length of the barn – remind her of a church. Tiles have come loose all over the place and, despite the spare tiles she's just seen, they haven't been replaced. In those spots, stripes of sunlight shine in.

Beneath her she hears the bull shuffling and groaning.

Dirk. A superfluous lump of meat. Otherwise it's quiet, as quiet as only a hot day in June can be. The swallows flying in and out are almost silent. She screws the cap back on the bottle, holds it up to see how much water is left, then lays it back down next to her. When the straw stops rustling, she hears footsteps. Very quick footsteps. 'Dirk!' she hears. Dieke. The child doesn't know her grandmother is up above her. A little later, when the footsteps have almost reached the barn doors, the child shouts, 'Uncle Jan!' Dirk starts to snort. Dieke says something else, but she can't make it out. Soon after, it falls quiet again. She leans back carefully and, once she's rubbed against it for a while, the straw is reasonably comfortable again. Inasmuch as anything other than a soft mattress can be reasonably comfortable when you're the wrong side of seventy. She gives her belly a slow and thorough scratch, then rubs her face with both hands.

What's that bull still doing here? Why doesn't Klaas sell that enormous beast? She stares at the outside world through the hole in the roof. A very small, rectangular outside world. For now, that's plenty. I'll never celebrate anything again. Ever. We're not cut out for celebrating. We always say exactly the wrong thing. The long faces of those boys as they tramped around the zoo. A daughter would have taken photos or said things like, 'Look, a baboon. My first ever baboon!'

Somewhere in the barn something creaks. It's a dull dry creaking, loud too. The timbers? The boards of the hayloft? The big doors?

Dust

There are six windows in the living room. Dieke looks out through the one with the crack. She's staring at the lawn that extends from the front of the house all the way to the road. In the middle stands an enormous red beech. The leaves of the tree aren't moving. The blades of grass in the unmown lawn are completely still too.

The crack bothers her. It has for a long time now. She's scared that the glass might fall out of the window frame, maybe while she's looking through it. Dieke sighs and walks out of the living room, across the hall and into the kitchen. Her mother is sitting at the kitchen table smoking a cigarette. 'What are you sighing about?' she asks.

Dieke doesn't answer. She goes over to the window and uses both hands to wave at her grandfather, who she can see on the other side of the yard, past the wide ditch and her grandmother's vegetable garden, standing at his own kitchen window. If there were sheets on the clothes line, or towels and trousers, she wouldn't be able to see him. He doesn't wave back. The sun's almost reached the kitchen. Her grandfather walks away from his window.

'Where's Uncle Jan?' she asks.

'Is Jan here?'

'Uh-huh,' says Dieke. 'He just came over the bridge.'

'I don't know, Dieke. Somewhere out the back, I guess.'

'What time is it?'

'Six o'clock.'

'Is it almost teatime?'

Her mother turns her head to look at the stove, which doesn't have any pans on it. 'Yes,' she says. 'Go and look for him.' She stubs her cigarette out in a brown ashtray that is already full to overflowing.

Dieke slides over the laminate floor in her socks. Her yellow wellies are on the coconut mat in front of the door. She pulls one on, then starts walking before she's finished pulling on the other and tumbles over. 'Doesn't matter, it doesn't hurt,' she says to herself, getting up again. It's cooler in the long corridor that separates the house from the barn, but the concrete floor is as dry as a bone. When the floor's damp it's going to rain, she knows that. It's not going to rain. She jumps into the old milking parlour from the corridor, over the two concrete steps. After the milking parlour comes the barn. She stands still for a second and looks up. 'Doesn't hurt, doesn't hurt.' It's very big and gloomy in here, even with all the doors opened wide like now. The biggest doors are at the back of the barn, thirty steps away or more, big steps. An enormous rectangle of light, so bright that when she looks back up at the roof, she can no longer see the giant beams.

She starts to run. Halfway she yells out at the top of her lungs, 'Dirk!' The bull turns his enormous body towards the sound, but Dieke doesn't even look at him. She keeps running. She stops in the doorway. In front of her is the shadow cast by the farmhouse, stretching almost to the sheep shed. One of the two doors is hanging crooked on its hinges. On one side of the sheep shed is the old dungheap, on the other a salt-stained, concrete silo. The dung left on the slab is as black as ink and teeming with fishing worms. There are elderberry bushes growing in the silo.

Somewhere out the back, that's what her mother said. But somewhere is a very big place. In the sheep shed? Past the heaps of silage? Or all the way out in the fields? 'Uncle Jan!' she bawls. Behind her, in the gloomy depths of the barn, the bull starts snorting. 'I'm not calling you,' she says, without looking back. She takes a couple of steps forward and calls again, even louder.

'Here.'

'Where's here?'

'Behind the sheep shed.'

She can choose: either cut through between the silo and the sheep shed – but there are tall prickle bushes there – or take the path alongside the wide ditch and then go a bit to the right. She decides on the path and kicks the dust up as she goes. 'Watch the ditch,' she tells herself. 'Watch the ditch, watch the ditch.' When she spots her uncle, she glances back. The cloud of dust over the path is taking a long time to settle. Her uncle is sitting on a causeway gate looking out over the fields. She grabs the top board and carefully puts one foot on the bottom board, then waits until she's sure she's standing firmly before lifting the other foot. Uncle Jan doesn't say a word and doesn't look at her either. He's not the kind of person to just launch into conversation. She's now standing with both feet on the second board and her upper body starts to lean forward. It's getting difficult. She has to keep her balance with her hands on the top board, but if she puts her feet up any higher, she'll topple over forward and land face first on the hard cracked ground on the other side of the gate. She stays there like that, wavering between carrying on, stopping and climbing back down.

'Can't you manage?'

'No,' she says.

Her uncle jumps down on the other side of the gate and grips her under her arms. When he lifts her up, she swings her yellow wellies over the top board and sits down. Just like Uncle Jan, who's climbed back up onto the gate, though his legs are a lot longer. His feet reach down to the second board, hers are up on the third. She holds on tight to stop herself from falling forward or, even worse, backwards. She lets out a deep sigh.

'Is it still too hard?'

'No,' she says.

'Hold my arm.'

She does and that's better. As long as she's holding on to Uncle Jan, she won't fall. She doesn't fidget or slide around because it's an old gate, a gate the cows have chewed on.

Uncle Jan stares into the distance. Grass, yellowish stubble in Brak's fields next door, blue sky. There are no cows out in the fields and no sheep either. There aren't any animals in the fields at all. A bit further along there's a second gate and beyond that a third. Between the gates, two dead-straight parallel tracks. Shadows are starting to appear where cows dropped their pats and the grass is a little longer. The blades of the big wind turbines past the third gate aren't turning. Dieke feels the evening sun on her neck.

'What are you doing?' she asks.

It takes too long, her uncle refuses to answer. 'Why are you sitting here?'

'Because.'

'Because what?'

'Just because. Because I like sitting here.'

'Oh,' says Dieke. 'Did you come on the train?'

'Yep.'

'From Den Helder?'

'Yep.'

'Did Grandma pick you up?'

'No, Grandpa.'

'Was it hot on the train?'

'Very.'

'And was it on time?'

'Course not. The rails expanded in the heat.'

'Oh. I went to the swimming pool this afternoon.'

'Have you got a certificate yet?'

'I'm only five!'

'Oh, sorry.'

'I've got a card.'

'What kind of card?'

'The card you get for swimming through a hoop under-water, with your head under and everything.'

'Excellent.'

'Yes,' says Dieke, who thinks so too. 'Evelien was too scared.'

'Who's that?'

'My friend.'

'Oh, her.'

Dieke can tell from his voice that he doesn't have a clue who Evelien is. 'Grandma's too scared to put her head underwater too.'

'Yes, that's terrible. Grandma's seventy-three and she still doesn't have a swimming certificate.'

'You don't have a driving licence.'

'You've got me there, Dieke.'

She waits. 'Grandma's stupid.'

'Is she? Why?'

'Because.'

There are no cows making their way into the fields, no hooves kicking dust up along the path, which is still lined with electric fencing. It's quiet; even the birds think it's too hot to chirp. Then there's a dull bang, wood on concrete maybe. Dieke jumps and squeezes her uncle's arm.

'What could that be, Dieke?' Uncle Jan asks.

'I don't know,' she squeaks.

Rot

Klaas was sitting in the old cow passage on an easy chair that an acquaintance had left there because the old cow passage is a cheap and dry place to store furniture. He was watching the swallows flying in and out and catching mosquitoes in their wide-open beaks. There were no noises coming from up on the straw. Unlike the bull's pen. Dieke just ran past it. She's terrified in the barn.

He *was* sitting there, now he's stood up. The sliding door is open and when he goes to close it a little, it tilts slowly forward and bangs down on the concrete. The wood hardly splinters at all, the boards simply disintegrate from dryness and wood rot. He pulls a tobacco pouch out of his back pocket and pokes what's left of the door with his foot while rolling a cigarette.

To his left is the old dairy scullery, rolls of sheep wire standing upright on the bone-dry floor. Houseleek is frothing out of the roof gutter like boiling milk, and under the roof gutter is the wheelbarrow with the dead sheep, four stiff legs sticking up in the air. He doesn't remember how long it is since he pulled the creature out of the ditch. He's forgotten why he didn't call the collection service. He doesn't know why he still hasn't. The sheep has been here so long it no longer stinks and yet it's still a sheep.

He sees his brother and his daughter sitting next to each other on the causeway gate. Jan's back is wet. Dieke is wearing her yellow wellies. Slowly he walks over to them. He lays his forearms on the top board.

'Hi, Dad,' says Dieke.

'Hi, Dieke.'

'Klaas,' says his brother.

'Jan.'

'Did you break something, Dad?' Dieke asks.

'No, Diek, it broke all by itself. Because of the weather, or because it was so old.' Klaas pulls pieces of rotten wood out of the gatepost and suddenly sees it on fire, years ago, after he and Jan had stuffed leftover crackers into it on New Year's Day. Lighting a cracker, watching the explosion, walking off, and half an hour later coming back with something else on their minds and seeing the gatepost calmly burning. Like a giant matchstick. Only now does he light his roll-up.

'You want to get down?' his brother asks Dieke.

'Yes, please,' she says.

Jan slides off the gate, lifts Dieke up and puts her down on the ground next to Klaas.

'Uncle Jan's really strong,' she says.

'What brings *you* here?' Klaas hears himself asking. It's something he almost always says, as if his brother would never come home without a specific reason. But he doesn't mean anything by it.

'Painting.'

Klaas looks at his brother. What's that supposed to mean? He doesn't pursue it. 'Come on, Dieke, it's teatime.'

'Are you going to eat with Grandma?' Dieke asks Jan.

'Today I'm going to eat with Grandpa.'

'Can he cook?'

'I don't actually know.'

'Where's Grandma?'

Klaas looks at his brother.

'She's not here just now,' Jan says. 'But I'm sure you don't mind that.'

'No. Are you going to be here tomorrow too?'

'Yep, sure am. All day.'

'Fun! Are you coming to the swimming pool?'

'No, I'm not going swimming. I'm working.'

'Did you go to the swimming pool a lot when you were little?'

'They couldn't keep me away.'

'Why don't you go now then?'

'I'm going to do something else.'

'Too bad.' Dieke turns and runs off.

Klaas turns away too. 'I'll see you.'

'No doubt,' says Jan.

Dieke yells out 'Dirk!' again as she runs through the barn. It sounds muffled, as if the emptiness inside the barn and the dust of almost a hundred years are smothering her voice. All the bulls have been called Dirk, as far back as Klaas can remember.

'I'll be there in a minute, Diek,' he calls out to his daughter, who has already reached the door of the old milking parlour.

She doesn't answer, rushing on in her yellow wellies. Dirk has stuck his square head out through the iron bars of his pen.

'Klaas?' he hears from above.

'Yes.'

'Have you talked to Jan yet?'

'Yes.'

'You have to tell him to stop.'

'Stop what?'

'Just stop. Stop it. I never see him, he just stays on Texel. Of course, if there's something to celebrate, he'll come, and then he trudges round the zoo looking completely miserable. You boys are horrible.'

Klaas looks over his shoulder. He's the only one here, isn't he?

'You still there?'

'Yeah.'

'You're all in league with each other. You and your father and Jan. And Johan too.'

'Johan?'

'Yes, Johan.'

'When are you coming down?'

'That's for me to decide.'

'Aren't you hungry?'

'No.'

'Well, I'm going to eat now.'

'Do what you have to do.'

Klaas stays standing there, waiting for more. He rubs Dirk between the eyes.

'I'm never celebrating anything again. Ever!'

After that, nothing. He throws his roll-up on the floor and carefully crushes it underfoot. Then he walks through the side doors and into the yard. A young woman rides past on a bike and waves hello. He raises his hand, even though he's too busy looking at her legs to see who it is as she flashes past. Rekel, his parents' chocolate Labrador, is sitting waiting on the other side of the ditch. As if someone has forbidden him from crossing the bridge. His tongue is lolling out of his mouth and his tail beats listlessly on the paving stones of the path that leads from the wooden bridge to the side door of the house. He can't see his father anywhere. When he walks over to the kitchen window to see if tea's ready, he bangs his head on the drinking trough his father once screwed to the wall as a planter for colourful spring flowers.

'Shit!'

There's been grass growing in it for years.

Gold

Dieke creeps down the stairs. She knows it's really early, that's why she's creeping. It's nice to be downstairs again. Not that she's scared upstairs, but once she's outside her bedroom there's a lot of empty space, with a couple of empty rooms and a high-peaked roof with a crossbeam and a bare bulb hanging down that doesn't give enough light.

The door to her parents' bedroom is wide open. Inside it's orange – that's the curtains. She stares at her father and mother, who are bobbing up and down slightly on the enormous waterbed as they sleep. Her mother almost completely under the duvet, her father only half. She used to have her mother to herself at this time of day. She tugs on the arm her mother has out on top of the covers.

'I already heard you,' her mother says. 'You don't need to pull my arm too.'

'Where's Uncle Jan?' Dieke asks.

Her mother looks at the alarm clock. 'It's six o'clock, Diek. He's still in bed, where else would he be? Everyone's still in bed at six o'clock. Except for farmers.'

'When's he going to get up, then?

'Later,' her mother sighs. 'You go back to bed now too.'

'I want to stay here with you.' Without waiting for permission, she climbs in next to her. A wave passes through the bed. It's almost like a swimming pool, and then being on a wooden raft, like the raft that floats in zone two, the part of the pool she's allowed in with water wings.

'But no wriggling, OK?' her father says.

'Can you do your legs?'

Her mother rolls over onto her side and pulls up her legs. Dieke slips her feet in between her raised thighs. It feels lovely, even now it's summer, with her feet warm almost all the time, but in winter it's even better and never gets clammy. She lies calmly on her back staring at the red curtain.

'Is he staying today?'

'Yes, Diek,' her mother says in a sleepy voice. 'I think he's staying all day.'

'Why isn't he coming to the swimming pool then?'

'Because he's got something else to do,' her father says.

'I think it's strange. If it's this hot, you go to the swimming pool.'

'Go to sleep, Diek,' her father says. 'Now.'

Dieke closes her eyes and folds her hands together on her stomach. Sleep, she thinks, now. And falls asleep.

Three hours later she's standing on the wide windowsill in the kitchen; her mother is down in the cellar. Even the brown tiles under her feet are warm. She hasn't got dressed yet, she's still in just knickers and a vest. There is one plant on the windowsill. It's a kind of cactus, she knows that, but it's a cactus that doesn't have prickles. She's waiting for her grandfather to appear. 'Where is Grandma? Where is Grandma?' she hums. 'Stay away. Stay away.' Keeping her balance by pressing her forehead against the window, she rubs her right shoulder for a second. It's still a bit tender. The grass in the rusty drinking trough isn't moving.

Then she sees her grandfather, fiddling with something on the sideboard under his kitchen window. Maybe he's going to put on some coffee. For Uncle Jan. She starts to wave, both hands at once, becoming more and more frantic. She only realises that her mother has come up out of the cellar when she falls over backwards and doesn't end up on the floor. She feels hands under her arms and sends the cactus without prickles flying with a kick of her right foot.

'Unbelievable!' her mother says. 'Why do you always stand on the windowsill?'

'Ow!' she yelps.

'What?'

'My foot!'

'Look at all those dirty smudges.'

The cactus has fallen onto the floor and Dieke doesn't even look at all the dirty smudges on the windowpane. There's something between the roots, something that was once shiny. She kneels down in the soil, avoiding the bits of broken pot, and stretches a finger out to it.

'And now you've got your knees dirty too!'

She's not listening to her mother, who sits down at the kitchen table to light a cigarette. It looks like a ring. She rubs off some of the moist soil and cautiously pulls it. Roots snap.

'Oh, go ahead, break it too. That Christmas cactus has been there since your father was a little boy.'

Dieke hasn't really started listening yet. She spits on the ring, then rubs it clean on her perfectly white vest. A gold ring, but not for a finger.

'Repotted just three years ago. As if I don't have enough to do. Old junk. Do you have to wipe that thing clean on your vest?' Her mother stands and, with the cigarette dangling between her lips, pulls the vest up roughly over Dieke's head. 'Back in the wash with this, then.'

'Ow,' Dieke says softly, but hardly feeling a thing. A gold ring. But not for a finger. Then she thinks, Christmas cactus. A plant like this is called a Christmas cactus.

Cuttlebone

Saturday, it's Saturday today. He sits on the side of the bed, hands on knees, whistling softly. It's ten to six. He looks down at his hands.

At five past six he pulls the bedding straight. The sun's already up, the tall trees in the front garden look grey and ominously still. Zeeger Kaan fluffs up the pillow and lays it on the duvet cover. He's had a window wide open all night, but you couldn't really say it's cooled off in the bedroom. It was a short night. Under the window the hydrangeas have started to flower. He walks to the toilet and sits down to pee. When he's finished he doesn't flush, but throws a few sheets of toilet paper into the bowl and closes the door as quietly as possible. The ticking of the inherited grandfather clock in the hall is loud and cavernous. He thinks of the tiled floor covered with walnuts. Some people eat their walnuts fresh; around here we always dry them for days on end first. Another four months or so and it will be that time of year again. No, more like five.

He doesn't go back to the bedroom to get dressed. The front door needs opening. He turns the key and unbolts the upper half. The air outside is as still as it is in the house. He goes upstairs.

Jan is lying on his back, legs wide, one arm over his stomach. The curtains are open, the window is shut tight, the duvet has slid down to the floor. Sweat gleams on his nose; a mosquito, fat and red, is sitting on his forehead. He's dumped his bag on a chair, his clothes are draped over the back. Zeeger Kaan stands there for a long time staring at his son, at the brown-checked curtains, at the trinkets on the coffee table, at the bed Jan is lying on, at the mosquito, which eventually takes slow flight and lands again on the sloping white wall.

At quarter to seven he gets the paper out of the letter box. There aren't even any dewdrops on the flap. Still dressed in just his vest and underpants he walks, newspaper in hand, up onto the road. Empty. The chocolate Labrador watches from the path. 'Food?' Zeeger Kaan asks. The dog barks.

He throws two mugs of dry food into the dog's bowl and goes into the living room with the paper. After reading the 'Town & Country' section, he lays the paper on the coffee table and notices the empty space under the bookshelves. 'What's she going to come up with next?' he mumbles. He goes into the bedroom to get dressed. He wants to go outside, into the back garden, but a basket full of colours keeps him in the laundry just a little longer. He fills the washing machine, sets the temperature to sixty degrees and presses the button. After the machine has been running for about a minute, he goes out through the side door.

At the side and front of the house there's lawn and trees; behind the house, perennials, and further into the garden, more trees. Anna's been nagging him about the chestnuts in the front garden for years. She wants him to cut them down because it 'gets so dark and gloomy' in the house in summer. Water flows over an algae-covered granite ball and disappears between rocks in the ground. 'Bloody slugs,' he says, passing the hostas. He stops under the walnut tree. The dog walks on a little and sits down by the side of the ditch. It's shady even there, from the row of pollard willows. Together they look at the farm. When a couple of jackdaws land on the roof ridge, a tile slides clattering down, catches the gutter and arcs down onto the gravel. If she wasn't awake, she is now. There isn't a single nut at his feet.

At ten to nine he fills the coffee machine with water and tips five scoops of coffee into the filter. He puts the glass jar of ground coffee back in the sideboard, then reconsiders. Jan likes it strong. When he looks up he sees his granddaughter standing on the windowsill and waving enthusiastically with both hands. His daughter-in-law appears, a plant slides out of view, then Dieke's gone too. He hasn't even had time to wave back.

A few minutes later Jan pads downstairs in his bare feet, looks around and grabs the paper from the living room.

'Good morning,' he says.

'Yep,' says his son.

'Coffee?'

'Yep.'

Rekel immediately creeps under the kitchen table to lie on Jan's feet.

'Sleep well?'

'OK.' His son rubs his forehead and opens the 'Town & Country' section. He doesn't ask *him* if *he* slept well. Alone. It seems some things are more or less normal, no matter how irregularly they happen.

'Food?' he says.

'Do you have zwieback?'

He gets the zwieback tin out of a cupboard and puts it on the table, drops a single sugar cube into Jan's coffee and starts to eat. His son eats too, but doesn't say anything, reading the articles Zeeger read earlier. *Pile-driving starts for modern school building, Blue-green algae in recreational lake, Cyclist hit by car in Den Helder, Local resident in finals of international swimming race.* 'I've got cuttlebone,' he says.

'What for?' Jan asks.

'To clean it.'

'How's that work? Rekel, get out of there.'

Sighing, the dog comes out from under Jan's side of the table and walks back under it on the other side, where he lies down on Zeeger Kaan's bare feet.

'Wet it, rub it, then wash it off.'

'Can I see?'

'Here.' He pulls his feet out from under the dog and walks through to the laundry, where he picks up the green bucket with the five pieces of cuttlebone. Jan's followed him and takes one out. He studies it, running a finger over the smooth shining side and pressing a hole in the soft side with his thumb. Exactly what *he* did when the man at the stone suppliers in Schagen handed the stuff over to him completely free of charge.

'Paint in the garage?' Jan asks.

'Yep. I'll come with you.'

'No need, I'll find it.' Jan takes the bucket and disappears through the side door. The dog ambles off behind him.

And now? What should he do now? Wait till Jan's gone. He looks at the breakfast table, the empty plates covered with zwieback crumbs, the half-full cup of coffee and the mild cheese that's started to sweat. Then he clears it all away.

A few minutes later Jan comes back, disappears into the bathroom, re-emerges without his T-shirt and goes upstairs. Comes back down again in shorts and worn trainers, and fetches his T-shirt from the bathroom. He smells of sunblock.

'You going?' Zeeger Kaan asks.

'Almost.'

'Found everything?'

'Sure. You've got a flat.'

'What?'

'Your back tyre's flat. On your bike.'

News to me, he thinks. He watches his son walk off, not to the garage, but over the bridge, holding his T-shirt loosely in one hand. Aha, he thinks. Then he unloads the washing machine and hangs the trousers, towels and shirts neatly on the line while looking around the garage in his mind's eye, trying to remember where he put the puncture repair kit.

Straw

A storm! No, not a storm. But why that tile then? She's slept, very deeply, but restlessly as well, and the tile sliding off the roof has woken her from her sleep or doze, or maybe it's just the memory of dozens of glazed roof tiles lying shattered in the yard.

An eternity ago, Zeeger's grandmother lay dead in her bedroom the morning after a November storm. The fire was cold, the paraffin lamp had gone out. Zeeger's father was in the yard clearing away the broken tiles and she was standing next to her brand-new husband, bare arm to bare arm. The night had been divided into rising wind, racket on the roof, fading wind. One of the boughs of the red beech in the front garden had snapped, and the bare twigs were scratching across a window at the front of the house. 'We'll have to change that pane,' her mother-in-law had told her father-in-law when he was finished with the tiles. 'It's dangerous.' Her father-in-law had pulled open the door of the cabinet. 'After we've cleared up,' he said, taking a gold medal from a shelf and buffing it up against his chest. She had looked at Zeeger, willing him to look back at her, but he just stood there as if he'd been nailed to the ground, staring at his grandmother's face. The Frisian tail clock on the wall ticked very loudly.

She doesn't know where she is, and when she realises, she doesn't want to know. She pricks up her ears. Was she really just woken by a falling tile? She looks up through the rafters, trying to see if there are more holes than there were yesterday afternoon. Beneath her: shuffling and snorting in the bullpen. A filthy light fills the barn, as if the day doesn't want to get properly started. She struggles up to a sitting position, rubs her sore neck with one hand and remembers the dull creak from earlier. Was that her? Are her bones creaking? The parade sword is lying in exactly the same spot as before; the smooth leather scabbard is warm and oily, nothing like her own dry neck. She tears open the packet of biscuits and eats one whole compartment. Then she unscrews the cap of the water bottle and drinks a few musty mouthfuls. She lies down again, on her right side this time, hoping to go back to sleep for a while.

Zeeger's face, half a century ago. She was so desperate for him to look at her. Shivering in that bedroom with the clivias and sansevierias on the windowsill, the resonant tick of the Frisian clock, the cracked windowpane that would never be replaced, her mother-in-law walking in and out. But no, he stared straight ahead at his dead grandmother. His place on the farm had come one generation closer.

Someone's walking around the yard. Jan, she thinks, because Zeeger and Klaas walk very differently, if only because those two almost always wear clogs. Is he coming into the barn? She clears her throat quietly. Not that she's planning on saying anything, but still. The footsteps move away again. She listens so carefully she can even hear Rekel shuffling along. She swallows. It's quiet.

Jan always does a circuit when he comes home. She imagines his route: past the dead sheep, a little further to the collapsed rabbit hutch with the leftover straw and rock-hard pellets, the cracked concrete slabs, a stack of half-rotten gateposts, past the back of the cowshed, then inside where there's still a mound of dry silage in the feeding passage, maybe he'll even pull open the toilet door and be surprised by the toilet bowl – unexpectedly clean – then through the feeding passage to the back of the barn, out again, past the old dungheap, behind the sheep shed, then left onto the dusty path along-side the ditch, with the silo on the left and Kees Brak's plum trees on the other side, then cutting across the yard at an angle to the big threshing doors . . .

He comes into the barn. She hears him walking up to the bullpen. Keep quiet, lie still. Horrible boy. Has he got some-thing to say? The bull snorts, she hears his horns clicking against the iron bars.

'I'm taking your bike!' he shouts.

Don't say anything, just lie still, let him see what it's like.

It stays quiet down below for a long time. Then he walks to the side doors. She doesn't want to say anything, she really doesn't, but when she's sure he's outside, she calls out, 'Don't change the computer!' She covers her mouth with one hand, laying the other on her stomach. A little later she hears something fall into the ditch, followed by thrashing and splashing. Jan says something she can't make out. Then there's just the swallows flying in and out constantly and the snorting of that superfluous lump of meat. How long before I start on the advocaat? she wonders.

Christmas Trees

Zeeger Kaan watches from the bench by the side door as his son picks up Rekel and carefully clambers down to the ditch. 'Swim!' Jan shouts, dropping the dog. His body is only visible from the chest up and now goes lower. 'No, don't get out straight away. You need to swim, and then lie down in the shade.' Jan turns and climbs back up the bank of the ditch. 'Stupid dog,' Zeeger hears him say. As Jan comes towards him, Rekel creeps up out of the ditch with his head hanging and his tail between his legs. He just stands there, without shaking himself dry, watching balefully as the man who just dumped him in the water walks away.

'I'm off,' Jan says. He goes into the laundry and re-emerges almost immediately with the green bucket.

'OK,' says Zeeger. 'I'll come and have a look a bit later.'

His son looks at him. 'She said something.'

He nods.

'I'm not allowed to change the computer.'

'Ha. The things she worries about.'

Jan goes around the corner of the house into the back garden. Zeeger waits, wipes his forehead with one hand and looks at the washing, which, if the wind gets up a little, might dry in an hour. Rekel comes over to him and only now shakes himself dry. 'Ah, nice,' he says. The dog whimpers and lies down against the leg of the garden table.

He crosses the lawn between the chestnut trees and looks down the road in the direction of the village. Jan is riding slowly, the bucket swinging back and forth on the handle-bars, banging against his knee. Then he brakes, gets off, puts the bucket on the pannier rack and pulls the straps up over it. He looks around for a moment before continuing on his way. Zeeger Kaan watches until he's become a blotch that turns left, into the village. To the north the road is empty, and when he looks in the other direction it turns out to be empty to the south too. Although it's still early, the countryside is shimmering: the trunks of the young elms diffracting in the bands of light. Even though he can't see the trees that well, he still shakes his head disdainfully. They're supposed to be resistant, this variety. Just like the last variety. Straight ahead is a wood. Owned by some guy from the city who, the first time Klaas spoke to him, said things like, 'Nah, you know, just shaking up the rigidity around here a bit.' And, later, 'Lovely, feet in the mud, just planting away. All this free oxygen.' Or, 'It's my way of getting a breath of fresh air to blow through this polluted world, know what I mean?' A wood, in the middle of the polder. Hopefully without any elms, because they'd all just die. Behind the wood, directly west, it's hazy: a broad strip of filthy-looking sky is advancing.

In the garage he's greeted by a voice from the radio that plays day and night. Zeeger Kaan leaves it on because he thinks music and voices scare off burglars. His wife turns it off now and then. She finds it 'lonely': a pointless radio playing for nobody. In winter, with a slight easterly, he hears it when he wakes up in the night through the window he keeps ajar. He doesn't find it 'lonely'. He investigates what's missing from his workbench. Jan's taken the white paint, a few sheets of sandpaper and a brush. Maybe a rag too, and ammonia, there's a very slight hint of a pungent smell and the red bottle has been moved. He pokes his nose out of the door to look around the corner at the outside tap. The bricks under it are wet. Jan must have moistened a rag. Rekel is lying in front of the open door, full in the sun. 'Go and lie in the shade, will you, dog?' he says. The animal beats the yellow clinker bricks with his tail but doesn't stand up.

'*Radio North-Holland goes classic*,' a woman's voice says in English, and then violin music really does come from the radio. He resumes his work from yesterday. A Christmas tree made out of seventeen wooden slats. A long vertical one, four for the base and twelve as branches, each circle of four a little smaller than the one below it. The glue is dry, now he can start attaching the aluminium candle-holders. In a corner of the garage there's a whole collection of Christmas trees: some untreated, some painted green. At least fifty of them. Attaching the candleholders is precision work, they're fragile and he wants them all in exactly the same spot. Fifteen minutes later he tacks the last one in position and puts the Christmas tree with the rest of the collection. In a week there'll be another car boot sale in Sint Maartenszee. There'll be Germans there and Germans always buy Christmas trees, even when it's scorching. Then he remembers the flat tyre. He takes the red tin with the puncture repair kit down from a shelf and whistles along to the violins.

Hydrangeas

The baker with the chapped face is standing in his neat front garden. A gravel path leads from the road to the front door and is flanked on both sides by low box-hedge squares. Insides the squares are hydrangeas, which he manages to keep blue with copper scrap and some other stuff he picked up in a garden centre. They're just starting to flower, but the leaves are drooping, they could do with a few watering cans.

'What are you doing there, twiddling your thumbs?' A fellow villager with a little dog.

'What about you?'

'At least I'm taking the dog for a walk.'

'I don't have a dog.'

'I know. Why don't you get one?'

'Yeah.'

'Then you'd always have a reason to go outside.'

'Aren't I allowed to stand in my own front garden?'

'Of course, why not? It's unbearable inside anyway.'

The men are quiet for a moment. 'Off on holiday soon?' the baker asks.

'Already been. A week in Burgh-Haamstede. Beautiful. You?'

'I might go yet.'

'Bye, then.'

'See you.'

On the other side of the street there are tall fences around the snack bar, the Eating Corner. Have been for months. The windows are boarded up too. According to the large sign on the patio, two new apartments are going to replace it. The baker sighs and goes inside. The radio in the kitchen is playing classical music. That's strange, Radio North-Holland never has violin music at this time of day. Although there's nobody in the house to change stations, he checks that the radio is still tuned to Radio North-Holland, then walks through the hall to the living room, where he stands at the large back window. Two or three kilometres away there's another road parallel to this one, recognisable by the young elms planted along it, and between his back garden and that road – the Kruisweg – nothing but drab green grass with a kind of desert sky above, that's how he imagines it. He has jammed some newspapers behind the pot plants on the windowsill. He doesn't know exactly what purpose they serve, but it's something his wife always did and that's why he does it now.

His daughter lives in Limburg. South Limburg. He's started to hum along to the violins. A dog. Why not actually? Not a big one, but medium-sized, one of the ones with a German name. A schnauzer, that's it. Or is that the kind of dog you have to get trimmed every couple of months? Suddenly he's had enough of the view. He goes into the hall and opens the door to the shop. It's darker here than anywhere else in the house, with yellowed lace curtains hanging in the enormous window. Nothing's changed in this room. The counter's still there; the cabinet that used to contain the zwieback, rye and gingerbread hasn't been moved. Everything's just empty. He flicks the lights over the counter on and off a couple of times. He reads *Blom's Breadery* in mirror writing through the curtains. 'Blom's Breadery?!' He can still hear his wife saying it, much too long ago. 'What's wrong with Blom's Bread and Pastries?' He'd mumbled something about the seventies being just around the corner. A new era, a different era, elegant lettering on the Volkswagen van. 'You're weird,' she'd said, but without any real spite.

A gleaming, light-grey 1968 Volkswagen van, Type T2a. Tailgate and sliding side door, packed full at the start of the round with bread and pastries, cakes and white rolls, and everything still within easy reach. The streamlined VW logo prominent on the front, beautifully central between the two headlights; the chrome hubcaps and door handles; the red leather seats and front-door lining. The dealer in Den Helder told him, not without pride, that the chassis had Y-shaped steel supports and that 'in the event of an accident' the steering column would fold forward to prevent him from being crushed. The Saturday farm run in particular was fantastic at the start. At the start. Fresh bread and fresh leather, as if the two smells belonged together and were inseparable, made for each other.

He flicks the lights on and off once again, then strides through to the kitchen, where he pulls the large watering can out of the cupboard under the sink.

While emptying it between the hydrangeas for the third

time, he sees a cyclist approaching on the other side of the canal that bisects the village. With difficulty, he straightens up; the watering cans are heavy and his back is old. A man with a green bucket on the pannier rack, wearing shorts and a T-shirt. Short red hair. Early forties. 'Hmm,' goes the baker with the chapped face, putting the half-emptied watering can down on the gravel. He keeps watching the red-headed man until he turns off and rides onto the grounds of the former Polder House, where he slowly rounds the rose bed on the left before disappearing around the side of the building. The baker sticks a hand into the watering can and scoops up some water, bends forward a little and rubs his face with it, even though it's no longer that cool.

'So! At least now you're doing something.' The villager with the little dog is on his way back home.

'What kind of dog is that anyway?'

'This? Jack Russell. Rough coat. Have I got you thinking?'

'Ah.'

'Jesus, man, the sweat's pouring out of you. I'd sit down if I were you.'

'Yes, I'm about to.'

'We're going to get some rain. At last.'

'You reckon?'

'I do. You can put that watering can away. We'll be getting gallons of the stuff and you won't have to pay a penny for it.' The villager walks on without saying goodbye.

Not one like that anyway, the baker with the chapped face thinks. Too small. He pours the remaining water out over the gravel path without noticing, then walks in through the open front door, puts the watering can on the draining board and sits down, both hands neatly placed on the table in front of him.

The old Queen. She was there once, in front of the Polder House, long ago, when the light-grey Volkswagen van was still gleaming. She was presented with two pygmy goats. By the district council if his memory serves him right. What happened to those goats? Did the driver stuff them in the boot of that big black limo? Did they spend years eating grass in the back garden of Soestdijk Palace? I've got photos of them somewhere, of that whole visit, he thinks. Lots and lots of photos. She was inside the Polder House too, of course. I saw the table, he thinks. White tablecloth, plates and glasses, vases with sweet peas. I delivered freshly baked bread there in the morning. Ordinary bread, nothing special, that's what the district clerk said. Brown and white rolls, fruit loaf. It was only after she left that I started on my round of the surrounding farms. Yes, there are photos. Later. Now I'll sit down.

He looks at the calendar, hanging between the two narrow windows. Saturday. There are words written there that he can't read from this distance, but he knows what they say. *Dinner at Dinie's.* He sweeps imaginary crumbs off the tabletop.

Coffee

'Look, Daddy, a gold ring!'
   'Nice,' says Klaas. 'Where'd you get that?'
   'From a plant.'

'A plant?'

'Uh-huh, it's broken now. It was there.' Dieke points at the floor.

His gaze goes from the floor up to the windowsill, where one of the Christmas cactuses is now in a plastic tub and listing to one side. Then he has a closer look at the large ring. It reminds him of something, something from the old days. 'You going to put it in your bag?'

'Of course.'

'Can I have a look in that bag sometime?'

'Of course not.'

'Why not?'

'It's my bag.'

'Can't argue with that.'

'Can I have it back now?'

He hands the ring back to his daughter and rustles the newspaper. When they've finished the paper it goes over to the other side of the ditch, and the newspaper from the other side of the ditch comes here. The breakfast things are still on the table, but the mid-morning coffee is already dripping through the filter. It's almost ten o'clock. A long way to go to midday, he thinks, and after that, a much longer afternoon.

'I'd still rather you didn't hide the bag so far in under your bed,' his wife says.

'Why not?'

'It's dusty.'

'So what?'

'Yes, what.'

'Otherwise people will look in it.'

'No they won't. Your father and I aren't going to look in it if you say we're not allowed to.'

'I don't want to go to the swimming pool.'

'What?'

'I want to go see Uncle Jan.'

'Where is he?'

'In the village. He just left. On Grandma's bike.'

'Haven't you arranged something with Evelien?'

'Doesn't matter. He had something hanging off his handlebars.'

'It *does* matter.'

'I don't like it at the swimming pool!'

'Yesterday,' Klaas says, 'talking to Jan, you were full of it.'

'That was yesterday! Now it's today.'

'Whereabouts in the village has Jan gone?' his wife asks.

I didn't ask him anything, Klaas thinks. I don't really have a clue. 'He's probably gone to the churchyard.'

'The cemetery.'

'Huh?'

'It's a cemetery, the church is miles away.'

'Yeah! I want to go there!' Dieke screeches.

'You think that's fun?'

'Of course! He said he was going there to work. I can help him, can't I?'

'And then every ten minutes you'll want to come home again I suppose?'

'Or start whining for Evelien? Wouldn't you be better off going to the swimming pool?'

'No!'

[54]

'Coffee?'

'Lovely,' says Klaas.

His wife pours the coffee. Big mugfuls. She opens a cupboard and gets out a packet of biscuits, tearing it open with one index finger. The mugs and biscuits go on the table, between the teacups, jam and chocolate sprinkles. Klaas takes milk and sugar, his wife drinks her coffee black. Dieke is quiet, letting the gold ring slide through her fingers and not whinging for a glass of lemonade. Klaas has put the paper aside and rolled a cigarette. His wife has already lit one. Now and then he looks at her over the top of his brown mug. She has a dour expression on her face and keeps her eyes fixed either on the tabletop or out of the window, maybe staring at the withered grass in the drinking trough. He doesn't know what she thinks about it, that grass. She doesn't seem to mind it too much; she's never attempted to fill it with a few violets or some ivy-leaved geraniums. The kitchen is blue with smoke.

'You'll take her?' she asks.

'Me?'

'Sure, why not?'

'I've got things to do.'

'Really? What, for instance?'

Say something immediately, don't wait, it doesn't matter what. 'Clean out the cowshed.'

'Oh.'

'See?'

She gets up, pulls the jug out of the coffee maker and tops them up. Then she stubs out her cigarette, stuffs a third biscuit into her mouth and looks menacingly at Dieke

– who is still being as quiet as a mouse. 'The cemetery,' she mumbles. 'What next?'

After the coffee, his wife and Dieke leave on the bike for the village. For appearances' sake, Klaas walks through the front garden to the cowshed, where he really doesn't want to be. Not that it's that much work: clear the mound of silage from the feeding passage with the tractor, muck out the calf stalls, give them a spray with the high-pressure hose and you're done. Monday, I'll do it Monday. It's the weekend now, and maybe in a couple of days it won't be so outrageously hot. He pulls open the toilet door. It smells fresh, of lemon, the bowl is spotless and there's water in it. He doesn't know who does this, who takes the trouble of coming here every now and then to flush the toilet and maybe even clean it with the brush. There are no spiderwebs in sight and even the light-brown tiles are clean. He unzips his flies, lowers his jeans, turns and sits down. He leaves the door ajar. After wiping his arse – there's even a roll of toilet paper under the calendar from the company that sold them the tractor – he tugs his jeans back up. The calendar's behind. He rips off the old days, tears them up and throws the pieces into the toilet bowl. He hesitates about whether or not to push the button on the cistern. In the end he does, but doesn't stay to watch the water gush through. He closes the door softly behind him.

On a shelf in the milking parlour is the old radio that used to go on twice a day. Sometimes he forgot to turn it on and the cows reminded him by getting restless. He turns it on. Classical music, violins. He twists the knob back a little too energetically and the radio tumbles off the shelf, landing corner first on the white-tiled floor and bursting open. The batteries skid into the milking pit, the volume knob rolls out through the open door and into the feeding passage. Klaas watches it roll away, then follows it without tidying up the mess.

Stepping out through the front doors onto the concrete path that leads to the road, he sees a hazy strip of clouds in the west. Rekel bumps up against his legs. 'Here, boy,' he says, leading the way through the front garden and back to the yard. There, he picks the heavy dog up and descends carefully to the ditch, near the bridge. With a slight swinging movement, he throws Rekel into the water, overbalances, comes close to falling in after the dog, but is able to grasp the bridge railing just in time to steady himself. The dog circles back, snorting, makes as if to climb up out of the ditch on Klaas's side, then changes his mind and swims over to the other side where the bank isn't as steep. He climbs up out of the water like an otter, his tail stuck to his belly and his head down to the ground, then shakes himself thoroughly once he's reached the top of the bank. Only then does he turn around. Klaas and the dog exchange glances. 'Why don't you do that yourself sometimes?' Klaas asks. Rekel just stares at him impassively, then saunters along beside the ditch to the far corner of the garden and starts an extended sniffing of the root of a willow. It's the last pollard in the row of five: runty and stunted for years now, with a small head, probably because it's too close to a much older pear tree and has never had enough light and air. Or is it because of that other dog? Is that what Rekel can smell, even though it was buried there some twenty-five years ago?

Shit

The woman who thinks she's responsible for the cemetery leans on her worktop with both hands to look out through her kitchen window and across her back garden at the hedge around the cemetery. The hedge is some kind of conifer and thick, except directly across from her back garden, where a section suddenly turned light brown two years ago. After which, council gardeners removed quite a few conifers. Without replacing them. Besides the hole and the headstones, the woman can't see a thing. She takes her hands off the worktop and shuffles through to the living room, glancing at the calendar on the way past. It's one she bought late last year with paintings by Ada Breedveld. Not that she'd ever heard of Ada Breedveld: the paintings just appealed to her. *Herm dinner* is written under today's date.

There are newspaper cuttings spread out over the coffee table. The light in the stifling-hot through room is yellow; she made sure to lower the awning early this morning. Apart from a bra, she's not wearing anything on her upper body at all. She sits down in one of the easy chairs and shuffles the clippings. She doesn't need to read them, she knows perfectly well what they're about. 'Yes, Benno,' she tells her dog. 'Yes, yes, yes.' Next to the clippings is the framed photo of her husband. 'We'll go over there again later,' she tells the dog, which is enormous, with a broad head and lots of fur. 'Have they gone completely mad?' Shit: that's what the clippings are about. Cow shit. And about 'an unidentified vandal or vandals' and 'an investigation that has been launched'. She hasn't seen a single police officer over there once. Now she stops to think about it, she never sees any police anywhere, not even cycling or driving past.

The dog, which has been staring out the window lethargically, walks over to the woman and starts to lick her knees. She pulls her skirt up a little and tucks the fabric into the waistband. 'Good boy,' she says. 'Your mistress is boiling.' She slips a thumb under a bra strap to wipe away the sweat. Just when she's about to get up to turn on the radio, she sees a woman passing on a bike with a child on the back. A red-headed girl who, judging by her mouth, is talking nineteen to the dozen. She's wearing a small ruck-sack. She doesn't know the woman; there are so many people she doesn't know in the village. She only moved back from Den Helder after her husband died, mainly because he wanted to be buried here. If it had been up to her, she would never have come back. People have left, died, been born, moved, disappeared. She has no desire to start over again. There are all kinds mixed up together on the new estate, even a Negro and a family of Muslims, though she doesn't have a clue what country *they're* from. She's standing there in her bra, her thumb now under the other bra strap, and she sees the woman and the child both look up at the front of her house. I'm virtually naked, she thinks to herself, only just realising. I'm standing here on display for the whole neighbourhood. Next thing, that Negro will come walking past! She tries to think of nasty things about Negroes – sneaking into other people's houses, stealing, lying, that little black kid, is he the Negro's son? – but doesn't get very far; she doesn't want the word 'rape' in her head, even if that's nasty too, but it's the one that sticks. She hurries into the hall and, from the hall, upstairs to put on a blouse.

Shells

Counting trees. That's what Dieke does until she gets to a number that's too big for her. She starts again, but is soon distracted by other things. Farms, the prospect of going to the cemetery, where she's never been before, passing tree trunks, her mother's hips that grow and shrink under her hands, grow and shrink, a grey heron standing in the ditch as still as if it's in a photo. When they pass the sign for the village, she says, 'Will you do the houses?'

'Dilemma,' her mother says. Big white house. Tall, more than anything, with a red-tiled roof.

'Moving On.' House with geraniums on the windowsills, and curtains.

'Let 'Em Talk.' Junk in the front garden, shopping trolleys, railway sleepers, no plants in the windows.

'Eben-Ezer.'

'What's that mean, Mummy?'

'You know I don't know what it means, Diek.'

'Why not?'

'I just don't. Why do you keep asking? I'll look it up for you one day. Hi, hello!' Her mother waves at a woman pulling up weeds in her front garden. The bike wobbles. Dieke grips her mother's hips extra tight.

The Eating Corner. Boarded-up windows, tall fences, weeds.

'That lady should work here,' she says.

'You're not wrong there. Do you want to go through the new estate or shall we go past the Polder House?'

Dieke has to think about that. Usually there's more happening and more to see in the new estate. The swimming pool is behind the new houses, near the football pitches. Her bottom's starting to hurt from sitting on the pannier rack, she wants to get off the bike sooner rather than later, but she doesn't know which route is shorter. And she thinks of Evelien, who might already be at the swimming pool.

'Well? We haven't got all day.'

'New estate,' she says.

'Linquenda.'

'Yes!'

'Yes, what?'

'Just yes.'

'Oh, that's all right then.'

'What's Linquenda mean?'

Her mother doesn't answer. Dieke feels her hips grow and shrink a little more urgently. In the new estate hardly any of the houses have names. There *is* one, just before they get to the cemetery. The Old Stamping Ground.

'What's a stamping ground?' Dieke asks.

'A place.'

'A place?'

'Somewhere you spend a lot of time. The old stamping ground means a place from the old days.'

'But this house is new, isn't it?'

'Yes, Diek.'

'It's not old.'

'Would you like to go back? You can ring the doorbell and ask what exactly they're referring to. Does that mouth of yours ever stop?'

'No! Don't go back!'

'That's a relief.'

'Don't you have to go to work?'

'No, otherwise I wouldn't be taking you to the cemetery right now, would I?'

'Yes,' says Dieke. Then she says, 'No.'

'And you do realise that you have to stay with Jan, I hope. I can't just pop back to pick you up, and if you want to leave, nobody will know.'

'Doesn't Uncle Jan have a phone?'

'I don't think so.'

'Doesn't matter. I want to stay there anyway.'

They arrive at the cemetery's rear entrance. A narrow gate, with two very straight trees next to it. Dieke jumps off the back of the bike and dashes onto the deserted lawn on the other side of the gate.

'Wait!'

She waits, without turning back to look at her mother. It's just like a football pitch. A bit further up there's a hedge, with an opening for the path. Uncle Jan must be behind that hedge. As soon as her mother has caught up, she walks on.

'What's this?' she asks.

'This is for when there's no more room on that side.'

When she reaches the opening in the hedge, Dieke recoils. In front of her is a wheat field of stones, stones everywhere. But there are also plants and bushes and shrubs. Uncle Jan is nowhere in sight. The path goes in two directions. She feels a leaf in the hedge. It's the same as along the side of the yard at home, only there it's not trimmed.

'Jan!' her mother calls, but not very loudly.

He appears in front of them, popping up between all those stones. 'Here,' he says, raising an arm in the air. They walk over to him, Dieke more slowly than her mother, listening to the shells crunching under the soles of her sandals. The shells under her mother's shoes crunch a lot louder. Uncle Jan comes out onto the path.

'Hi, Jan,' her mother says.

'Hi,' he says.

'Dieke wants to be here with you, she doesn't want to go to the swimming pool.'

'Why not?'

'She goes there every day. She gets bored.'

Dieke keeps quiet, twisting the toe of one sandal down into the crushed shells and not looking at her mother or Uncle Jan. Her face is blank.

'She can stay here then. It's fine by me.' He looks at her. 'I'll take care of her. Will you be careful too?'

'Uh-huh,' says Dieke.

Her mother starts to turn away. 'I'll come back to pick her up a bit later. You can count on her wanting to go to the swimming pool in half an hour.'

'I won't,' Dieke says.

Her mother walks past her without looking at her. Crunch, crunch, crunch and she's gone.

Dieke keeps staring at the path.

'Is your mother a bit cross with you, Diek?'

'I broke a plant,' she says.

'Did you?'

'And I got up too early. She said.'

'How early?'

'Five o'clock?' she tries.

'That is *really* early. But it was probably light by then too. It hardly gets dark now.'

'I don't know.' She looks up. Uncle Jan looks a lot like her dad, but at the same time he doesn't look like him at all. 'You haven't got a top on.'

'No, I was hot.'

'Is that your T-shirt on your head?'

'Yep.'

'Look. I've got my grey dress on.'

He clears his throat.

'Sleeveless.'

'Smart thinking.'

'With purple flowers.' Dieke looks around cautiously. Now she's here, she sees that it's not just stones standing up, there are stones lying flat on the ground too. They're like radiators, she can feel the heat coming off them. The cemetery is more or less completely flat. It only has one tree, but it's a very big one.

'What have you got in your rucksack?' Uncle Jan asks.

'A drink.' Dieke unzips the rucksack and pulls out a Jip and Janneke drinking cup. 'See?'

'Aha.'

'And two apples and two bananas. They're for you too.'

They've already had a really long talk and Uncle Jan started it.

Now he steps off the path and goes over to a small stone in the second row. He kneels down next to it.

Dieke doesn't know what to do. First she puts the cup back in her bag. Then she takes three steps towards Uncle Jan, and that takes her up to a stone in the first row. She lays a hand on it, but jerks it back straight away. Too hot. There's a tin of paint and a green bucket with a wet rag draped over the side on the ground next to her uncle, along with a few sheets of paper and some white things she doesn't recognise. A paintbrush just like the ones she uses with her watercolours is balanced on top of the tin. Her uncle picks up a screwdriver and starts using it to chip away at the white paint on the stone. Something goes wrong: the end of the screwdriver makes a scraping noise and Uncle Jan starts to swear.

'You're not allowed to swear,' she says.

'Who says so?'

She takes another step forward. 'What are you doing?' she asks.

Blouse

It takes a while for her to find an appropriate blouse. She's not looking for an appropriate blouse at all. She shakes her head, but that doesn't help get rid of the Negro and the word 'rape'. She has to stretch out on the bed for a moment, closing the bedroom door first to keep Benno out on the landing. Her bra straps are pinching, that thing has to come off, and while she's removing it, both hands accidentally touch her breasts. She does her best to think about the baker with the chapped face – it's Saturday, they'll be seeing each other this evening – but fails. He has a name, just like everyone else, but she thinks: baker. There's an open window but the warm air isn't stirring.

The Negro climbs in through the open window like some kind of big African cat. Her skirt and girdle are pinching too, they need pushing down. Why is it so hot? It's June but it feels like an oppressive day much later in the summer, as if there are already brown leaves littering her front garden. He's wearing a kind of apron, a loincloth but otherwise naked. Naked and gleaming with sweat or oil, some magical African lotion. Benno barks. The Negro's lips part, revealing teeth and an astonishingly pale, pink tongue. Dinie Grint opens her mouth too and lays her hands by her sides. After stretching out beside her on the bed, the Negro tears off his loincloth and she feels his penis pressing against her thigh. 'I don't want this,' she mumbles. 'No, no.' The Negro shuts her up and she grabs at his penis, which, in contrast to the rest of his body, is matt, not gleaming. Her mouth fills with saliva that tastes of bitter leaves, her fingertips glide over veins that . . . Benno barks. 'Quiet!' she shouts. The Negro was gone for a moment, but now he's back again, bigger and harder than ever. Swelling, pumping male blood under her fingers, yes. It's as if she's offering her throat to this African feline, her throat, her lower body, pushing up and forward, she wants him inside her, she wants to grab and pull and guide, but instead she grips the side of her double bed with one hand and he's in her anyway, he can manage that fine by himself. She's happy for him to go very deep and fast, or slow, whatever he likes, and he doesn't need to be told twice – God, he's so big – and now she wants him to get out of her and stick it in her mouth. He does that too, of course. But not right away. Slowly he crawls up on all fours. 'No, don't,' she murmurs. 'Stop it, now.' The Negro has become his penis, a penis with heavy balls dragging over her nipples. The head already pushing against her lips. The baker, she thinks. The baker.

Not the baker, her son. He's lying on his back, his underpants down around his ankles, one knee raised, the other on the floor, the jeans with the leather knee patches in a heap next to him, black pubic hair that comes as a shock to her, and the Kaan boy, the redhead, and her own head, of course, sticking up through the trapdoor in the floor of the garage attic, thinking, I don't want this, look away, go back down the ladder; and not reacting to that, continuing to stare at her son, that beautiful black-haired boy with an erect penis amongst that unexpected pubic hair, and that red-headed Kaan, naked, with his head on her son's beautiful belly and his hand on his own crotch, and still her own head sticking up through that hatch, and the thought of that bloke of hers, the hopeless drip who never paid her any attention but preferred to go out and play pool or spend the whole evening slumped on the sofa staring at a conveyor belt with prizes on it, and a strange longing for her very own son, so young still, so unspoilt, but that longing comes up in her so intensely and so suddenly that she blushes and when that cheeky red-headed Kaan stares back at her – but probably doesn't even notice her because her son's penis is between them, the penis she doesn't want to see, but can't avoid seeing – the thought: get out of here.

She sits up much too quickly, the blood rushes to her head, making her dizzy. The Negro dissolves in the hot air, but his tongue and penis have left their mark. She doesn't want to think about her son when the Negro's here. That's not right. It's not allowed. She suddenly feels sick. Not bitter leaves – bile. She no longer grabs at heavy balls, but at her bra, lying on the carpet next to the bed. She puts it on quickly and pulls her girdle and skirt on even faster. Despite the dizziness, she jumps up off the bed, pulls open the wardrobe door and grabs a blouse without even looking. Benno barks. She opens the door, pushes the big dog out of the way with one knee and goes into the bathroom. The first thing she sees is her raven hair in the mirror. The second is the wild look in her eyes. On the shelf under the mirror is a pot of Wella Dark Brown. Not Wella Black, that makes her look ridiculous. She bends forward and turns on the cold tap.

Straw

She's heard him all right. Maybe he took off his clogs and is now standing on the concrete in dusty socks. He must have been there at least five minutes; is he staring the bull down to keep it quiet? She might as well say something for a change. 'You never think of Mother's Day.'

Silence.

'Do you even know when it is, Mother's Day?'

'December?'

'The second Sunday in May!'

Silence.

A daughter knows things like that. A daughter would visit in May with presents, or at least ring. *She* would have come. She scratches her stomach again. Is it the straw that's making her itchy? Her stomach's never itchy otherwise. Or is it the heat? 'What time is it?'

'You really want to know?'

'No, of course not.'

'Ten thirty.'

She can't help it, she has to laugh. To herself. She pictures him standing there with his head back. 'Where is everyone? Have they all gone to the churchyard?'

'The cemetery.'

'Huh?'

'Is there a church there?'

She's still smiling. 'You know that better than anyone.'

'Yes.'

Ten thirty. Way too soon to come down off the straw. 'Have you been stirring them up?'

'Of course not.'

'Don't lie.'

'I never lie. And who exactly do you mean by "them"?'

'Jan, of course. And Johan.'

'Johan?'

'Why does everyone down there keep shouting out "Johan" as if they're so surprised?'

'He's not even here.'

'No, not yet. But soon enough.' She drinks some water. The bottle is starting to get quite empty. 'So, where's Klaas?'

'I don't know.'

Swallows flying in and out. Spiderwebs, very old ones, like grey wool. And then suddenly the sound of concentrate sliding in the wooden silo that forms one pillar-like corner of the straw loft, even though it's been a very long time since there was any feed in it at all.

'And another thing, you're not my mother.'

'I'm your children's mother.'

'You're not *my* mother.'

'Ah, man, go back to your Christmas trees.'

That's shut him up. For a moment.

'You coming down?'

'No.'

'Aren't you hungry?'

'Of course I'm hungry!'

'Come down then.'

'No.'

Now it's finished. She waits. Tilts the water bottle; the water sloshes back and forth, growing warmer and mustier. More sliding in the wooden silo. Is there a rat in there? The noise is drowned out by the swelling roar of a jet fighter. During exercises, the pilots do their best to fly as low over the trees and farmhouses as they can, and for a second Anna Kaan is scared the plane's going to go straight through the barn. It doesn't.

'Talk to me!' He's waited until the sound of the jet has died away completely. She tilts the bottle one way, then the other. Beams, spiderwebs, a swinging rope that hasn't been used for years, cane, tile laths.

'Have you got the parade sword up there?'

And of course the peepholes to the outside, even if there's nothing out there to see.

'What do you intend to do with that?'

She takes one of its two red tassels in her hand. Nothing, she thinks. Or can she do better than that?

'I'll think of something. You'll see.' Oh yes you will, she thinks.

'I'm about to go. I've fixed my tyre. Then you'll be stuck here alone.'

I'm already stuck here alone.

'Talk to me!'

It's hard not to say anything. She has to be firm. Now he starts to sigh. The bull, which has been silent until now, joins in by snorting. It's almost too much. And all that when she's not even a hundred per cent about being up on the straw.

'When's Father's Day?'

She knows, but she's not going to take the bait.

'I'm going now,' Zeeger calls.

No, stay. Sit down somewhere, on a leftover bale of hay, on a sack of pellets, on the old workbench, on the tray of the hay wagon. On the concrete floor if necessary. Zeeger, don't go.

'If I'm not here, I'm off with Jan.'

Anna Kaan stops tilting the bottle. She rests it on her

stomach and stares at the rectangle of light over her head. Then she starts to count the tiles, first to the left of the gap, then to the right.

'June!' Zeeger calls up, already outside and with his clogs back on. 'The third Sunday in June!'

Birds

Dieke thinks about what *she* says when someone like Grandpa asks her what she's doing. It depends what she's doing, of course. If she's drawing, she'll say, 'I'm drawing.' But sometimes she's really deep into her drawing and then she doesn't say anything, if only because the tip of her tongue is in the way. Grandma's never once asked her what she's doing. But it's not a hard question. Uncle Jan could easily come up with something. His shoulder blade goes up and down, he keeps scratching and poking, he keeps swearing under his breath. She takes a couple of careful backward steps until she's back on the path with the broken shells. She squeezes her eyes half shut. There's her rucksack. First, a drink. She gets the Jip and Janneke drinking cup out of the bag and shakes it from side to side before taking a couple of sips. The water's already warm. An apple? No, she'll save that for later. Anyway, she wants to eat the apples with Uncle Jan, not by herself. The bag shouldn't be on the path, she needs to put it somewhere tidy. She looks over at the big tree. There's a bench under it, in the shade. That's a good spot.

It's not really that much cooler by the bench, but the

white shells don't hurt her eyes here and the wooden seat isn't hot to touch. She thinks of her red sunglasses, lying around somewhere at home, although she can't quite remember where. On the back of the bench there's a metal plate with writing she can't read. She sits down next to her bag and takes her time to look around. All she can see of Uncle Jan is his head with the T-shirt wrapped around it. He's talking to himself, but she can't hear what he's saying. Now he scratches his head with his fingers in his hair. She rubs her knees, which are still slightly black from the soil in the pot with the . . . 'Cactus,' she says. 'Cactus, cactus . . .' No matter how hard she rubs, her knees won't come clean. 'Christmas cactus!'

She looks up at the tree. Sitting next to each other on a low branch are two small birds. From this angle she can only see their heads. She stands up to get a better look. Both of the birds have their beaks wide open and she can almost hear them sucking the air in and blowing it out again. Are they sparrows? Or starlings? They must be a mummy and a daddy. Do they live in this big tree? She can't see a birdhouse hung up on it anywhere. She takes another mouthful of warm water. As she's carefully putting the cup back in her rucksack, a jet fighter tears overhead. She looks up at the birds in fright, but they don't do a thing, not even rustling a feather or snapping their beaks shut. It's like they don't even hear the roar of the plane. 'Hmm,' she says, wiping her forehead with one hand and heading off to investigate the surroundings.

There aren't actually many paths in the cemetery. One long path from the Polder House to where she's standing, and then a square that leads to the one she and her mother came in by. Uncle Jan is at work on the square. There are wide stones, tall stones, white and black stones, a blue stone, a stone the light shines through. Sometimes there's only a thick stone lying on the ground. Cemetery. What does that mean anyway? A little bit further along there's a big hole in the tall hedge, on the side with the new estate. She doesn't know if she's allowed to just walk between all the hot stones, but she still wants to go over to look at that hole. Just before she gets there, she accidentally kicks over a vase on the side of a rectangle with little stones in it. There's a bunch of flowers in the vase, very old flowers, because when they fall onto the ground they crumble into dust. She looks around, picks up the vase and puts it back where it was. There's only a very small chip out of the top. Nothing too bad.

She reaches the hole in the hedge and looks out over a lawn and a wide ditch along the back gardens of a row of houses. The houses are a good bit lower than the cemetery. There's someone standing at one of the windows, a woman with black hair. She starts tapping on the window. With a ring, Dieke thinks, because it makes a loud ringing sound. Is that for her? She doesn't think so, and because she doesn't think so, she doesn't do anything. She just keeps standing where she's standing and staring at the woman.

'Dieke!'

She turns and walks, even more carefully than before, between the stones to the shell path. 'Yes!' she calls.

'Where are you?'

'Here!' She walks back past the bench, the birds and her

bag to where Uncle Jan is working. 'Do you want an apple?' she asks.

'No. Later.'

'What are you doing?' Just try again.

'I'm doing up this headstone.'

'Cleaning it?'

'That too. And then I'm going to make the letters white again. With paint.'

'I like painting!' She lifts up a leg, lets her foot hang limply and starts to shake her leg.

'Shells in your sandals?'

'Uh-huh.'

'Can you do something for me, Diek?'

'Sure.'

'Could you fill this bucket up with water?'

'From the ditch?'

'No, of course not. From the tap.'

'Where's the tap?'

'Over there.' He points to a small house near the entrance behind the Polder House. 'There's a tap on the outside wall. It's the cemetery worker's tool shed. Can you manage that?'

'Of course,' she says indignantly.

'OK, fine. I didn't mean to offend you.' Uncle Jan hands her the green bucket.

Dieke takes the bucket and walks over to the little house with the long name she's already forgotten. The tap is at the front next to a door. Before turning it on, she pulls on the door to see if it's locked. It doesn't budge. Next to the door there's a window. She turns the bucket upside down on the paving bricks and climbs up onto it, holding

the window ledge to keep her balance. Even before she's
had a chance to pull herself up far enough to get a good
look at whatever's inside the house, she's shocked to see a
bird strung up on a piece of string. A dead black bird,
blurry behind spiderwebs and dirty glass. She jumps down
off the bucket. Takes a moment to get over the fright, then
puts the bucket under the tap. It's not that hard to turn
it on, you just have to try. If it doesn't work in one direction, it has to go the other way. The water starts to flow
and splashes up, the drops turning into dark spots on her
grey dress with purple flowers. Now it's time for her to
turn the tap off again, but no matter which way she turns
it, the water keeps coming, pouring over the rim of the
bucket and wetting her bare toes. Her heart is pounding,
but she doesn't want to start bawling straight away. She
tries again first.

'Uncle Jan!'

'Couldn't you remember which way to turn it?'

'No.' She sniffs.

'It doesn't matter, no problem. It's off now.'

'Yes.'

Uncle Jan half empties the bucket between the shrubs in
front of the tool shed. Then unties his T-shirt and dips it
in the water that's left. He wrings it out and ties it back
around his head. He takes her by the hand. 'Come on,' he
says. 'Now we're going to scrub it.'

'Scrub it?'

'Clean it.'

'Bananas first?'

'Mm, yeah, a banana. I feel just like a banana now. On the bench under the tree?'

'Yes.'

They walk over to the bench. Dieke gets the two bananas out of her bag and gives one to Uncle Jan. After peeling hers, she points out the birds.

'Ah, blue tits.'

'They're hot.'

'There's a bucket of water right here.'

'That's way too deep.'

'True. They'd drown in that.'

'Are they a mummy and a daddy?'

'I haven't got a clue, Diek. You can't tell with tits.'

Dieke's finished her banana and hands the peel to Uncle Jan.

'What am I supposed to do with this?'

'Put it in the rubbish.'

'Oh.' He stands up, takes a couple of steps towards the hedge and tosses the banana peels over it. There's a splashing noise and now Dieke knows that there's a ditch on that side of the cemetery too. The cemetery is almost an island.

'What is this place?' she asks. 'A cemetery?'

'Well,' says Uncle Jan. He comes back to the bench and sits down. But he doesn't say any more.

Straw

Anna Kaan and Rekel stare at each other. Anna looking down, Rekel looking up. They've been at it for quite a while.

Anna is lying on her stomach with her head sticking out over the side of the straw; Rekel is sitting motionless on the hard concrete. Every now and then she says, 'Come on, boy,' and Rekel slaps the concrete with his tail without moving from the spot. Dogs aren't as thick as you'd think, she thinks. By the looks of him he's just been for a swim in the ditch. The Barbary duck waddles in through the big barn doors. Anna sees it out of the corner of her eye. There used to be more of those ducks, but there's only one left. A big drake. Now it's going to get interesting. She keeps her eyes fixed on the dog and can tell from his eyebrows that he's wavering. When Dirk starts snorting too, Rekel gives in, stands up and barks once at the duck, which is gone again through the doors in a flash. Dirk falls silent. The equilibrium in the barn has been restored but when the dog sits down again Anna Kaan has already disappeared.

She crawls back to the spot she squashed down flat, where the straw isn't as hard, and grabs the bottle of advocaat. It must be afternoon by now. Straight out of the bottle? That's the problem with advocaat: it's thick, you can't really drink it. When she grabbed a few things yesterday – just after Johan rang – she didn't think of taking a spoon, let alone a glass. The viscous substance slides into her mouth – too thick to drink, not thick enough to eat. She feels a tremendous craving for *metworst*, the dry sausage she used to buy in the old days when they still had a real butcher in the village. She would get it on Saturdays, or send Klaas or Jan to get some. She squishes the advocaat up against the roof of her mouth with her tongue. The old days.

She screws the cap back on the bottle and stands it up

next to the water bottle, the open packet of Viennese biscuits and the parade sword. Swallows flying in and out. Rekel, slowly starting to whimper. What is it with dogs? Do they sense your hostility? Do they like getting kicked? If she'd had her way, they would never have had another dog after Tinus. The last bit of advocaat is stuck at the back of her throat. She hawks it up and spits it out straight ahead. It disappears below the edge of the straw. That's for Rekel.

She lies down again and imagines herself sitting up nice and straight at a birthday party, surrounded by a gaggle of neighbours. That makes her laugh, coming immediately after letting fly with such a heartfelt gob. She has another shameless scratch. Is that it? she wonders. Is that why she's up on the straw? Married fifty years, when did that happen? She holds both hands up in the air with the backs turned towards her. It's too dark in here: she can't see the veins, liver spots and loose skin.

The old days. Orchards with quinces and Notaris apples, test fields with linseed or buckwheat. Down the road there's a farm, now renovated, made spacious and bright, where they once took photos of prize bulls and 100,000-litre cows, where the farmer had sons who spent their weekdays at agricultural college in Wageningen but were still happy to turn their back on the city and return to the country after years of study, where the magnolias in the garden weren't shrubs but trees, and where they had books with fancy blue-linen dust jackets that stated *this polder measures 1,800 morgens and 580 rods inside dyke length*. And on this farm, girls also preserved everything there was to preserve and lined the jars up on wooden shelves in the cool cellar. Here, her mother-in-law had the farmhands and their wives over for coffee in their Sunday best once a year, presenting them with homemade biscuits on the fancy tray. All long before bakers bought new Volkswagen vans, friends had their bathrooms renovated and Beentjes Bros. of Assen began installing one Mueller bulk tank after another. Saturday. Brown beans or marrowfat peas. Klaas or Jan off to the grocer's for a jar of apple sauce. Washing the car, doing the laundry, mowing the lawn.

She groans. Where in her head had those precise numbers been hiding? 'Klaas!' she shouts. Breaking her silence wasn't the idea. Dirk answers her call. The useless lump of meat. No, she'll never celebrate anything again.

Two or three weeks ago they had all driven in a minibus to a zoo in the east of the country. After a considerable delay, because Jan had to come from Texel and Johan forgot. As soon as they arrived, the misery began. The driver said there were two locations, the old zoo and the new park. Half the minibus wanted to go to the old location, the other half preferred the new one. 'We're going to the butterfly garden!' Zeeger shouted, and because he was the loudest, the old zoo won. No sooner were they were inside than it turned out the two locations were connected anyway, so the driver had caused all that discord needlessly. Johan got lost almost immediately, and when Anna's brother, Piet, went off to look for him, he got lost too. Jan walked around with his shoulders hunched and a scowl on his face. Klaas's wife didn't look friendly either and Zeeger got into an argument with his sister – in the hot, humid butterfly garden of all places. Since Johan had the shopping trolley full of food and drink with him, and the drive had taken more than two hours, everyone got hungry and thirsty but Zeeger refused to buy anything. After an hour and a half, Dieke and Klaas found Johan with a squirrel monkey on his head that had been there, according to Johan, 'f-or at l-east an hour' and was holding on tight to his ears with its little hands. That was why he'd just stayed sitting where he was. Then it took a while to get everyone gathered around the shopping trolley with the food and drink and, for the quarter of an hour that followed, the Kaans themselves were an attraction for the other zoo visitors. Anna Kaan had tried to keep her spirits up, but when, separated from the group, she arrived at the baboon rock, it was too much for her. Everything was so far from how she'd imagined this day that her legs went weak and she had to sit down on the massive stone wall that surrounded the enclosure.

Never again, she thinks, I'll never celebrate anything again. We're incapable. She stares straight up at the sky through the hole in the roof. She can't tell if it's blue or not, just like you can't tell from a paint swatch what the colour will be like on a whole wall. She sits up and reaches for the water bottle. After drinking a few mouthfuls, she eats three biscuits and lies down again. Next time I'll bring some pillows, she thinks.

Zeeger had booked a table at a restaurant, not in the city with the zoo but in a village close to home on Lake Amstel. During the drive back, Klaas, Jan and Johan ate everything there was to eat – crisps, Mars minis, almond cakes – and then nodded off deliberately in protest at the lack of beer. Anna's brother Piet and his wife, and Zeeger's sister and her husband, stared out at the landscape for two hours, while the driver whistled along softly but badly to the radio, which was turned up fairly loud. First they had to take photos on the dyke behind the restaurant. When Anna picked up the prints she could hardly bear to look at all those aggrieved, dissatisfied faces. The photos are still in the envelope. The meal itself, served at six o'clock sharp, was a disaster. Weekend staff brought it out to the table and Zeeger and Klaas's wife insisted there was a stand-in chef in the kitchen too. Everything had been ordered and arranged in advance, and of course the menu didn't satisfy anyone. Plates were pushed back and forth across the table and it wasn't long before chips were flying through the air. Jan kept ordering more drinks at the top of his voice, although that too had been arranged beforehand. Johan matched Jan glass for glass, even though he can't hold his drink at all, and Klaas and his wife lit up while others were still eating and that annoyed Jan even more, which got Klaas's back up so much he started chain-smoking just to be difficult. Zeeger spent ten minutes shut in the toilet because the lock was broken, and nobody even noticed until Dieke had to go too and couldn't get in. Anna began getting visions of a daughter who squatted down next to her chair to ask softly if she was enjoying herself, before handing out sheets of paper with a song she'd written for the occasion, a song to be sung 'to the tune of', the same daughter who had earlier exclaimed cheerfully how lovely it was to finally see baboons in real life.

Then someone started off about the grave. She's not sure who – probably Zeeger, he's the one who extends the leases on the plots every ten years. Jan picked up on it and said he'd do the painting. In a moment of quiet she said, 'No question of it,' which nobody reacted to, except perhaps Johan who said that he wanted 'to d-o some thing too'. After she had again categorically stated that she wasn't having it and, without pausing to take a breath, finally told Zeeger that as far as she was concerned they didn't need to extend the lease again either, even Klaas and his wife butted in. Zeeger was making trouble on purpose, everyone was winding everyone else up, for a moment they stopped drinking and throwing chips around. She felt alone, as if everyone had been waiting for that opportunity to join forces and turn on her.

And then Dieke, sulking over a pudding she hadn't ordered. It was unbearable. Anna Kaan had grabbed her tightly by her upper arm, perhaps a little too tightly, and said, 'Eat it!' Klaas and his wife were sitting further up the table, puffing away as if their lives depended on it. 'This isn't what I wanted,' Dieke sobbed. Anna squeezed her arm even harder. 'Eat it, you ungrateful little brat!'

She grabs the advocaat and forces down a few globs, which isn't easy, as she already has a lump in her throat from that last image. And what were they doing, celebrating their golden wedding anniversary in June when they got married in April?

'I have to catch the last ferry,' Jan had said. Although they'd already made up a bed for him and left the window of the spare room ajar. They finished up quickly. Her brother Piet, who lives in Den Helder, gave Jan a lift to the ferry. Everyone left in their own vehicles. Anna and Zeeger didn't say a word during the drive home from the restaurant, almost fifteen minutes. She sat there wondering what had been the most painful thing to have happened that day. As they were getting into bed, Zeeger said, 'So, the day went quite well, I think.'

And maybe that was it: the most painful thing.

She screws the cap back on the bottle and checks how much is left. About half. She lays the bottle down next to her and crawls over to the edge of the straw. Something beneath her is shaking. Shaking worse than it should from just her crawling. When she reaches the edge and looks down, the concrete floor is completely empty. No dog, no Barbary duck, no Zeeger. Even Dirk is keeping quiet. Please don't let me start thinking about earlier celebrations, she thinks. Lying back down in her old spot, she realises that her feet are cold.

Capitals

'Did you drop her off?'
   'There's a heap of silage in the feeding passage.'
   'What?'
   'What are you kneeling down here for?'
   'I'm trying to see if the carpet's already started to wear.'
   'I thought you were going to muck out the stalls?'

'Yes.'

'And?'

'Didn't Dieke want to go to the pool?'

'No.'

'What's she doing now, then?'

'How would I know? I didn't stay there. Has that brother of yours got a mobile?'

'Doubt it.'

'Is that brother of yours all there?'

'And you?'

'Why are you kneeling down here instead of working in the cowshed? You're not checking whether I keep it clean, are you?'

'No. It's too hot.'

'I'm hot too.'

'You're not mucking out the cowshed.'

'It can't go on like this.'

'What?'

'This. Everything.'

'Why aren't you at work?'

'It's summer, everyone's on holiday.'

'But a butcher's always got work. Your brother's shop is always packed.'

'It's summer! Everyone's gone!'

'Calm down.'

'What does Eben-Ezer mean?'

'Huh?'

'Forget it.'

'If everyone's on holiday, there's people on holiday in Schagen too and your brother's as busy as ever.'

'What?'

'You have to learn to think the other way round sometimes.'

'What?'

'All those Germans. In Schagen.'

'I don't speak German.'

'Anyway, if it can't go on like this, you'll have to start working more than one day a week at the butcher's.'

'Oh, so you do understand what I'm getting at. Have you already called a land agent?'

'A land agent?'

'Don't play dumb.'

'What was Jan doing?'

'He was kneeling down, like you, only not in his daughter's bedroom. Between the headstones.'

'What was he doing?'

'Klaas, I dropped Dieke off and left again.'

'Where have you been, then? Riding there and back can't take more than quarter of an hour.'

She doesn't say anything else, just turns and walks out of Dieke's room. Halfway down the stairs she does say something, *just* loud enough. 'I'd rather be out on my bike, even if the tyres are melting, than stuck here.' Silence. 'Will you go and pick Dieke up in a minute? She won't last more than half an hour there.' The staircase door closes quietly.

Klaas stands up. Dieke's treasure bag was under her bed. Not in a blanket of fluff, but on spotless carpet. He didn't look in it. When he straightens his back, the window cracks. For a fraction of a second he feels it in his lower back, then wonders how something like that can happen out of the blue. The heat? A structural defect? The crack is in the outside pane of the double glazing and will be sure to cause condensation in autumn. He does some calculations. The window was fitted almost forty years ago. Old age? He pulls on the mechanism to see if it still opens and closes properly. Just before closing it again, he thinks he hears his mother's shrill voice calling him. He shakes his head, but can't block out a muffled echo of his name.

Three years ago he resumed work where his father had left off, removing thick layers of dust and grime with a vacuum cleaner and a soft broom. His wife never came upstairs. There was plenty of everything. Wall planks, laths, skirting boards, and more than enough nails. No floor covering. He drove to the Carpet Giant in Schagen and Dieke went with him. With a very determined expression, she pointed out a roll of light-green carpet. Zeeger Kaan would have varnished the planks, everyone did that in the late sixties, but Klaas painted the bedroom lime green. In four weekends he was finished. His father didn't lift a finger. He came to have a look now and then, mumbled something or other, but didn't do a thing. That must have taken willpower, because he's the kind of father who can't bear to stand by and watch. The sight of his children repairing punctures made him huff and puff until he snatched the puncture repair kit out of their hands to do it better and faster himself. Once the bedroom was finished, he showed up with five letters, capitals he'd sawn out of a piece of wood in his shed. The letters were different colours and he'd screwed eyelets into the tops. Dieke moved from Klaas and his wife's bedroom to the new room, after he'd installed a gate at the top of the stairs first.

DIEKE slept in the new room for the first few weeks, but after that it was always someone else, because she had found a box on the landing she could stand on. *IKDEE* slept there for a while, and so did *IDEEK*.

Nobody asked why he had finished off the third bedroom when the two old bedrooms at the front of the house had been empty for years.

Before leaving the bedroom, he takes *DEKIE* off the door and rehangs the letters in the right order. Very far away, he can still hear his mother calling his name right at the back of his mind. It could have just as easily been five other capital letters, he thinks. In black. Or grey. No, four others. He walks past the stair gate to the front of the house and has a quick look in the other two bedrooms. In each room there's a bed with just a mattress and a pillow without a case. Nobody ever stays overnight. In the largest room, with the balcony, the air is thick and there's too much sunlight. He opens the balcony doors, steps out onto the green-stained rectangle and plants his hands on the rail. The crown of the red beech in the middle of the lawn is thinning. That's something he hasn't noticed before. The wrought iron of the railings is crumbling under his hands. Cautiously he steps back into the bedroom, where he closes the balcony doors again, equally cautiously. He pulls off his shirt and dries his face with it. Motes of dust spin in the thick air. Thick, he thinks. Nobody breathes it. I'll go and get Dieke.

Shit

What's that girl doing there? Why doesn't she react to my tapping? She picks her glasses up from the worktop and puts them on for a better look. The girl has turned around and is walking off between the headstones. Red hair. Isn't that the girl I just saw on the back of that bike? What's she doing at the cemetery? Where's her mother? What's going on? 'Benno!' she calls.

Fifteen minutes later, she's on her way. She curses herself for having pulled on a jacket. It's a summer jacket, but this is weather for being out in a billowy dress. Actually, it's weather for floating in the sea or lying in the back garden under a beach umbrella. If there weren't houses left and right and the tall hedge around the cemetery, she'd probably see the sky shimmering. Benno is hardly moving. She tugs on the leash, but it doesn't help. Every few steps she has to push up her glasses.

The girl and the man are on the ground behind the first row of headstones. They're busy with water and something – sponges, perhaps? The girl turns, sees the dog, jumps up and runs off. She stops a bit further away, near the monument to the four English airmen whose plane crashed. Her light-grey dress has dark patches on it. Benno ignores her.

The man, who was hunched over, has now raised himself onto one knee. He looks at the girl. Dinie sees who it is immediately.

'You're a Kaan, aren't you?'

'Yes,' the man says with a sigh. 'I'm a Kaan.'

Benno raises his big head and, without her urging him on, takes a few steps towards the man. She gives him some slack. 'I thought,' she said, 'I'll come and have a look. I saw some movement and there's been some nasty goings-on here recently. I live there.' She points at the hedge and realises that from here, nobody can see her house. The Kaan boy doesn't even look in the direction she's pointing.

'And I keep my eye on things a little. If I don't, who will? They don't do anything here at all! There, that hole in the hedge, it's been there two years now. My husband's buried here too, over there.' Now she points at her husband's grave, a tall narrow headstone topped with a granite weeping willow. She's got lots more to say, but for the moment she can't bear to look at the Kaan boy, and keeps her eyes fixed on the stone willow instead. 'What if the little bastards knocked over his headstone? They were in here again last week. They didn't knock over any stones, but they smeared filth all over them. Shit! Cow shit! Isn't that disgusting? At least it was easy to clean off. Fortunately they didn't touch my husband's grave. It was in the paper. Didn't you read about it? No, you don't live here, you probably read other papers, ones that don't have that kind of petty village news. Nobody's been arrested. They don't know who it is. I'm sure they haven't spent much time on it, either.' Now she has to look at him again. 'If I see anything out of the ordinary, I come and have a look. With the dog. I saw a girl, and I thought, let's go.' She pushes up her glasses and wants to take off her jacket, but can't, because there's no reason to, besides her feeling hot, at least. 'Or are you cleaning that stone because there was filth on it too? It's your little sister, isn't it? I haven't forgotten, such a little girl, buried here amongst all these adults. Look, um . . . Over there they've made a special children's corner, that's much better . . . I just mean, all those children together, with cheerful teddy bear headstones and little suns and stars and . . .'

'Can you get this dog out of here?'

She's changed the subject to the children's graves, but she thinks of the baker. In his brand-new, light-grey Volkswagen van. She'll have to tell him about this tonight. Or should she keep quiet about it? Drool drips off one of the Kaan boy's knees. Benno is standing very close to him, he must be able to feel the dog's hot breath. She feels like turning around and leaving the cemetery. The dog could just stay standing there. Benno's a softie, but people don't know that. They see an enormous beast, a kind of mountain dog with lots of fur. Let that Kaan boy sweat for an hour, or longer. 'Benno, here!' she says.

The dog comes back to the shell path and immediately lies down, without taking his eyes off the Kaan boy for an instant.

'But you're not knocking over any headstones,' she says.

He finally stands up. 'No,' he says, 'I'm not going to knock over any headstones.'

He could have just as easily have said 'Yes, I'm a Kaan' again, it sounds exactly the same. Is he making fun of her? She looks at him. Shameless. Topless and wearing shorts in a cemetery. And what's he got tied round his head? It looks like a T-shirt. Those pale eyes, hard eyes. No, no – don't think about before, her son's big penis, his cheeky face; no, not even cheeky, it was more unseeing, as if she didn't exist, as if she was irrelevant.

'Dieke, come back here. That dog's harmless.'

Really? You think so? She looks at the mess on and around the child's grave. A screwdriver, a bucket, a wet rag, and what's that other thing? It looks like cuttlefish. There's a big scratch on the headstone. The gravel is wet and dirty, a dirty green. What's going on here? She doesn't trust it, she doesn't want to trust it. The girl has come up next to the Kaan boy. What an ugly little red-headed brat. 'Who's that?' she says. 'Your daughter?'

He doesn't say anything, just gives a wry smile and takes the hand the girl is holding out to him.

'You've both got such red hair.'

'I'm Dieke,' the girl says.

'Yes,' he says. 'This is Dieke, she's helping.'

She tries to look as neutral as possible, but it's not easy. She breaks the spell of her revulsion for that bare body, those pale eyes, by pushing her glasses up again. He must see who I am? Why didn't I walk off right away, without Benno? 'Fine,' she says.

'Fine?' he says. 'Who are you? The cemetery attendant?'

If this child is his daughter, was the woman on the bike his wife? Is he really being as contemptuous as he sounds? To her?

'He's not my father,' the girl says. 'This is Uncle Jan. Who are you?'

Yes. Jan Kaan. The green filth on the gravel is drying to a crunchy crackling layer. Benno is panting. The sun is shining, but not as fiercely as earlier.

'I'll be heading off then,' she says.

'Yep,' he says.

'Bye!' says the girl.

She hauls the dog up onto his feet. 'Will you keep an eye out?'

'What for?' she hears the girl saying, before she's even taken a step.

'Nothing,' Jan Kaan says. 'Do you know who that woman is, Diek?'

'Nope. Just a woman, I think. A granny.'

'Do you think she dyes her hair?'

'Dunno.'

'Come on, back to work.'

They're doing it deliberately, she thinks, as she walks back down the shell path agonisingly slowly. This bloody dog! He's acting like he's twelve already! Through the gate with the two evergreens next to it. She looks back over her shoulder and sees that the dog's tail has left a trail in the grit. She yanks off her coat and removes her glasses.

Water

'But,' says Dieke, 'what *is* this?'

'Cuttlebone,' says Uncle Jan. He doesn't look at her, he's staring at a headstone and rubbing his chest with one hand.

The dog lady pointed in that direction. 'What?' he says, after a while.

'You were the last one to say something, not me.'

'What did I say?'

'Cuddle bone.'

'Cuttlebone.'

'What is that?'

'It's from a cuttlefish. That's a kind of squid.'

'Aren't they all soft and slimy?'

'Yes. But these ones have a hard bit too.'

'Where?'

'On their back maybe.'

'I don't get it.' She rubs her finger over the worn, soft part of the cuttlebone.

'Me neither. It's rubbish anyway, it doesn't help at all.'

'It's all dirty.'

'Let's get some more water.'

'OK.'

'Or would you rather go to the pool?'

'No!'

On the way to the little house with the long name, Dieke looks around. There are dead people buried everywhere, that's what Uncle Jan said. But not all dead people come here, some prefer to be burnt. He said other things too, and she was glad when they started scrubbing the stone, and secretly she thought about the swimming pool after all, and Evelien too.

'Do you want to do it?'

'No.'

Uncle Jan turns on the tap and waits with his hands on his hips until the bucket's full.

'There's a bird in there,' she says.

'Hmm.'

'On a string.'

'Hmm.'

'It's dead too.'

Uncle Jan turns the tap off again without any trouble at all. She watches him closely and can't work out why she couldn't manage it before.

'Why?' she asks.

'What?'

'That bird?'

Only now does he look in through the window. 'That's a magpie.'

Dieke sighs.

Uncle Jan empties the bucket over the stone in a few splashes. He chucks the bits of cuttlefish into the bucket, together with the sandpaper and the wet rag, uses the screwdriver to lever open the paint and stir it. Then he gets the wet rag back out of the bucket and wipes the screwdriver clean. Wet rag and clean screwdriver go into the bucket, which he puts down on the shell path. 'So,' he says. 'Now we'll just wait till it's dry again.'

'OK,' she says.

'Do you know what a bogeyman is?'

'No.'

'Neither do I. In the old days Grandma and Grandpa used to tell us stories about the bogeyman to scare us. They said he lived in the ditches. That's how they kept us away from the water.'

'Why?'

'You can drown in water. They were always scared of us drowning.'

'Didn't you have swimming lessons?'

'Of course, but not till we were about five or six.'

'What's a bogeyman?'

'A great big monster that grabs you if you get too close to a ditch. In the ditch between your house and my parents' house, there's a spot where there's always bubbles coming up. Do you know where I mean?'

Dieke thinks about it. 'I don't think so.'

'That's marsh gas, but my father always said it was air bubbles from the bogeyman.'

'Grandpa?'

'Yes, your grandpa.'

'Was it really air bubbles? Is that where the bogeyman lived?'

'No, of course not.'

'It's a bit scary.'

'Yes, that's why he said it. And do you know what happened the first time Johan went to a swimming lesson?'

'No.'

'He asked the pool attendant if there was a bogeyman in the swimming pool. "What's that?" the pool attendant asked. "He bites," said Johan. He was terrified. The pool attendant laughed and said that the only thing that might bite him would be water fleas and they were so small you wouldn't even feel it.'

'Do they bite?'

'I don't think so. Have you ever felt them biting you?'

'No. How old was Uncle Johan then?'

'Five, I think. The same age as you are now.'

'And you?'

'Seven. And once we were there when lightning struck.'

'Really?'

'Yep. The whole swimming pool was full of people and then there was a thunderstorm. The pool attendant blew his whistle three times and everyone got out of the pool straight away. Johan and I went to sit in a changing cubicle. Johan was really scared and kept asking if the storm was going to go away again. He was as bad as Tinus, the dog we had back then; once he crawled into the cellar during a thunderstorm. We started counting.'

'Counting?'

'Yep. If you see the lightning and the thunder comes nine seconds later, then the thunderstorm's three kilometres away. The less seconds, the closer it is. When there was hardly anything left to count, I pulled myself up on top of the cubicle door and, just when I had my head up over the door, the lightning hit the water.'

Dieke thinks of Evelien and hopes a thunderstorm doesn't come now.

'It was like a blanket of light over the water. Everywhere, from the paddling pool to zone four. I got such a fright that I let go of the top of the door.'

'And then?'

'It was like I'd seen the swimming pool's skeleton.'

'Huh?'

'As if the swimming pool had been turned inside out.'

'And Uncle Johan?'

'He was sitting on the bench shivering.'

'Inside out,' says Dieke. 'I don't get it.'

'I didn't get it either. It was weird.'

'Why wasn't Daddy at the swimming pool?'

'He already had two certificates. He preferred to go swimming in the canal. He thought the pool was childish.'

'If lightning hits the swimming pool does it kill you?'

'Yes, I think it would.' Uncle Jan slides the T-shirt on his head back and forth a couple of times, as if it's itchy underneath. 'That headstone'll be dry now, don't you think?'

'Is that your wife under the ground?' Dieke asks.

'You what?'

'Your wife?'

'I don't have a wife. Never have.'

'Why not?'

'Because.'

'Oh,' says Dieke.

'This is your auntie buried here.'

'I don't have any aunties.'

'Um, no, you don't. Because she's here.'

'Who?'

'Oof,' says Uncle Jan. 'Hang on a sec.' He tips everything out of the bucket and walks over to the little house with it. Then he comes back and puts the bucket, which is filled up almost to the rim, down in front of her. 'Dip your head in here if you get too hot.'

'Do it yourself,' she says.

'OK.' He kneels down, puts his hands on the ground either side of the bucket and sticks his whole head in, T-shirt and all.

After a while, Dieke starts whistling. Sometimes things go faster if you whistle. 'Uncle Jan!' she calls. But he can't hear her, of course. What else did he say a minute ago, when they were sitting on the bench? That when you're dead, the world doesn't exist any more? She pulls on his shoulder, which is oily, her hand slides off. She grabs the knot of the T-shirt and pulls her uncle's head up out of the bucket.

'At last,' he says.

'Not funny,' says Dieke.

'I was only joking. I was waiting for you to rescue me.' He leaves the soaking T-shirt where it is, tied around his head. Water trickles out of his nose. 'Ow,' he says, brushing bits of shell off his knees. 'Why don't you go see if those blue tits are still in the tree?'

She bends forward, thinking of the day she got her swimming card, takes a deep breath and plunges her head into the bucket. She'll show *him*. She can already feel the hand reaching to pull her out again, her shoulder's itching a little. She opens her eyes and quickly closes them again. Why doesn't Uncle Jan help? She's had her head stuck in this bucket for at least a minute now. I should have breathed in more first, she thinks. Just a little bit longer now. She can do it, even if her chest already feels like it's full of cotton wool. Come on, pull me out! She jerks her head back up and feels her wet hair slap her on the back. 'Why didn't you do anything?' she bawls.

Uncle Jan stands there very calmly and looks down at her with his arms crossed. 'You don't want the world to stop existing yet, do you?' he says.

*

He kneels down in front of the headstone and picks up the brush and the tin of paint.

'What do I do?'

'I just told you. Go and have a look at the blue tits.'

She waits a very long time before turning around and reluctantly setting out for the tree and the bench. She closes her eyes tight and pretends the world no longer exists. When she thinks she's made it to the tree, she opens them again. Yes, the birds are still sitting on their branch, sucking air in and blowing it out again. She feels sorry for them, but she can't do anything to help. The zip of her bag is open, she sticks an arm in and grabs an apple. 'Do you want an apple now too?' she calls.

'Sure.'

She gets the second apple out and walks back. When Uncle Jan goes to take the apple, she pulls it back. 'Never do that again,' she says.

'I promise.' They eat their apples on opposite sides of the grave, facing each other.

'The birds were still there,' she says.

He doesn't say anything.

'How old is this auntie?' she asks.

'Two.'

'Two? She can't be. How old are you? Thirty?'

'Ha! Forty-six. You understand that this auntie was one of Grandma's children?'

'Huh?'

'I'm one of Grandma's children too, right?' He spits out a bite. 'Yuck, that was a bad bit.'

'Um . . .'

'Don't worry about it. We have to think of something for you to do. Or would you rather go home?'

'No.'

Uncle Jan looks around. 'Would you like to clean some of the other stones?'

'Sure.'

'Good.'

'Do I have to do it with the cuddle bone?'

'No, just water will be fine.' He walks over to the path, picks up the wet rag and shakes out the shell grit. 'Here's a rag. Is there enough water in the bucket?'

'Yes,' says Dieke.

Uncle Jan comes back to the shell path and points out a stone, one that's lying down, completely smooth and brownish.

'Who's under here?' she asks.

'Do you really want to know?'

'No.' She dips the rag in the water, wrings it out and starts to rub the stone clean, the tip of her tongue soon appearing between her almost clenched teeth.

'Daddy!' He'd walked up without her noticing.

'Hi, Dieke.'

'There's lots of dead people under here!' she shouts excitely. 'I'm cleaning them.'

'No.'

'I am.'

'Did your uncle tell you to do that?'

'No, I thought of it myself,' she lies.

Her father walks over to Uncle Jan. She stands up and follows him. He puts his hands on his hips and watches Uncle Jan at work. 'You shouldn't do it that way,' he says.

'What do you mean?'

'You have to lie the stone down flat. That'd be a lot easier.'

'Can we do that?'

'We can try.'

Her father and Uncle Jan take hold of the headstone and wobble it back and forth a little until they're able to lift it up. They lay the top part of the stone on the raised edge of the grave.

'Are you taking it apart?' she asks.

'We'll put it back later,' her father says. 'It's not a problem.' He sits down on a nearby grave, pulls his tobacco pouch out of a back pocket and rolls a cigarette.

She looks closely from one to the other. They really do look a lot like each other, but at the same time not at all. Her father's older, at least she thinks he is, and that's strange, because her uncle looks older. Uncle Jan dips the brush in the paint tin and bends over the stone. Her father lights his cigarette. One smokes, the other paints. She was cleaning and she goes back to that. Neither man says anything, but it's still a lot nicer now. There's something beautiful about working in silence; she can sense that. It means something. When, after a while, Uncle Jan says, 'It's no good like this, we have to stand it up again,' she doesn't even react. She only looks up when she catches sight of someone coming down the shell path. 'Dog!' she shouts. And that big lady with black hair. The dog and woman march past her without a word.

'What's the meaning of this?' the woman says. She talks loudly and the dog starts barking. 'Quiet, Benno! You're wrecking the place. I knew it. I was on to you. Do you plan on knocking over other headstones too?'

Dieke has stood up, but stays close to the stone she's cleaning. Uncle Jan and her father are standing between the graves with the stone in their hands. The woman sounds angry and the dog's not listening to her. He's still barking.

'This is our grave,' her father snaps. 'You keep out of it.'

Dieke's shocked. The way he's said it sounds really rude.

'I'm going to report this! And what's that girl doing? To that stranger's grave! She's dirtying the stone. Have you got a tub of cow shit here somewhere too? What are you doing? Benno, quiet!'

The dog barks, Uncle Jan and her father slowly lower the stone. 'Up a little,' her father says, 'there's some pebbles on the concrete.' Uncle Jan bends down and brushes something away with his free hand and the stone moves down out of sight. Then the men straighten up, her father with a red face.

'Well?' the woman says.

Dieke looks at her father. Is he going to be rude again?

'Go away.'

'What?'

'Just mind your own business.'

Her father stares intently at the big dog, and after a while it stops barking and skulks back behind the woman's legs.

'I *have* business here,' the woman says, pointing at the tall narrow headstone she pointed out to Uncle Jan earlier.

Her father turns and looks carefully in that direction. 'We're not doing anything against the rules,' he says slowly.

'We'll see about that,' the woman shouts, now staring at Uncle Jan. 'And you . . .' she says.

'Yes?' says Uncle Jan.

It looks funny: Uncle Jan bare-chested with that T-shirt tied around his head, the woman and her dog on the shell path. Only now does she notice that the woman doesn't have her jacket on. And wasn't she wearing glasses before? Dieke is curious what she's going to say to Uncle Jan. It's gone very quiet, so quiet she thinks she can even hear the panting of the two birds. The woman doesn't say another word. She just spins around and strides off. When she passes Dieke she gives her a dirty look. 'Horrible boys,' she says.

Dieke gives her a sweet little smile. 'I'm a girl,' she says cheerfully. 'Bye-bye!'

The dog drags on the leash.

'I actually came to pick you up,' her father says a little later.

'Did you?' she says.

'Yep. You ready to go home?'

'No.'

'Don't you want to go to the swimming pool?'

'No.'

'We could go to the beach instead.'

'Yuck.'

'When are you going to have lunch?'

'I've already had a banana. And an apple.'

'Me too,' says Uncle Jan. 'Let her stay if she wants to.'

'Fine.' Her father sticks his hands in his pockets. 'You heading off again tonight?'

'Yeah,' says Uncle Jan. 'What would I stay here for?'

'Maybe we could do some fishing?'

'In weather like this?'

'Sure, why not? A worm's a worm, or do fish stop biting when it gets too hot?'

'Yay, fishing!' Dieke shouts.

'Have you already decided what you're going to do?' Uncle Jan asks her father.

'What do you mean?'

'Have you sold the land yet?'

'No.'

'But what are you going to do then?'

'I dunno. It's not your problem.'

'No,' says Uncle Jan. 'So towards evening we'll go fishing.'

'We'll see,' her father says. 'I'll see you in a bit, Diek.'

'Bye, Daddy.'

Her father strolls down the shell path to the Polder House. He walks a bit crooked, she notices. Almost like Grandpa. Quickly she throws the rag into the bucket, which is almost empty. 'My water's finished,' she says.

'I'll get a new bucket. Shall I fill your drinking cup while I'm at it?'

'Yes, please.' She sits down on the stone she's cleaning, although that doesn't feel quite right. It's not nice that her father's gone again. She feels a bit lonely and wonders why she said no. Because now she *is* thinking of the swimming pool. And of Evelien, because she's sure to be having fun there right now. Maybe with Leslie, though he hasn't been to the pool that much lately. Of course, somebody else might come here, like Grandpa, and then she can go home with them. And then she can lie down in her big blow-up paddling pool. If a thunderstorm comes she'll be able to get out of that a lot faster than the swimming pool. Even Grandma would be OK, although Dieke's been doing her best to avoid her ever since that visit to the zoo and the dinner afterwards. It hurt like anything, her pinching her arm like that. The church bell rings.

'What's the church clock say, Dieke?' asks Uncle Jan, coming back with a full bucket.

'A lot.'

'Twelve.'

Straw Book

I need new underpants, Zeeger Kaan thinks as he takes the dry washing off the line. He tosses the clothes in a laundry basket and sets it on the kitchen table. That's as far as his duties go. He's never folded them up or done the ironing. Rekel has followed in at his heels and stretches out under the kitchen table. Zeeger looks at the clock. Twelve thirty. Summer days can take forever. Klaas is back home. The car, filthy and clapped out, is parked next to the barn. He suspects that his oldest son has been to the cemetery. He goes over to the sliding patio doors and stares out at the garden, which has grown fuller and fuller over the years. All kinds of plants are in flower, not a single perennial clashes with the perennial next to it, but still it looks somehow drab on a day like today. He'd like to turn on the sprinklers, but doesn't, because he doesn't want a scorched lawn. The large leaves of the pipevine are dull and dusty. Already, and it's not even July yet. He crosses the room and studies the front garden. Anna's right, it's gloomy, even now, at the start of summer. Early this morning it was already grey. But for some reason he finds it impossible to cut down things he planted himself. Anna's not the only one to complain; Klaas has taken to commenting too, not that he pays him any attention: he doesn't keep the farm garden up at all. He just lets things go to rack and ruin, not even taking the trouble to plant a few violets or African marigolds in the drinking trough next to the back door in spring.

He gets the exercise book out of the desk in the small room, intending to take it through to the living room, but changes his mind. Why not just stay here? It's pleasant enough and has more or less the same view as the one through the sliding door, just a couple of metres further along. He opens the door to the garden. Not because he thinks it will make it cooler, but so he can hear the radio in the garage. Rekel starts to whimper; he doesn't like being alone. Zeeger walks into the living room and says, 'Come on, then,' to Rekel, who's standing with his front paws on the last row of kitchen tiles. That's his limit, he's not allowed in the rest of the house. Head down and tail between his legs, the dog comes up to him. He's doing something that's forbidden, but he's been ordered to do it. That confuses dogs. He slips into the small room and slinks straight through it. He exhales deeply and slumps against the open door to the garden. 'It's not easy for you either, is it, boy?' says Zeeger Kaan, who sits down on the desk chair and rubs his knees. Sometimes he has to tap his left knee when he wants to stand up, as if the joint won't work without a jolt to get it going.

The fairly thin exercise book has a grey marbled cover. The label on the front is blank, he hasn't given it a name. It's not a diary, it's a straw book. Before he starts writing, he leafs through it a little. The pages feel dry and brittle, but in other seasons they're limp and clammy.

Thursday 9 October 1969. Anna's back up on the straw. For the second time. Just after the funeral Jan and Johan couldn't find their mother. Me and Klaas went looking. She was up on the straw. I asked her to come down but she didn't say anything and wouldn't come down. Mother-in-law came. On Saturday 5 July (1969), mother-in-law cooking, she came down. She sent her mother home. Yesterday (8 October) I leant the ladder against the loft. She kicked the ladder over when I was about halfway up. Broken wrist. Can still milk, but with difficulty. Plaster got dirty and wet. A few hours later she came down. No comment.

23 December 2003 (Tuesday). Klaas's wife tried to get Anna down off the straw. She stood there yelling like a fishwife. Anna said nothing, as always. She took her duvet, fortunately. It's bitter cold. When Klaas's wife walked out of the barn she said something after all,

'*Go to your child.*' *Hours later she came in, it was already dark. She was very angry and asked me why I hadn't decorated the Christmas tree yet.*

21 March 2004 (Sunday). It was to be expected. The old Queen is dead. Instead of plonking down in front of the TV (the whole damn day), she was up on the straw. What's left of it anyway, there's only about three layers. Today too there was all kinds of stuff on TV. There's been fifteen months between the last time and now, although until December 2003 I thought she'd never do it again. After all, the time before that was the end of June 1994. 'So,' she said when she came in this afternoon. And later in the evening there was more. 'Everyone and everything's starting to die off now. Just me left to go.'

30 March 2004 (Tuesday). My heart was in my mouth but Anna didn't make any trouble. She just sat in front of the TV watching the gaudy purple coach and kept watching until someone drew the curtains in front of the hole in the church floor. Then she put the kettle on.

Despite the brevity of his notes, the exercise book is almost half full because he eventually started using it as a gardening book too. Careful records of everything that's died in the garden. First everything around the farmhouse, then, after moving to the other side of the ditch, in the garden here. Two elms blew over on 24 December 1977, several hostas

didn't come up in the spring of 2001, a pear tree fell on 1
April 1994, both the buddleias froze at the end of March
2002, a conifer turned brown after the summer of 2003
(*inexplicable, mould?*), the orpine (*fell apart*) was removed
in the autumn of 1993. And in between the downfall of trees,
shrubs and plants, the occasional death notice:

*12 October 1981. Klaas had the vet look at Tinus. Addled
with cancer, he said. Give him a shot, said Klaas. In
the afternoon the collection service came to pick up a
dead calf. Klaas wanted to give them Tinus too. I
wasn't having it. Dug a hole at the base of the last
willow and buried the dog there. The ground was still
loose. Klaas snorted a bit, Anna seemed almost relieved.
She always told the dog off, she kicked him, but he
was her dog. The whole time I was digging she stood
there right behind me. I think she felt like ripping the
shovel out of my hands.*

*May 1984. The back willow isn't really taking. I've
pollarded them twice now, the other four have formed
a nice head. Leave it for now, it's not dead. Tinus?*

'Should I start writing now, or wait a little?' Zeeger Kaan
asks Rekel. He's sick of all those old things, the whole
exercise book, but still feels obliged to keep it up. There's
not a single bird singing in the garden, which seems crushed
by the heat. It's no longer violin music coming from the
radio, but talk, too soft to hear what it's about. Now and
then he makes out a word or two: *Maartenszee, shipyard,*

volleyball. Rekel has sighed once, after hearing his name. He takes a pen from the pen cup, turns it between his fingers, taps the point on the open exercise book, then puts it back in the cup, which falls over, sending a few pens rolling over the desk. A couple end up on the floor. He closes the exercise book and puts it back in the drawer, then walks out into the garden in his socks. 'So,' he says, 'come on, you.' Rekel stands up and follows him reluctantly, as if he senses what's about to happen. Zeeger slips his feet into his clogs at the side door, then lures the dog to the bank of the broad ditch between his house and the farm. He sits down and pulls the dog up onto his lap, then slides down until his clogs are resting on the wooden shoring. With some difficulty, he slides Rekel, who's damn heavy and not cooperating, off his lap. The dog falls into the water sideways and goes under. Zeeger Kaan rubs his knees and leans back. Just to lie down for a moment. He doesn't care that Klaas and his wife might be able to see him through their kitchen window.

Pygmy Goats

The baker with the chapped face is getting ready to leave the house. He wants to go. He doesn't want to go. He puts it off. Radio North-Holland's culture correspondent is discussing forthcoming events. Next week there'll be a car boot sale in Sint Maartenszee, tonight there's outdoor cinema at the old national shipyard in Den Helder, fairs in Harenkarspel and Middenmeer, a volleyball tournament in Schagen. Nice, he thinks. Lively. He puts his empty water glass down on the sink and goes through to the living room. The coffee table is covered with photos; the ashtray, table lighter and plant have made way and are now on the window-sill. In front of the dried-out newspapers.

He filled the time between looking at the calendar and spreading out the photos by going through the classifieds in the local paper. Under the heading *PETS AND ACCESSORIES* he couldn't find a single puppy. Two old dogs for sale, *because of the home situation*. 'Not them, then,' he mumbled. He also drank a good few glasses of water, standing at the kitchen window looking out at the Polder House. Behind the Polder House there are several large chestnuts. The tall conifer hedge blocks his view of the cemetery.

He sits down with one hand on the small of his back, like a heavily pregnant woman. He never got round to putting the photos from the Queen's visit in an album. The envelope that contained them – he can still see his daughter's hands reaching out to grab it – is still the one from 1969, usually slipped between the pages of a reddish-brown photo album. He did stick in other, later photos, including those from the holiday in Schin op Geul: late August 1969. It wasn't a relaxed or light-hearted holiday, despite the beau-tiful weather. Every day sun, and every night a gigantic thunderstorm. Only their daughter smiling – in two or three snaps. The album is lying on one of the easy chairs; the envelope, now torn, is on top of it. He can't remember when he last looked at this album. Sad pictures, each and every one, and later they only got sadder, because his wife and daughter were no longer there to look through them, giggling and whispering.

He looks at the clock and thinks, what do I care? Then takes a bottle of lemon brandy out of the sideboard and pours himself a drink. This time he doesn't sit down like a pregnant woman; he has to concentrate on his balance to keep the spirits from spilling down the side of the small glass. One of the photos even shows those bloody pygmy goats. He'd forgotten that. Over the years he'd even begun to wonder if he hadn't just imagined them. A farmer in spotless overalls is holding them tight while accepting the old Queen's expressions of gratitude. The goats are eating a bunch of Sweet William, inadvertently dangled in front of them by a woman who is staring at the Queen with big excited eyes. Lots of pictures of his daughter and the butcher's son, together holding an expensive floral arrangement. He takes a sip. There's only one other shot of the Queen, seen from behind on her way into the Polder House, passing between two lines of children with flags. Jan Kaan is in the photo: sulking, with his belly pushed forward, flag hanging. He's wearing a grey cardigan with black trim and silver buttons. A brand-new cardigan. He appears twice, both times with that scowl on his face. Why? The baker takes another sip, then puts the glass down between the photos. His daughter's beaming. She seems really happy. The butcher's son looks bored, with one leg bent casually, as if he's indifferent to the whole event. Yet he's the one who gets to present flowers to the Queen. The baker studies Jan Kaan again. Was he jealous? Is that why he looks so angry? Had he sat up straighter than straight in the class-room with his arms crossed, hoping to be chosen? Or did he just think he looked ridiculous in that Norwegian cardigan?

The baker picks up the second photo with Jan Kaan in it off the table. Standing next to him is Dinie's son. Teun, he thinks. What's happened to him anyway? Dinie never says a word about her son. It's actually a bit strange: Teun is a few years older than Jan Kaan, what's he doing lined up there? They're standing hand in hand. Wherever the Queen might have been in the instant he took the photo, Teun is definitely not looking at her. He's looking slightly sideways, at Jan Kaan. The baker takes another mouthful, tipping the lemon brandy down his throat in one go. Teun Grint looks like someone who can't keep his eyes off a deformed leg, even though he knows it's not polite to stare. This evening he'll have to ask Dinie what's become of her son. His head starts to spin.

In one movement he slides all the photos together and dumps them into the album. He crumples up the envelope and tosses the ball into the bin. Then he takes the ashtray, the plant and the table lighter from the windowsill and puts them back on the coffee table. He pours himself another glass of lemon brandy and knocks it back in two gulps. After a couple of drinks, an old body doesn't feel as old; it feels looser, freer.

Hanging on a wall in the empty shop is a large picture in a black frame with non-reflective glass. The light-grey VW van. Parked in front of the bakery. Blom's Breadery. Him, his wife and their daughter at the rear of van. Beaming. With his left hand he carefully pulls the bottom of the picture away from the wall while holding out his right hand, but the photo that was wedged in behind the frame still floats down to the floor. He bends over – which really is a little easier after two glasses than it was earlier when he was doing the watering – and picks up the photo. This one is very special. But also unbearable to look at. And what good is hiding something if you know exactly where you've hidden it?

He'd made the delivery to the Polder House early that morning. 'Nothing fancy,' they'd told him. 'Just plain loaves, bread rolls, fruit loaf. The Queen needs to eat and drink like everyone else. Just as long as it's fresh out of the oven.' He dropped the order off in the new van, wanting as many people as possible to get used to the name *Blom's Breadery* painted on the side. The van was actually meant for the surrounding area. His elderly father did the village round on an equally elderly tricycle with a walnut box with the old name on it: *Blom's Bread & Pastries*. He'd joked to his wife that they could, in all honesty, now add *by appointment to Her Majesty the Queen* under the shiny new letters on the window.

Later that morning he dropped a large quantity of white rolls off at the notary's, from which he deduced that he hadn't been invited to dine with the Queen and decided to organise a festive lunch of his own. He hadn't looked in the wing mirror before opening the door and a boy shouted out 'Hey!' as he whizzed past on a bike. Startled, he jerked the door shut again. The boy straightened up and looked back over his shoulder as he rode off. It was Jan Kaan, the second son of Zeeger and Anna Kaan. The baker raised a hand in apology just before Johan Kaan raced past on a scooter, trying to catch up with his brother. Driving back very slowly to the bakery after carrying in the bread rolls, it took him a while to get over the fright: his knees were weak and changing gears wasn't going very smoothly either. The farm run would have to wait until later in the afternoon, the Queen was about to arrive. He parked the light-grey van at an angle in front of the bakery, and admired it from across the road: the Queen couldn't miss it. There were already quite a few people in front of the Polder House and he could hear excited children in the distance. Half the village could think of nothing but the lunch. He went into the shop, said hello to his wife and fetched his camera from the living room.

He followed his daughter, one of the two chosen children, and pressed the shutter in the instant that she, completely overcome by nerves, handed the Queen the flowers. And again when she, relieved, stepped back into line. Jan Kaan was there too, a scowl on his face. The Grint boy was standing next to him, holding his hand. The West Frisian dance group started up, and he took photos of them too, and of a friendly-looking Queen watching the folk dancing, and of old Van der Hoes with his violin, eyes and mouth screwed up in concentration. That'll be a good one, he'd thought. Afterwards he spoke to people, shook hands and enjoyed the beautiful June weather. People complimented him on his new van, and Blauwboer told him that the Queen's secretary really had made an arrangement about when to pick up the goats. He kissed his daughter. There were less and less people in front of the Polder House; he stayed on. And because he stayed, he managed to take the most beautiful photo he could have hoped for.

'What are you beaming about?' his wife asked, when he was finally eating his own lunch before setting out on the postponed delivery round.

'I'm happy,' he said. He had never said anything remotely like that before.

His wife sniffed and walked through to the shop; the bell had rung.

Bread and leather. The baker had installed a radio in the van and it was playing. Music, window down, the smell of fresh bread and new leather. A west wind, he thought, looking at the elms along the long road. Always a west wind. He drove past the labourer's cottage next to the Kaan farm. There was nobody there, they were on holiday. RC too, and maybe not even interested in the Queen because of it? For his part, the baker never felt much need of a holiday; the village was lively enough for him and, anyway, how could he relax in a holiday home in Overijssel or Drenthe while somebody else baked and sold the bread? Even if that somebody was his father? He turned into Kaan's yard, parked the van in front of the new milking parlour, hopped out and slid open the side door. A loaf of brown and half a loaf of white. Behind him, something made a thwacking sound. He jumped and looked around. A wet sheet on the clothes line. He went into the milking parlour and walked through to the kitchen door. He didn't close the door behind him, he wouldn't be long. He laid the one and a half loaves on the table with a flourish. 'Here they are again,' he said.

Anna Kaan looked up. She'd been standing at the window staring out at the washing.

'Anything else today?' He always asked and the answer was almost always no. Very occasionally a roll of zwieback or a packet of Frisian rye. Once in a blue moon, Zeeger Kaan wanted six almond cakes.

'No,' said Anna Kaan.

'Not even on this special day?'

'No.'

'What was the Queen like?'

'Special.'

The look on her face told him he wasn't going to get anything else out of her. The baker jumped again, this time from a loud banging overhead. 'What's going on up there?' he asked.

'Zeeger's making a bedroom in the attic. For Hanne.'

'Is she going upstairs? Is she already two?' The baker knew that all the Kaan children slept downstairs for two years, in the bedroom next to the living room. After years of going to people's houses you knew everything about them.

'Just,' Anna Kaan said. 'And afterwards we're getting rid of the wardrobes and the sliding doors.'

'That'll give you a really big living room.'

'Yes.'

The young Irish setter came into the kitchen from the hall. Tinus. A strange name for a dog. The baker squatted down to pat it and let it lick his face. The sound of sawing was now coming from upstairs.

'That will all take a while. The bedroom has to be finished first.'

'Everyone seems to be renovating these days.'

'And buying,' said Anna Kaan. 'Nice van.'

'Thanks.' It was the first time she'd mentioned his new acquisition.

He pushed the dog away, stood up and turned to leave without saying goodbye. He didn't consider it necessary: he went into so many houses, in and out, in and out, there'd be no end to it. Whistling, he left the kitchen, closing the door this time. On his way to the van, he used a gnawed pencil to note the loaf of brown and half a loaf of white in his book. He could do that, the baker with the chapped face: walk, whistle and write at the same time.

Almost subconsciously he was whistling 'Oh Happy Day'. He'd just heard it in the kitchen on a radio that looked brand new. It was a tune that stuck in your head. He backed out of the yard and only then did he think of the car door and Jan Kaan and that he should have mentioned it to Anna Kaan. Oh well, it wasn't really necessary. His knees had stopped trembling. Between the Kaans' and the next delivery he saw a bird of prey in the air. A buzzard, he thought. Or a harrier? He wasn't sure, he'd have to look it up in his bird guide: how to tell the difference. A few more farms and then home. There are three kinds of harriers, he thought. Marsh harriers and hen harriers and another kind that's named after somebody, so being able to tell the difference between buzzards and harriers isn't enough. He started whistling again, changed gears smoothly and tried to think where in the bookcase he'd put the bird guide.

Half an hour later he passed the Kaan farm again, now going in the other direction, taking it easy on his way home. He was still thinking about buzzards and harriers and that's why he was driving sedately, not paying too much attention to the road. It was very quiet, only a single car had obliged him to move over onto the verge. Then just before the causeway he hit something. He bent forward over the steering wheel, his foot pressing lightly on the brake. There wasn't anything on the road in front of him. In the wing mirror on the right he could see something brown. A dog, Zeeger Kaan's young Irish setter. Had he hit it? But if he had, how could the animal be sitting up like that? He felt the fright through his whole body once again, his knees started to shake. He slowed down and turned off the radio, still staring in the wing mirror. His left hand slid over the wheel. When the van came to a halt it was almost at right angles to the road. Silence. The smell of new leather and fresh bread. An unexpected gust of wind almost ripped the door out of his hand. The elms on the roadside bent towards him. *Blom's Breadery*. Even before he'd rounded the van, he loathed himself for that lettering, hearing himself gabbling on about the seventies being just around the corner, about a new, different era.

There was nothing wrong with the dog. It hadn't moved. It was sitting, but seemed to be pointing, as if the child lying half on the road was some kind of game. As the baker had driven on for quite some distance and was now hardly able to walk, it took him a while to reach the child and the dog. A wispy shadow slid over the road, the elms bent down lower over him, without rustling. The child looked unharmed. She was still, that was all, and her eyes were closed. When he squatted down, the dog thought he was doing it for its benefit, jumped against him and started licking his face. The baker pushed the young animal away roughly. A thin line of blood trickled out of one of the child's ears. The dog started barking, shrill and piercing. The side door – which was actually a front door, as the door in the front wall of the farmhouse was blind – opened. The baker stood up. Anna Kaan took a few steps into the yard and stopped. 'Zeeger!' she called. The young dog fell silent.

The baker's eyes moved up the facade from the blind door. A few metres above the balcony he saw for the first time – despite knowing everything that happened in the house – a plaque. *Anno 1912.*

'Zeeger!'

The dog began to whimper softly.

That night he didn't go to bed. He sat in an armchair he'd slid over in front of the big rear window and didn't even move when he heard his father starting work in the bakery – how had *he* got in? The bird guide was lying on his lap; he stared at the newspapers his wife had placed behind the pot plants. He now knew the precise difference between a buzzard and the three kinds of harriers. Montagu's harrier, that was the name he hadn't been able to dredge up earlier in the day. No, it was already yesterday. He didn't care any more. And even if he did, the 'dark bar across the base of the secondaries' was something he'd never be able to spot in flight. Especially not if he was driving. At four thirty – it was now Wednesday 18 June – his daughter came downstairs.

'What are you doing?' she asked.

'Sitting,' he said.

His daughter pushed hard to slide another armchair over in front of the window and sat down too. Then immediately fell back to sleep.

Is this what I'm going to remember? How to tell the difference between birds of prey? He looked at his little girl. Her cheek was still glowing from the touch of the Queen. Hanne Kaan's cheeks would never glow again for any reason. He stared outside, where it was already light and lines of mist were marking the ditches.

That was how his wife found him, after she too had come downstairs. She came over to stand behind his chair.

Their daughter woke up. 'What's wrong?' she asked.

His wife told her what had happened.

'I have to go there,' the baker said. He thought of his van. Just thinking of the smell of new leather and fresh bread made him feel sick. He saw himself making the journey to the Kaans' on his bike.

'Not now,' his wife said.

'No,' he mumbled. 'Not now.'

Yes, he thinks, a dog. A schnauzer maybe. He looks at the photo in his hand. Finally he wants to go. He doesn't want to go. He puts it off.

Piccaninny

'What's that?'

Uncle Jan feels his forehead. 'A mosquito bite, I think,' he says.

'Oh.' It really is starting to get a bit boring here. The bucket's empty again and Dieke doesn't feel like asking Uncle Jan to fill it up. She doesn't feel like doing it herself either, because then she'd have to think way too hard about which way to turn the tap off. The wet rag isn't wet any more, it's draped over a stone where it dried in a couple of minutes; she could see it getting lighter and lighter before her eyes. She walks around Uncle Jan until she's standing right behind him. Unbothered, he keeps filling in the letters with white paint. He's already finished one word and started on the next. There's a bald spot on the back of his head. No, not bald, it just has less hair than the rest of his head. His T-shirt is still damp. Because it's rolled up, of course. Her father doesn't have a bald spot like that. Uncle Jan hasn't said a word for a long time and now she has to do her best to follow what he's saying.

'Do you think it's boring not having cows any more?'

At least he's talking again. 'No.'

'Why not?'

'I don't like cows.'

'Don't you want to be a farmer when you grow up?'

'Me? Of course not!'

'Why not?'

'I don't know how to drive a tractor.'

'You could learn.'

'No, not me.'

'Even I can drive a tractor.'

'Really? Without a driving licence?'

'On Texel, I drive one of those little tractors.'

'Oh, that doesn't count.'

He draws the brush back out of a letter, dips it in the paint and starts on the next one.

'What letter's that?'

'This is an "l". It says "little". An "l" is easy, but the "e" is quite difficult.'

Dieke sighs. Very deeply.

'Or would you rather work at a butcher's? Like your mum?'

'No, it's smelly there.'

'What do you want to be then?'

'A painter.'

'Like what I'm doing now?'

'No. Paintings.'

'Fancy.'

She sighs again and goes for a little walk. It's like she can hear the noise from the swimming pool, far away in the distance. Shouting. What's Evelien doing now? Is it no fun at the swimming pool because she, Dieke, isn't there? Or is she not thinking of her at all and floating around next to Leslie with her water wings on? Maybe Leslie's not thinking about her either? No, Leslie's probably not at the pool anyway. When she arrives at the bench and sees her bag, she wonders what's happened to her cup. Uncle Jan was going to fill it up again, wasn't he? 'Where's my cup?' she bawls.

It takes a while before the answer comes. 'It's still over at the tool shed.'

Oh no, does she have to walk all the way over there again? It really is boiling. She kicks the shell grit up as she goes. At the little house it's a teensy bit cooler. The Jip and Janneke drinking cup is under the tap, but when she picks it up her arm feels funny, because the cup is still empty. 'Ow,' she says softly. And now? She walks a little bit further and looks around the corner of the house, where she finds a box, a fairly solid box. She picks it up, goes back to the front and puts it down on its side under the small window. Now she hardly needs to pull herself up on the ledge at all: the box is a lot higher than the bucket. There's the bird. It's spinning around in a very slow circle. What kind of bird was it again? A magpie. The kind of bird grandpa catches in a steel cage that's already got one inside it. The decoy bird, that's what Grandpa calls the other magpie. The bird spins back in the other direction, even more slowly. It's dead. Dead as dead. But still moving. Otherwise there's not much inside the little house. She can see a few shovels, some fence posts, a big wooden hammer and a kind of table with handles sticking out. She looks more closely at the magpie, sees that its legs are tied together, and follows the string up to the beam where it's looped around a nail. Then she jumps down off the box, brushes the dust off the front of her dress and kneels down at the tap. First turn it on a tiny little bit, and then turn it off again straight away. Then a bit more and remember, with her hand on the tap, which direction's off. When the cup is overflowing, she turns it off, clockwise, without having to think about it any more.

'But you could marry a farmer instead. Then he'd drive the tractor.'

'Nope,' she says.

'OK,' says Uncle Jan. 'I won't mention it again.'

'We have to leave.'

'The farm?'

'Yes.'

'Who says so?'

'Mum. She says the house is falling apart.'

'Is that so?'

'One day a bit of the balcony fell off.'

'That's dangerous.'

'No it's not. Nobody ever goes out on the balcony!'

'Would you like to try to do some painting?'

'After a drink.' She drinks half the cup in one go. It would have tasted a lot better if Uncle Jan had said something about it. Oh well. She's a bit scared to say that she wants to leave. She puts the cup down next to the grave and steps up onto the scraggly pebbles. Uncle Jan hands her the brush. Kneeling down, she notices that her hand is shaking. Quickly, she stands up again. 'It's too scary.'

'That's OK. I'll do it.'

He picks her up under the arms and lifts her over to the

dry earth next to the grave. Yes, she really does want to go now and she's starting to get hungry too. A banana and an apple, that's not enough to keep you going. Uncle Jan is sitting down again, painting again, he's started humming. She wants to go so much, she wouldn't care even if it was Grandma who came to take her back home. Then Uncle Jan starts singing.

'*Piccaninny, black as black, took a walk without a hat, but the sun shone bright and yella, so he put up his umbrella.*' He finishes a letter and starts on the next one without looking up. 'Do you know that song?'

'Nope.'

'It's about a little black boy.'

'Leslie?'

'Is he in your class at school?'

'Yep.'

'Then it's about Leslie.'

'He's at the pool now. I think. Evelien too.'

'And maybe now you wouldn't mind heading over there too?'

'Mm,' she says. 'Leslie's got a really big dad.'

'What do you mean?'

'Big. Tall.'

'Oh?'

'Yep.' Dieke starts singing softly and drawing circles in the shell grit with the toe of her sandal.

'I think Grandpa will come soon. Then you can go home with him.'

'Hm,' she says.

Gravel

The guy from the garden centre had asked him something
really hard. Something about surfaces. So much by so much,
so he could work it out for him. 'N-ormal,' Johan Kaan had
said. 'What fits on t-op of a little kid.' After that it took a
very long time before the garden-centre guy had figured it
out, and after *that*, they had to fill a bag, separately and
just for him, because they didn't usually stock the kind of
stones he wanted in bags. He had money, yes, of course he
had money. Otherwise you can't buy anything. 'D-you think
I'm c-razy or what?' The guy had started speaking slower
and slower – slower and louder.

Now he's walking down long straight roads with the
bag on his shoulder: first one shoulder then the next,
sometimes draped across both on the back of his neck
and, when it gets too much, very briefly clamped to his
stomach. He doesn't know how heavy the bag is,
he's forgotten what the guy said in the end, but it's just
as well, because what difference does it make – a number,
an amount – if you still have to carry the bag? It's really
quiet, except for just now, on the stretch of bike track
right after the white bridge over the canal, where a few
cars passed him. He knows these long straight roads, and
that one winding road before the white bridge too. He

knows where the junctions and bends are, he knows the roadside ditches like the back of his hand. In the old days, yeah, in the old days, he'd ride long stretches with his eyes shut, keeping it up as long as he could, and then a bit longer. The Zündapp between his legs like a . . . well, like a moped. Since the day he turned sixteen, he hadn't ridden a bicycle once. Out drinking in Schagen: sober on the way there, drunk home. He knows the roads in storms and in hail, misty, hot and cold, under a full moon, with the tang of ditchwater in spring, the sour smell of poplar leaves in autumn, a hint of metal when it rained (was that the Zündapp or did the rain itself smell of metal?), a sense of animals resting in the dark (along the winding road there were always sheep). And belting along, always. Never going off the road, never smashing into the rail when he crossed the white bridge they repainted every five years, never ending up in a ditch. No, not until he started jumping with as much control as possible over cars and tree trunks and slabs of . . .

He starts singing. Very loudly. There was something in his head just now that needed drowning out. The bright-blue stones are leaving dents in his flesh; that helps too. Along the side of the road are a few big trees, with yellow dots painted on two of them. Between the big ones there are smaller ones with shrivelled brown leaves. It's getting too heavy, he has to put the bag down for a moment. Next to a causeway gate he takes off his trainers and sits down on the end of a culvert that runs under the causeway. He sees steam rising from his bare feet. In his head. He's stopped singing and for a second forgets where he's going. He pulls a pack of Marlboros out of the back pocket of his cut-off jeans; the cigarettes are squashed flat, but unbroken. On his right is the road, with patches of melted tar; on his left a field, two birds with long curved beaks walking in it. They pretend they haven't noticed him. 'Currrr-lew!' he calls, and even then they don't take off. Stupid things. Or is it too hot to fly today?

Today. Isn't it today that Jan . . . ? He thinks. He tries to think. He pictures Toon. Maybe that will help him get the day worked out. Did Toon say something before he left? No, because he made sure Toon didn't see him go. He draws on the cigarette. He slaps the soles of his feet against the water in the farm ditch. Jan lives on Texel, he thinks. Boat. Seagulls. The cigarette's finished, he draws on it once too often, the filthy taste of the filter gets stuck in his mouth. He slides down off the culvert and stands up to his thighs in the water, which was clear, but isn't any more. He scoops up some water and uses it to rinse out his mouth. The filter taste is gone. Climbing back up out of the ditch he kicks the sludge off one foot and then the other, then uses his white socks to dry carefully between his toes before putting them back on, filthy and damp. Shoes too, and then he has an elaborate scratch of the crotch, it's all a bit sweaty down there. Bag back on his shoulder. 'Currr-lew!' he calls again and walks on, in the middle of the road. A few minutes later a car beeps him over to the side. It's like a giant apple driving past; never before has he seen a car this colour, a strange kind of green, it hurts his eyes. The car doesn't brake; it wouldn't have occurred to the driver to give him a lift. Johan Kaan rests his free shoulder against the trunk of an old elm. He looks up. Dead, he thinks. 'Stone dead!' he shouts.

Ledge

Yes, the red beech has had it. The tree is just short of a hundred. Probably planted in 1912, just after the farmhouse was built, in the middle of the newly sown lawn. Directly in front of the blind door and the balcony over it. Zeeger Kaan looks at the tree through a kitchen window that gets no sun, because of the three chestnuts he planted in his own lawn. One of which is already showing signs of that new disease, bleeding dark sap from little holes. What's it all about? he wonders. All these diseases trees get? What purpose do they serve? Shall I ride or drive? Taking the bike is good for his knees, but the car's better on a day like today, it's got air conditioning.

While backing up the drive a little absent-mindedly – earlier that day he hadn't seen a soul on the road – he has to suddenly brake hard for a car that's going at least thirty kilometres an hour over the limit. Stunned, he follows the green blur with his eyes. What kind of idiot buys a car that colour? He himself drives calmly up the road in the settling dust. In the village he slows down even more. Here and there he raises an index finger to people painting their eaves or letting out the dog, the odd cyclist. It's only when parking the car next to the Polder House that he starts to notice the air conditioning. Stupid, he thinks, painting eaves in weather like this. They'll have blisters in the fresh paint by evening.

'Hey, Grandpa!'

'Hi, Diek,' he calls.

'We're over here!'

'I see you.' Dieke is standing on the path at the entrance to the new part of the cemetery. Every time he comes here it seems smaller and more cramped. Jan is sitting in front of the headstone. He's finished *Our little* and is already working on the *s* of *sweetheart*. 'It's coming along.'

'Yep,' says his son.

'Hungry?'

'Nah.'

'Dieke! You hungry?'

'Yes,' Dieke shouts. 'Grandpa,' she then adds, as if she hasn't said hello to him yet, 'come and have a look here.'

He walks away from his son. Dieke shouldn't stay out in the sun much longer, her arms are already turning red. She points. Three large herring gulls are standing in a circle and stamping on the dry grass, staring down at their feet. They want worms, but on a day like today they'll be waiting a long time. Even the red dots on their yellow beaks – here it is, come and get it – won't lure any worms up. 'Gulls on land, storm on strand,' he says.

'What?'

'It's a saying.' He looks to the west. The hazy air is advancing, the sun no longer quite as bright.

Dieke whispers something.

'What'd you say, Diek?'

'I'd like to go home after all.'

'Then you can come with me in a minute, OK?'

'OK.' They walk back together, holding hands. When they reach Jan, Dieke lets go of his hand and carries on to the bench under the linden. She picks up her cup and starts to drink. 'Phew,' she says, screwing the lid back on the cup.

'That cuttlebone . . .' Jan says.

'What about it?'

'What's it for?'

'To get it nice and clean.'

'It's useless. The stone's way too rough.'

'OK, we know that for next time then.'

Jan pulls the brush back out of the *w* and looks at him. After a while he says, 'Yep.'

It's not always easy, watching your children. They resemble you so much. Sometimes they come so close it's frightening. Jan especially can get a look in his eye that makes Zeeger Kaan feel quite uncomfortable.

'There's an auntie of mine over there,' Dieke yells from her bench. 'Under the ground.'

Sometimes their faces merge and he'll suddenly see Jan in Klaas, or Klaas in Jan, and have to close his eyes to get it right again. At other times he'll see himself, and that gets stronger as they grow older: bags under their eyes, lines at the sides of their mouths, creases in their foreheads. Not with Johan of course, he's the exception to every rule. Since the accident he's developed into the best-looking Kaan by far.

'Is "Piccaninny black as black" a boy or a girl?'

He looks away, opens his mouth to answer his son, then closes it again and hums until he gets up to '*so she put up her umbrella*'. 'She,' he says. 'She's a girl.'

'You sure?'

'Yep.'

'Hey!' Dieke yells. 'Can you hear me?'

'Sure. Is it warm enough for you?'

'Warm's not the right word,' Jan says.

'I think it'll be better tomorrow.'

'I won't be here tomorrow.'

'We're going fishing tonight!' Dieke calls.

'You don't even have a rod,' says Zeeger Kaan.

'*You* do!'

'Careful, that "e" isn't going right.'

Jan stands up to hand him the brush.

'No.'

'Yes. Go ahead.'

'Don't start.'

'Maybe you can do it better yourself.'

'No.' He pushes his son's hand away.

'What are you doing?' Dieke calls.

'My knees hurt.'

Jan lowers himself back down until he's sitting on the gravel with his legs either side of the raised edges. 'You asked me to do it. If you go on at me like that, I'll just stop.'

'OK,' says Zeeger Kaan. It's true, he thinks. I did ask him. He's the best painter, he does the maintenance on all those holiday homes over on Texel, and he always used to criticise me when I was painting. And rightly so, I loathed all that scraping and sanding. But I never painted full in the sun.

Zeeger Kaan goes for a wander around the ever-shrinking cemetery. He runs a hand over his short hair, he rubs a knee.

'You going already?' Dieke screams.

'No,' he calls back. 'Just a little longer.'

'Don't forget me, OK?'

Children's graves are marked with stuffed animals that were once rain-soaked and swollen and are now dry, lumpy and flocky. He looks at the names and years on the headstones. Three mayors buried in a row. All three of them alone, without wives. One of them was mayor when the old Queen came to visit. Knowing him, he probably said something grovelling like, 'This way if you please, Your Majesty. Lunch will be served here inside,' before they disappeared into the Polder House. A bunch of daffodils at the foot of the monument to the English airmen is completely withered, just this side of crumbling to dust. He walks on into the older section, behind the Polder House.

'Are you going?'

'I'll be back in a minute, Diek!'

'Are you in such a hurry to go?' he hears his son ask.

'Not really,' Dieke says.

He stops at his parents' grave: *Jan Kaan* and *Neeltje Kaan-Helder*. A grave that's much newer than the one Jan's working on. A grave whose lease, as he now remembers, needs renewing for another ten years sometime soon. Lying next to them are his grandmother and grandfather: *Zeeger Kaan* and *Griet Kaan-van Zandwijk*. Always strange to see your own name on a headstone. He never knew his grandfather, who died young. But his grandmother didn't die until she was ninety-five, on a stormy night in November. Dozens of roof tiles in the yard, fallen trees, no electricity, a big crack in one of the front windows. And early in the morning, a dead grandmother in the three-quarter bed. He stood there, studying her face for a long time, making out what he took for a last trace of resistance. Anna stood next to him, squeezing his hand so hard she was almost crushing it, and he wanted to look at her and smile, but couldn't tear his eyes away from the dead woman. In the days that followed, his father and mother had a massive clear-out, with virtually everything going onto a huge pile behind the farmhouse that they weren't able to light for two or three days because of the constant easterly. The old kapok mattress smoked and fizzed for a long time before it finally caught fire, the sansevierias exploded damply.

He walks on quickly to the gravediggers' shed, where he turns on the tap, cups his hands and splashes water on his face. Then he sees his father, who after clearing the broken tiles from the yard, went directly to his mother's cabinet and took out his medal. A gold medal, won with the sleigh on Kolhorn harbour one freezing winter. His father was very good with horses. Rubbing the medal on his chest, puffing on it and cleaning it again, while behind him his mother lay dead in her three-quarter bed. The farm was finally his.

He looks in through the window. A shrivelled magpie is hanging on a string. There is a heavy mallet. An old-fashioned bier. Spades and shovels, posts. It must be suffocating in there.

Going back to get Dieke, he realises that there is a whole village under his feet. No, several villages. And still, the older he gets, the smaller and more cramped this place becomes. Will there be space for me? he wonders. Nellie, that was the name of the horse his father won the medal with. Bloody hell, that just popped up out of nowhere.

'We're off.'

'Yes!' says Dieke. She jumps down onto the ground, grabs her rucksack and heads straight for the gate.

'We have to say goodbye to Jan first.'

'Oh, yeah.'

Jan is up to the second *e*. Zeeger notices how muscular his back is: although he's bending forward, his backbone is still in a furrow, not sticking out at all. 'You should take that T-shirt off your head and just put it on.' A muscular back and thinning hair.

'Do you know what I thought of this morning, riding past the Polder House?'

'What?'

'Uncle Piet, and how he stood on that black ledge.'

'What do you mean?'

'At the funeral. He stood on that black ledge without holding on to anything.'

'Ah, son, come on. That's not even possible.'

'Are we going now?' Dieke asks.

'It's still true.' He's talking without looking up. He dips the brush into the paint again and puts the tip in the *t*.

Zeeger Kaan sighs. What an imagination. He takes Dieke's hand. 'Come on.'

When they're seven or eight graves away, Jan calls out to him. 'Did Mum say anything?'

'No,' he lies.

'Did you try to get her down?'

'No.'

Dieke tugs on his hand. 'Grandpa . . .'

'When did she actually go up there?'

'Just before I left to pick you up from the train yesterday, Johan rang. He wanted to speak to her. When we got home, she was up on the straw.'

'And now?'

'Grandpa!'

'Yes, Diek. Nothing.'

They walk on. It's very quiet. Without speaking, Dieke points out two small birds perched on a low branch of the linden. Blue tits, their beaks wide open. The shells crunch underfoot. He looks at Anna's bike, which Jan has leant against a chestnut tree. There's the black-painted ledge that runs all around the base of the Polder House. Seven centimetres wide at most. Black varnish, that's what it's painted with. Just to be sure, he inspects the wall, which is painted off-white. Maybe there's a ring somewhere his brother-in-law could have held on to. Nothing. Dieke has walked ahead to the car. He opens the door and she jumps onto the seat. 'Oof!' she says.

'Wait a sec,' he tells her. 'I just have to . . .'

'It's boiling in here.'

'Leave the door open. I won't be long.'

He walks around the car and opens the door on the driver's side as well, turns the key in the ignition and switches the radio on. He stops to listen for a moment. A reporter from Radio North-Holland has gone to the seaside: *'It's chock-a-block down here, the beach restaurants are doing a roaring trade and that's a real turnaround from last year when the summer was a complete washout. I'm now walking down the ramp . . .'*

'Boring,' says Dieke.

'There'll be music in a minute.'

He walks back to the black ledge, but changes his mind and carries on. Past his wife's bike, now in the shade of the chestnuts and the gate, which he fortunately didn't close behind him, so he can go back into the cemetery without making a sound.

He can't see anything. His son is hidden behind the head-stones. Maybe working on the *h*, or even the third *e*. The herring gulls, which he had forgotten, laugh as they take wing. Jan sits up a little to look at the birds as they glide over his head and disappear behind the hedge, tumbling over each other as they fly west. To the beach. Then the cemetery seems deserted again. He turns and walks over to the black ledge, stands with his back against the wall and steps up with one heel on the ledge. When he tries to put his other foot up there too, he immediately loses his balance. He tries it again, this time with the other foot first, and again fails. 'Strange boy,' he mumbles.

'Grandpa!'

Radio

Klaas is back in the easy chair in the old cow passage. Not because he wants to take it easy, but because he can't get his mother's voice out of his head. He still doesn't know if he imagined it or if she really did call him. He stares out, which means staring at a square in the distance where the sliding door was yesterday evening. Sitting on top of the white-brick wall that forms a partition in the L-shaped cow passage is another radio. In the old days you used to walk out of the cowshed to the sound of music and be greeted by the same music a bit further along. Now the only radio you hear is the old thing in his father's garage. He turned this one on not expecting it to work, but it did . . . *'I'm now walking down the ramp and onto the beach, let's see if anyone's here . . . Could you tell me if . . . Wait, this is a German family, they don't understand me of course, and if they say something in reply, you won't understand them. Unless I translate it on the spot, but it's much too hot for that, ha ha ha. I'll just walk on a bit and – Ah, yes, here are two dyed-in-the-wool North Hollanders. Ladies, are you enjoying your day on the beach?'*

'It's glorious, but now the sun's gone, so we're not going to get much browner. But we're not going home yet! Rie and I just love swimming, so we'll be going back in for another dip!'

'You heard it, listeners, this is the place to be right now. What was your name? . . . Jenneke and Rie are in their element. The sun really has disappeared for the moment, so let's switch to our weatherman, Jan Visser. Jan, can you . . .'

The wooden silo starts creaking. Like an upside-down iceberg, only a small part of it is visible from here, the lower section that emerges from the attic and tapers down to form a chute you can open by sliding up a steel door. First it creaks, then something falls against the door. Then it's quiet again, except for the drivel coming from the radio.

*

Have you sold the land yet? That brother of his – who spends all his time over there on Texel and never lifts a finger here, who never even shows up for the haymaking, when Johan is up on the cart before the first bale has rolled out of the baler, although it isn't really responsible, letting him help with something like that – that brother asks if he's sold the land yet. 'Tsk,' he says. He stands up and turns off the radio. Dust billows from the sheet covering the easy chair.

Why do we always try so hard to get Mum to come down? he wonders. What's the point? In the end she always comes down of her own accord. Once she'd taken his father's shotgun up with her and even fired it. She'd aimed at a swift, she admitted to her husband much later, and missed it of course. For some reason, his mother isn't really fond of animals. The next day he and Jan had tied all the ladders they could find together and climbed up to replace the dozens of wrecked roof tiles. Her shoulder was bruised for weeks. Klaas can't remember when that was, the early eighties maybe. It's getting more and more embarrassing, especially now she's in her seventies. Her dragging that old body up the ladder and laying it down on the hard straw; her shrill voice, muffled by a hundred years of dust.

He walks out and gives the door lying flat on the concrete another kick. There's that dead sheep again. How did they do it in the old days? Did they just bury the dead animals in a field? He remembers one of his grandfather's stories, about a mass grave on the edge of the farm after the anthrax epidemic of 1923. Hundreds of cow bones at the bottom of a field. He remembers so many things. He starts whistling and, like yesterday evening, walks to the causeway gate and rests his forearms on the top, badly chewed board. Two hares are sitting in the field about fifty metres away. Their ears are trembling. They're facing each other and staring into each other's eyes like two competing hypnotists. It's strange. You often see a single hare or two together, but very rarely do you see a group. They ignore his whistling.

Where the wooden silo comes down through the ceiling there's an access hatch. An open access hatch. Klaas pulls a rusty bike off a pile of rubbish and leans it against the white wall, grips the top of the wall, steps up onto the bike seat and uses the momentum to raise his hands to the bottom of the hatch. He steps up onto the wall from the bike seat, then hoists his upper body into the space, swinging his legs in the process and kicking the radio off the wall. It definitely won't work now.

It's gloomy; at the back of the barn there are just two small skylights. The straw is almost three metres high. He hears Dirk snort. He hasn't got rid of the bull yet; once he has, the place will be completely dead. Not that he costs much: a few handfuls of straw, a couple of scoops of concentrate now and then, a bucket of water. There's no ladder leaning against the straw. His mother wasn't born yesterday. One more thing: that old body hauling up the ladder. And she's not that clever anyway, because it's not the only ladder. The others might not be particularly solid, but they're not totally rickety either. One's leaning against the old milking parlour; another, aluminium, is lying on the floor at the front of the barn, where they used to keep the hay. If he wanted, he could get up there in no time, even without a ladder.

He leans on the bales of straw, still panting a little from the climb. He wants his mother to say something friendly to him, if only to get that softly echoing 'Klaas' out of his head. He hardly gets a friendly word out of his wife these days. She makes demands, she gives commands. He's forty-bloody-eight years old and he wants his mother to say a kind word. Maybe he even wants her to tell him what to do.

Straw

After hearing something fall and smash below, Anna Kaan turned over onto her stomach. Had he put on the radio specially for her? She pictures the 'dyed-in-the-wool North Hollanders', Rie and Jenneke. She's finished the Viennese biscuits. Together with the lukewarm water and the advocaat, they've made her a little queasy. She feels like something fresh: a sour apple, crispy French beans. That's easy enough, that last one, later – the vegetable garden is full of them. She hears Klaas panting. She knows he wouldn't have any trouble at all climbing the straw without a ladder. She's also realised by now that her heart's not really in it; she can't even look at the parade sword without feeling hotter than she already is. Strangely enough, her feet are still cold and there's a numbness in her calves. She feels embarrassed. She's up here because it's something she's been doing for almost forty years; she does it as a reminder, out of habit.

I'd be better off lying on the beach next to Rie and Jenneke, she thinks. Going for a swim together. What do I care that the sun's disappeared?

The three of them are stuck here together: her, Klaas and Dirk. And the swallows of course. She lets her oldest son wait a while first.

'Klaas?'

'Yeah?'

'What are you doing?'

'Standing here.'

That has her stumped. She turns over onto her side; her neck is stiff and her arm hurts. She rubs her breastbone, the nausea is already starting to fade a little.

'Did you just call me?'

'No,' she lies. 'Why would I call you?'

'Because you need me.'

'I don't need anyone.'

'Why don't you come back down?'

'Mind your own business.' She hears Klaas let go of the bales, the straw rustles, and then she hears him take a few steps across the wooden floor. Towards the hatch? 'You have to get Jan away from the cemetery.'

'Why?'

'No, just do it. Johan will be there too.'

'Johan? What makes you think that?'

The first time Johan was lost he was lying under the platform Zeeger had built for the washing machine. In the new milking parlour. It was a Miele top-loader.

Apparently Miele was the ultimate when it came to washing machines, but this one was constantly broken. The repairman would drive up in his van with *Miele, nothing better* written on the side. 'Humph,' she says now, almost forty years later. They shouldn't have been allowed to drive around in a van like that. And just like the baker used to call out 'Here it is again!' ad infinitum, laying the bread on the kitchen table with a flourish, the Miele man always used to say, 'Ready to wash, Mrs Kaan.' Until the next time it broke. She found Johan when she went to put on a load in between searching. He was lying on his side under the platform with his knees pulled up. A year or two older and he wouldn't have fitted. 'I wanted to go away,' he said, when she asked him what he was doing there. She asked him why. 'Because,' he said. Later, he often crawled in under the washing machine. Sometimes she pulled him back out, sometimes she left him lying there until he'd had enough.

'"Humph"?' Klaas asks. 'I asked why you think Johan will be there too.'

Oh, Klaas, that's right. 'I *know* he's there.'

'Johan's in Schagen. How would he get here? I don't think they're allowed to just up and leave.'

'As if he'd pay any attention to that.' She turns onto her back and spreads out her arms. She catches the smell of her own body and thinks of the beach again, the sea. 'You going?'

'Maybe.'

'I'm your mother!' She scowls. And she's heard something

in his voice that's aroused her suspicions. 'Or have you already been?'

'Of course not. What for?'

'You going?'

'Yes.'

'Right now?'

'Yes. Or soon.'

'Then you'll be doing something useful at least.'

Klaas doesn't say anything else. She hears him climb down through the hatch, then something else falls – strangely enough it sounds like a bike – and going by the noise, Klaas hasn't landed on his own two feet either. 'Oh, fucking hell,' he swears. The way him and his wife just sat there looking miserable and puffing away through the whole dinner just to wind up Jan. The food lying on the table instead of on the plates. Johan, who had started throwing chips – and earlier in the day sitting there like an imbecile, with a monkey on his head. It wasn't even anything new, they'd always fooled around with their food. If they were angry they'd turn tins of treacle upside down on each other's heads, or stick a carefully licked finger in someone else's custard. Zeeger, ending the festivities with his 'So, the day went quite well'. If she's not very mistaken, he even let out a sigh of satisfaction.

It's quiet again down below.

No, she'll never celebrate anything again.

And yes, that was where she found Johan. Under the washing machine. But that was later. On the day itself, he and Jan were at Tinie and Aris's. She'd rung herself, even though she can hardly believe that now. When did she find the time? Was it before or after she called an ambulance?

And Klaas, where was Klaas? The baker kept coming in that horrible light-grey van. He just gave up his cheerful 'Here it is again!' Of course he kept coming, it was his job, and he could hardly employ someone else just for them. When Blom's Breadery closed down because there was too much competition from the supermarket in Schagen, the whole village was up in arms. Not that they had any right to be, seeing as everyone realised it was their own fault. The whole village except her. She was relieved. There was a load of washing on the line too: whites, sheets flapping in the June wind. Maybe her mother brought it in. And someone – no idea who – turned off the radio. That was good because they kept playing that horrible song every hour or so.

Anna Kaan picks up the bottle of advocaat, unscrews the cap and lets the thick drink slide down into her throat. It makes her drowsy. At birthday parties she limits herself to one or two small glasses. When the big creaking starts – What is that? Is it the main timbers? The beams? Or is it something in her own body? – she screws the cap back on. A quarter left. Is the wood, all the wood, expanding because it's so hot? Or is it shrinking? She looks up through the hole in the roof at the sky, which does seem to have turned white now, or grey at least. Her time on the straw is almost over. A raindrop, she thinks. When I feel the first drop, I'll seize on it to go back down. She takes a few more mouthfuls of warm water to wash the sweet taste out of her mouth and shakes her legs to make her calves wobble. The numb feeling doesn't go away.

Walking Stick

The walking stick with the ivory knob. That will give him the support he needs. The hydrangea leaves are looking a little better, at least they're not limp any more. The gravel crunches under his feet, the point of the walking stick pokes holes in it. He'd rather not bump into anyone on the short walk from his house to the cemetery. He wants to walk purposefully, and the walking stick helps with that too. He thinks about Dinie's dog; but that's going too far in the other direction. It's big and sluggish and never seems that interested in what's happening around it. Its name is well chosen though, Benno. No, a schnauzer, he wouldn't mind that, with a short sharp name.

He takes the bridge over the canal and from there it's only a short distance to the Polder House drive. The point of the stick taps on the pavement. One, two, three. One, two, three. He interrupts the rhythm by reaching for his left rear pocket and touching the sealed envelope containing the photo. He slipped a piece of cardboard in to stop it creasing. It's much too hot for a jacket, otherwise he would have put the envelope in the inside pocket. The back of his shirt was wet the moment he stepped out the front door. The Polder House looks strange to him, so soon after looking at the photos of the Queen's visit, and after quickly gulping down a third lemon brandy before grabbing the walking stick. There used to be trees here, elms, and old-fashioned lamp posts, and next to the door a sign saying *Office hours: 9.00–12.30. Closed in the afternoon.* That's where the Queen, the mayor and a man he didn't know stood to watch the folk dancing, with that ancient violinist standing next to them playing, his lips thin and tight. He's buried a hundred metres further along by now, of course. Just like the mayor. The old Queen is interred in Delft, in that big crypt. They stood in the shade of the old linden espalier. He turns around, because he can see that image before him so clearly he almost expects to see his light-grey Volkswagen van outside the bakery on the other side of the canal. It's not there, of course. Someone is approaching on a bike and he hurries past the Polder House to the cemetery gate. It's wide open, as if somebody just left.

The baker hardly ever visits the cemetery. His parents were both cremated and he has no other family buried here. Dinie once brought him here to show him her husband's grave, leaving him to stand there awkwardly while she attacked the headstone with a dishwashing brush (he hadn't seen a fleck of dirt), threw away some old flowers and put some new ones in their place. The dog lay a few metres away looking in the other direction.

He has a slight headache, which is hardly surprising after three brandies in the middle of the day. He has a hat on the hat rack at home – he can picture it hanging there – but unfortunately he didn't put it on. More than just protecting your face from the sun – something that's not necessary now because the sun is hardly shining – the brim of a hat also casts a shadow over your eyes. Just act like you come here often, as if the cemetery is part of your regular afternoon walk. He looks at the inscriptions without reading a single letter. The shell grit under his feet sounds very different from the gravel in his front garden and he's glad he brought the walking stick; he really is leaning on it now. There's a bench over there, under a big linden. And now he sees Jan Kaan, or at least a gleaming back and a head with a cloth tied around it. He lowers himself onto the bench, in the middle at first, but there's a brass plate that jabs him in the back, so he slides across to one side. He stands the walking stick between his legs, both hands on the ivory knob.

Then it gets so quiet he imagines he can hear panting. It seems to be coming from above. Damn it, there are two little birds in the linden. Two little birds that are really hot. If he's not careful, one will topple over onto his head any minute. He slides back to the other side of the bench, drawing a line in the shell grit with the point of his stick. Jan Kaan rises up a little and looks in his direction. They look at each other, creating a brief possibility of speech, of greeting each other – then the moment is gone. By the time the baker decides to raise his stick up in the air, Jan Kaan is already sitting down again, hunched in front of the headstone.

Oh Happy Day

Dinie Grint is sitting on the sofa in her living room. She's lowered the awning even further, making it *even* yellower inside the room, despite the main window no longer being in direct sunlight. Her bare feet are resting on a leather footstool and Benno is sitting in front of it, licking her heels. She's crying. She's already reached out to pick up the phone three times, and three times she's pulled back her hand. You can't call the police when you're crying, they won't understand what you're saying, and if they do, they'll think you're soft in the head. 'Yes, sweetie,' she sniffs. 'At least you're nice to your mistress.' The dog looks at her and stops his licking. 'No,' she says. 'Don't stop.' The dog obeys.

People at the cemetery are generally nice and friendly. Sometimes they're not very talkative and she understands that. Sometimes they're the opposite and then she has to dam their flood of words, so she can have her say too. The council neglects its duties; she's the one who has to keep her eye on everything, clearing away wilted flowers now and then, with Benno's fat tail smoothing out the shell grit in the paths as a free extra. Those horrible Kaan boys sent her away from the cemetery. The red-headed monsters!

'Bah!' she says, pushing Benno away. She stands up, turns on the radio and looks at the clock. Yes, it's the *Golden Hours*. Non-stop hits. She sits down again, swinging her legs back up onto the footstool. They just chased her off. What did they say again? 'Just go away!' And, 'Mind your own business!' But she does have business there, and she knows what sorrow is. And that cheeky little girl – Dieke, who on earth came up with a name like that? – with her stomach pushed forward and those bright eyes under pale eyebrows. The tone of that 'Bye-bye!' of hers was outrageous. They were wrecking the place, whether it was their own grave or not. For the fourth time she reaches out to the telephone. She's stopped crying, but still doesn't pick up the receiver. Even if there is someone at the station, they'll only laugh at her, she knows that, her voice hasn't calmed down yet. 'Yes, sweetie,' she says soothingly, to herself *and* the dog. She hikes her skirt up a little, then stares at the radio, stunned, as a familiar tune begins and the Edwin Hawkins singers launch into 'Oh Happy Day'.

She closes her eyes and, instead of Benno's tongue, feels the draught on her knees in the white ticket booth; the wind blowing in through a hole under the counter, mostly warm, but sometimes biting cold. This song, all through that long summer, and it didn't bore her for a single minute. The smooth gospel flowing out over all of the heads in the swimming pool, singing about Jesus washing sins away and making no distinction between Christian and non-Christian heads. It was the first summer the radio had been connected to the speakers on the corners of the ticket booth. She sold singles, checked the season tickets, and fished sticky one- and five-cent coins out of children's hands in exchange for yet another piece of liquorice, another marshmallow.

It was only when she hadn't seen her son on the diving board for a while that she lifted herself up off her chair to get a better view out over the water, and then she immediately sneaked a glance at Albert Waiboer, standing in the paddling pool with his daughter, his back bent, his feet planted firmly on the bottom of the pool, muscles tensed. She used to daydream about Albert Waiboer. Him doing things to her that her husband couldn't even imagine. If Albert Waiboer wasn't there, and he didn't come often, there was always some other man to look at. And yes, she'd smoked a cigarette now and then, even though that wasn't strictly allowed; she just set the door slightly ajar and the smoke soon drifted out through the opening. The two little Kaans always came together, and she always greeted them with a cheerful, 'Ah, if it's not the Kaan boys again.' One always pulled a bad-tempered, surly face and the youngest one always swore. They were always unfriendly, they were never fun, not happy or carefree like other kids. And Teun dived off that board so beautifully in his yellow swimming trunks. She didn't see much of the oldest Kaan at the swimming pool, but the other one, Jan Kaan, who later . . . in the garage attic . . . with her son . . .

The song finished and they cut straight to another golden oldie. She's glad to reopen her eyes.

The Kaans. Once she rode her bike past their farm in winter and there they were, the oldest son and Zeeger in the middle of six or seven nasty-looking men, shotguns broken over the crooks of their arms. Lying on a white tarpaulin were rows of hare, pheasants and ducks, poor creatures. The hunters were knocking back little glasses of schnapps with their free hands, out in the open air, in broad daylight! Strange people. She hardly knows Anna Kaan, but she must have a screw loose too.

Teun. Her hand wants to move towards the telephone again. 'Benno, that's enough now,' she says. The dog doesn't listen. Instead of the police, maybe she could call Teun? And then avoid saying 'Teun' by accident, but use the right name, otherwise he can get so angry. The baker: she could call him too, he's always home. He'd be sitting in his back garden under an umbrella, a crossword puzzle on his lap. No, there's no point, she'll see him in a couple of hours. She starts crying again, this time more because she feels so helpless. It took all of her powers of persuasion, but she managed to get away from the village, the son respectably married in Den Helder with two children, and then he gets divorced. What's more, he no longer wants to be a fitter, but retrains as a youth worker and ends up running some home for 'difficult' youths. And just hangs up if she phones him and accidentally lets slip with a 'Teun'. But you are your name, surely? She and her husband didn't call him Teun lightly. Names are important, that's why it's so horrible when people have an ugly name. Dieke? Terrible for that girl, somehow. She thinks of calling her ex-daughter-in-law, but rejects the idea, because she has a new husband now and there's a chance he might answer and he doesn't know her at all. Oh, yeah. 'Does she dye her hair, do you think?' That's what that red-headed Kaan said to that ugly child. And he'd asked, 'Do *you* know who that woman is?' as if *he* didn't see who she was. If I recognise him, he must recognise me too, surely? 'Benno,' she says quietly, so that the dog doesn't even react.

Den Helder. Almost all of the shrubs and perennials they'd dug up out of the front garden froze that first winter, the furniture looked wrong in the small living room and her husband was completely miserable. Once, when everything was more or less sorted, just once, she called her son a nincompoop, which he accepted impassively. He'd started at a new school after a week or so and otherwise didn't seem to have a problem with the move. Her husband had a new, wide-eyed expression, as if he was constantly asking himself how he'd ended up somewhere so windy. Because of her, of course. She'd set the transfer in motion. He kept that strange look in his eyes until just before he died. It was only after she promised to bury him in the village that he finally started looking a bit normal again.

Don't call anyone then, because only weirdos call people when they're crying. 'Benno!' she exclaims. The dog stops licking. She stands up and walks over to the window, stares down at the dry grass. The dog comes over next to her and barks at a sluggish thrush in the garden. Long strands of drool drip from his jaws onto the rug. She should get started on dinner, put a bottle of white wine in the fridge. They're fond of a glass of white, her and the baker. The baker is nothing at all like the Negro who slipped in through her bedroom window this morning. He'd let dark ale run down his chin and drip onto his bare chest without any embarrassment, after which it would make stripes all the way down to his navel, or maybe even lower. She sighs. The Negro, of course, is also much younger than the baker.

Walking Stick

The baker hits the trunk of the linden with his walking stick to avoid losing face. For a moment he's afraid he's disturbed the birds, but they don't fly off. Just stroll over, have a look what he's doing, then comment on it? His mouth is dry from the lemon brandy, dry and cloyingly sweet. The stick is back between his legs and, putting his whole weight on it, he manages to stand up. Stroll, he thinks, don't walk. To his left there's a radiant gravestone that looks like it was lowered into place just yesterday. Jan Kaan is painting. A small tin of white paint, a brush. The baker isn't right behind him and has a clear view of what's written on the headstone. Four words in fresh paint. Jan Kaan has just started on the year of birth. The baker closes his eyes, he doesn't want to read the rest. 'Hi,' he says and then he's at a loss. Can he say 'Jan'? 'Kaan' is what he comes out with. 'Hi, Kaan.' Only then does he open his eyes again.

The red-headed man turns halfway towards him.

'It's turning out well,' the baker says.

'Hmm,' says Jan Kaan.

'And coming along nicely.'

Jan Kaan doesn't reply. He puts the tin of paint down on the ground and lays the brush across it, gets onto his knees, unties the cloth tied around his head, shakes it out and pulls it on. It's a T-shirt. He stands up. 'I'm going to go and sit on that bench for a bit,' he says.

The baker smells him as he passes, eyes fixed on the bench. Not unpleasant: sunscreen and perspiration, maybe a bit of something like deodorant mixed in. He's aged, of course, and has already started walking with his father's and grandfather's stoop, but the seven-year-old kid is still in him. And the twelve-year-old. The baker tries to remember when he last saw Jan Kaan. Really saw him. Maybe when he was about eighteen. After that, once or twice, three times at most? He must have been in the kitchen sometimes – on a Saturday – when he delivered the bread? He's sat down on the bench and is tugging at the short sleeves of his T-shirt. The baker takes his words as an invitation to go and sit next to him. He needs his walking stick to cover the fifteen metres. Exhaling deeply, he sits down on the bench for the second time. A bit of small talk first, he thinks. 'Where are you living these days?'

'Texel.'

'What do you do there?'

'I run a holiday park.'

'Oh,' says the baker. 'What's that involve?'

'Painting, mowing the lawns, talking German, cleaning up rubbish.'

'And you had the day off?'

'I'm just the assistant really.'

'Ah. But it is high season now?'

'Yeah.'

The baker thinks hard. The man next to him is answering his questions, sure enough, but he's not taking the initiative.

He's sitting there like Dinie's dog, Benno; it undergoes things passively like this too. 'Married?'

'Nope.'

That's a shame, because a wife would have to come from somewhere, and you can always find something to say about children.

'No wife, no kids. I don't have anything at all.'

'Oh,' said the baker, 'I'm sure that's not true. How are your parents?'

'Fine.'

'Both still in good health?'

'Yep.'

'Are you hungry? Should I go and get you something?'

Jan Kaan looks at him. Piercing eyes and light eyebrows. 'Why would I be hungry?' Again he reminds the baker of Benno, he's raised his chin slightly as if he's caught a whiff of something and is trying to optimise the position of his nostrils.

'Well, maybe –'

'I'm not in the least bit hungry. And if I was thirsty I'd walk over to that tap there.'

'I'm sure.'

'Have you been drinking?' Jan Kaan asks.

'Ah . . .' What am I doing here? the baker wonders. He wipes his forehead with one hand while gripping the ivory knob of his walking stick tightly with the other. He dries his damp hand on his trousers. 'I was just looking at some old photos, back home.'

'Hmm.'

'From when the Queen came.'

'The seventeenth of June, nineteen sixty-nine.'

'What?'

'That was when the old Queen was here.'

'Do you remember it?'

'Not at all.'

'Oh. You're in them actually. The photos.'

'I know.' Jan Kaan stands up. 'I'll get back to work.'

Jan Kaan walks away from the bench.

The baker stands up too quickly and one of his hands, the one he just used to wipe the sweat off his forehead, slides off the ivory knob. He falls to his knees. It hurts terribly. All those sharp shells. Jabbing into his hands too. Jan Kaan turns back to look at him, apparently wavering. The baker realises that he can't get up again without help. Help either from the man opposite him or from his stick. He gropes around for the stick. Jan Kaan takes a couple of steps towards him. 'No,' says the baker. 'Just let me sit down for a minute.' He sees the scene from above, as if he's one of the two birds in the linden tree. Old man on his knees. Much younger man, in T-shirt and shorts, looking down on him, ordered not to lend a helping hand. 'I wanted . . .' says the baker.

'Yes?' says Jan Kaan, in a tone that isn't even unfriendly.

'No . . . I . . .'

'Do you want me to help you or not?'

The baker stares up at him without answering.

'Look, um . . .' Jan Kaan is clearly trying to decide what to call him.

'Just call me . . .' Call me what? Mr Blom? Herm? Blom? Baker? 'I actually want . . .' He's got hold of his walking stick now and, planting the point in the shell path, slowly pushes himself up. With a pounding in his temples, he is now standing more or less straight, longing desperately for his hat and a large glass of cold water. He goes to brush the grit off his knees, then leaves it. Then he says, 'Here,' pulling the envelope with the photo and the piece of cardboard out of his back pocket and pressing it into Jan Kaan's hand. He doesn't care any more, he can tear the envelope open right here on the spot if he wants to. 'My wife left me,' he says. 'A long time ago now.' As if that explains the picture. He can leave the envelope sealed too if he likes, and look at the photo later. Jan Kaan stands there, hesitating, the envelope in his hand. The baker realises that he doesn't have any pockets, not on the T-shirt and not in his shorts, which are the kind people wear for running. 'She couldn't take it any more, living with me.' Now I'll turn around, the baker thinks, and then I'll walk to the gate, remaining calm and collected the whole time. I can manage that, especially if I use the stick properly. One, two three, swing; one, two, three, swing.

'Where is everybody?'

He turns back. Where is everybody? Jan Kaan is standing just like before, staring at the envelope he doesn't have anywhere to put. 'Everybody who?'

'In the village.'

'What do you mean?'

'It's like it's deserted.'

'It's not that bad, is it?' What does he mean?

Jan Kaan walks back to the grave and lays the envelope on the edge. He runs a hand over the back of his neck and sits down again. The baker swings his stick. One, two, three, swing. When he hears Jan Kaan say, quietly but clearly, 'Thanks,' he doesn't slow down. One, two, three, swing. But that doesn't mean he didn't hear it.

Chestnut

Klaas's wife is standing on the far side of the ditch. 'Mr Kaan!' she shouts. 'Do you know what Eben-Ezer means?'

'Eben-Ezer? That's what Kager's house is called, isn't it?'

'Yes, but what's it mean?'

'Not a clue. Does it have to mean something?'

'I was just wondering. And Linquenda?'

'You ask some difficult questions.'

'So you don't know either?'

'No.'

She goes back into the house, as if she came out especially to ask him. He's put the chainsaw down on the lawn for a minute. After getting it out of the garage he'd carried it through the back garden on his way to the side of the house, counting six more trees on the way that could come down too. To think that earlier in the day he'd smirked about that guy from the city planting his wood. 'Rekel, get out of here,' he says to the Labrador, which had sat between him and his daughter-in-law during their conversation, turning his head faultlessly to look at whoever was speaking. The dog only half obeys him, sitting down again where Zeeger was standing, while Zeeger moves on to the bleeding, patchy chestnut. It's the middle one, the biggest of the three. A letter arrived from the council, quite a while ago now, urgently advising people to leave infected trees alone. So Zeeger Kaan is not cutting down a sick tree, no, he's felling a tree he sees as a weed. A tree that's growing somewhere it's not wanted. Rekel bumps into his legs. 'Get, I said!' The dog whimpers and reluctantly retreats to the corner of the house, where he sits down on the brick path.

Zeeger has filled the tank to brimming with the fuel mixture, the oil tank is full as well, and he's even cleaned the air filter. He pulls out the choke and presses the hand guard with his wrist but the brake is already on. With one foot in the handle to keep the saw on the ground, he pulls the starter and immediately groans. Incomprehensible, these machines. One day the saw kicks over immediately, another you have to keep pulling it. He's also never sure whether to pull out the choke or press it in. Now he pushes it in and pulls the starter again. No, that's not right, he hears that immediately. He has to have the choke out. After three or four tugs, the engine starts. Rekel tries to stay sitting there, but then the racket gets too much and he stands up and retreats to the bridge. Zeeger pulls the hand guard back and the chain starts to turn. Long ago he did a one-day course. He no longer knows exactly what all the different parts of the felling process are called, but he does remember that he has to cut a triangle out of the trunk on the side he wants the tree to fall, and then cut the bark on the sides of the triangle before starting to really saw into the trunk from the other side at the height of the cuts in the back – the felling cut. The tree must be a good twelve metres tall: he has to make it fall diagonally, between the corner of the house and the third chestnut. The other direction isn't an option: half the tree would end up on the road. Fortunately, most of the strawberry plants in the vegetable garden are bare. I must be mad, he thinks when he has to put the chainsaw down on the lawn halfway through the felling because the sweat has started to run into his eyes. He pulls a hanky out of his pocket and tries to dry his face. He sees Rekel sniffing around near the open barn doors. The trees have been here almost forty years now. When he planted them, the labourer was still living here. 'You really want to?' said the labourer. 'Yes, I really want to,' he answered, and dug three holes. The labourer's two children thought it was fun, they watered the three saplings faithfully for weeks. He scrunches away his hanky, disengages the brake and sticks the blade in the cut he's already made. Soon the wood starts to creak. He takes a quick step back and to the side. The chestnut tips slowly through the warm air and slams down onto the ground with an unexpectedly loud crash, while twigs and brown leaves swish up. Shame about the French beans that were left, he thinks, turning off the chainsaw and going into the house. And the last few strawberries too, of course. In the kitchen he has a good look around. It's lighter. 'Hmm,' he says. It could be even lighter. Before going out again, he fetches a towel from the bathroom and drinks two glasses of water. Rekel is already waiting for him on the back doorstep. 'No, Rekel, I'm not finished yet,' he says. He waves the dog away with the towel. 'Go over to the other side of the ditch.'

Straw

Now everything's finished. The biscuits, the advocaat, even the water. The advocaat ran out after Dieke had stood downstairs for a while, calling up. When was that? An hour ago? Half an hour? Things about Jan, who 'was painting a stone with a really little brush' and about 'an auntie, but I don't get that'. About someone called Leslie and Jan saying that Leslie is 'a pick ninny'. Dieke herself had 'cleaned all these stones with dead people under them' and that had 'felt a bit funny'. She hadn't said anything in reply, of course, and eventually Dieke went away again. Dirk snorted for a while, then he too fell silent.

Anna Kaan has crept over to the edge of the straw and tries to look out through the open barn doors. He's cut down a tree, but which one? She can't see anything except a rectangle of gravel. And Rekel of course, hanging around the doorway: a paw on the concrete for a while, then a paw on the gravel. If she really wants to know what Zeeger's up to, she'll have to get down, and her whole body's itching, she's that keen. I'm not going, she thinks. Not yet. That raindrop. That's what I've decided on. They can wait a bit longer.

Again she hears the chainsaw starting up. Another tree? A little later, Rekel reappears at the barn door. Why doesn't that dog just come in? What's all this indecision about? She rubs her hands to warm up her fingers. It's because of lying still, she thinks. Her blood's not flowing properly.

Fortunately no memories of earlier celebrations have surfaced. She had dozed off and was half asleep when her granddaughter woke her. The old Queen's hat had appeared before her. It was a beautiful hat with a broad round brim, and made of fabric that complemented her dress. A dress with flowers on it, stems included. Leather gloves, but not for the cold, because it was beautiful early-summer weather. And the one glove she pulled off, and the words she said. The cheek she touched, briefly, with her bare hand. The two women behind her, one very posh with a yellow pillbox hat, and one who kept studying the Queen from close quarters, almost shamelessly. The one glove held loosely in the other, gloved, hand. 'The Queen touched her,' she was mumbling, as if it had just happened, when Dieke shocked her awake with a blaring shout of 'Grandma! What are you doing up there?' Incomprehensible, that child still wanting to talk to her, hoping for an answer.

Chestnut

Klaas is sitting on the lawn next to the big plastic paddling pool, keeping an eye on his daughter. The pool is on the south side of the house. By the sound of it, there are two trees down already, but he can't see from here. He's dying to know what's happening, but Dieke's in the pool and although she already has a swimming card, water's dangerous even when it's less than knee-deep. The screech of the chainsaw is hellish in the quiet afternoon. Apparently there's a third tree that needs cutting down.

'What's Grandpa doing?' his daughter asks.

'Cutting down trees.'

'Why?'

'Grandpa thinks trees are stupid.'

'No!'

'No. I think Grandma must have complained, Dieke. That it was getting too dark in her kitchen.'

'Why does Grandma go up on the straw?'

'Why don't you ask her?'

'I did. I said, "Grandma, what are you doing up there?" but she didn't say anything.'

'Maybe she'll tell you one day.'

'Has she got something to drink?'

'I hope so, otherwise she'll be getting pretty thirsty.'

'When's she coming down?'

'Oh, it won't be long now.'

'I don't care if she stays up there.'

'Dieke, it's not that Grandma dislikes you. You know that, don't you?'

She doesn't answer, she's too busy staring down at the warm water.

He watches her and wonders when people lose the ability to take things in their stride like that. She's already forgotten about the trees and now, in front of his eyes, she's forgetting her grandmother.

'Daddy . . .' she says.

'Yes?'

'Why does Uncle Johan talk so funny?'

'Do you think he talks funny?'

'Yes. Slow.'

'I've told you before, haven't I?'

'Mm.'

'I told you. About the accident he had on his motorbike . . .'

'He rode over cars.'

'See? You do know.'

'I kind of forgot.'

'It's called trial riding. And one day he fell off one of the obstacles.'

'Obsta . . . ?'

'It was a lot of tree trunks piled on top of each other.'

'Oh, yeah. And then it was like he was asleep.'

'Yes, for about ten days. Wait a sec, will you, Dieke? I'm just going round the corner to see what Grandpa's doing. I'll be right back. Will you stay sitting there like that? Exactly like that? Not lying down?'

'No,' says his daughter.

'What do you mean, no? Do you mean you *are* going to lie down?'

'No, not lying down. Will you get in the swimming pool too?

'Yep. I'm boiling.' He stands up. Before disappearing around the corner of the house, he quickly looks back. His daughter is doing her best to stay sitting exactly as she was sitting. As he walks under the balcony he looks up. Knowing his luck, a beam or a chunk of concrete will crash down just when he's walking under it. But the balcony doesn't drop anything. The privet that separates the lawn from the yard is much too high to see over, it hasn't been pruned for years. The smell of the flowers is unbearable. Stupid, he thinks, if I cut the hedge it will stop flowering. He goes up next to the hedge and breathes through his mouth. The middle tree is lying angled into the vegetable garden; he must have cut that one down first. The second is lying in the middle of the front garden; that makes sense, because the tree that was there is now gone. And he can tell from where his father is standing that the third tree is going to come down on top of the second one. He's only cut them down, he hasn't stripped them yet. This was the coarse work. Klaas's heart misses a beat: his elderly father, bent over next to the third chestnut with a potentially lethal machine in his hands. When the third tree falls, he's had enough and shuts off the chainsaw. Rekel, sitting in the middle of the bridge, immediately stands up and pads over to his master. Klaas turns and heads back past the front of the farmhouse. He looks in each window and doesn't see his wife through any of them. Dieke hasn't moved a muscle and looks at him contentedly.

'Is he finished?' she asks.

'Yep. He's finished.'

'Are you going to get in too?'

Klaas pulls off his shoes, socks and trousers, and steps into the pool. The water stopped being cool long ago. He can't quite stretch out full length in the pool. Dieke sits on his stomach.

'You're an island,' she says.

'Yes,' he says. 'I'm an island. With underpants.'

She's forgotten Grandma, she's forgotten Jan at the cemetery, she's forgotten Johan and now she's forgotten the chestnut trees too. 'Texel,' she says. She hasn't entirely forgotten Jan, then.

I'll just lie here like this for a bit, Klaas thinks. Breathing in the old-fashioned plastic smell: pungent, like water wings and inflatable beach balls in the old days. Then I'll go.

'Dad?'

'Yes?'

'That auntie, at the cemetery . . .'

'Yes?'

'Why is she dead?'

'Dieke . . .'

'Aren't I old enough?'

'Yes. Let's leave it at that, shall we?'

'Where were you?'

'Where was I?'

'Yes, when she died.'

'Oh, that's so long ago now. I don't remember.'

He was standing at the side window, two metres from where he is now lying in the pool.

He'd skipped school that morning as he had no desire to stand in front of the Polder House holding hands with his classmates or waving a stupid little flag. 'If I want to see the Queen, I'll watch TV,' he'd told a friend, and together they'd ridden their bikes to the canal to go for a swim near the white bridge. They knew the Queen would be coming from Slootdorp and it was no coincidence they were standing on the railing in sopping-wet trunks and that both jumped just when the big car was crossing the bridge. They'd agreed that neither of them would look, that they'd act as if they were just going for a swim like any other day. They didn't manage it; their curiosity got the better of them. Klaas saw the Queen sitting in the car, a woman with a little hat on top of her head. Afterwards he'd gone to his friend's house for something to eat and then he went home, where he made sure his mother didn't see him.

That afternoon he was sitting under the workbench in the barn, fiddling around with nuts and bolts, bits of wood, chicken wire and nails. He wanted to make something, but didn't know exactly what. The three young bulls were standing with their heads against the bars of the bullpen; a ginger tom was lying next to him on an empty burlap bag. It ended up being a kind of cart, with twine spools as wheels. Then he heard his mother scream, 'Zeeger!' That was no teatime call. He jumped up, banging his head on the workbench. The tom shot off, the young bulls took a step backwards. He didn't take the shortest route – through the barn – but went out around the back. By the dairy scullery he heard his mother call his father again. He made his way through the vegetable garden at the side of the farmhouse to the front garden. He stopped at the side window, where he could look straight through the house and see the road framed by the front windows, above a row of cactuses and the privet. In the distance he saw the baker's Volkswagen van.

He didn't move. He saw his mother, his father, he heard Tinus yelp once, as if he'd been kicked. The baker got out of his van; they bent down – behind the hedge – and they talked, but they were too far away for him to make out any words. He heard a siren, the baker disappeared, the van stayed where it was, half on the road, an ambulance manoeuvred past it and then a police car drove up as well. Men in white coats in the yard, men in uniform standing on the causeway and next to the baker's van, and Klaas still didn't understand what was going on. His mother called his name a few times.

Eventually, only the Volkswagen van was left, though he wasn't sure if the baker was still sitting in it. His eyes were fixed on the cactuses, the grey woolly ones with vicious barbs on them. Something bumped up against his legs: Tinus. Together they walked straight through the vegetable garden to the back of the house; he heard the beans cracking under his boots. He arrived at the barn, not knowing what to do, walked into the cowshed and pulled the door of the calf pen open. Tinus stumbled in behind him, and just before he closed the door the ginger tom slipped in too, frightening the calves. After he'd sat with his back against the wall for a while, the calves came up and started to sniff him cautiously. Tinus licked their wet noses. No longer standing with their heads pointing into the barn, the three young bulls pushed against the bars on his side. He stuck his hand in a calf's mouth and a little later he stuck his other hand in a second calf's mouth. He thought of a brochure from the Stompetoren Artificial Insemination Station his father had recently given him. It included a bull called Blitsaert Keimpe. Blitsaert Keimpe! That was a cut above Dirk. Dirk followed by a number, the name shared by all three of the young bulls. It was a long afternoon. The tomcat spent hours dozing in a corner, even Klaas nodded off for a moment. Tinus was restless. Then the cows came into the shed. Was his father going to do the milking? Was everything back to normal? Slowly he climbed up onto his feet – not wanting to wake up Tinus, who had fallen asleep with his head on his thigh – and opened the door of the calf pen. Grandpa Kaan was standing there. 'Ah, there you are,' he said.

Gravel

Shoes off, thinks Johan Kaan. Socks too. And fast. Somewhere, far away, somebody's making a racket with a machine. In the village there's a woman riding a bike and a man walking a dog. The man with the dog says something to him, but he doesn't understand. It's like he's speaking a foreign language. There are tables and chairs set up in front of The Arms, nobody on any of the chairs. Three wasps are buzzing around an empty glass on one of the tables. He walks into the cemetery, holding the bag, on this final stretch, clamped against his stomach. It's so heavy his shoes leave deep grooves in the grit on the paths. He can't see anybody.

'Hey! You here for me?'

He looks to the side. His brother emerges from behind a small building. 'Hel-lo, Jan,' he says, and stops still. Jan comes over to him. 'What were you doing there? W-anking?'

'No, of course not.'

'Why you got a h-ard on then?'

'I had to piss.'

'I'm not b-lind, am I? And you're all wet with sweat.'

'Water. There's the tap. What have you got there?'

'Are y-ou blind? S-tones, can't you see that?'

'What for?'

'I had a hard on yes-terday too. In the living room. And then Toon said, w-ant me to get rid of that for you? You'd be f-ine with that, huh?'

'Jesus, Johan.'

'No?'

'I don't even know who Toon is.'

'Y-es, you do. He's a good looking guy, j-ust your type, and he's got a v-ery big dick. That's what you like, isn't it?'

'You've told me that a hundred times.'

'See. You do know who he is.'

'What are you doing with that bag of gravel?'

'For Han-ne. Here.' Johan pushes the bag into Jan's hands. Finally he's rid of it. He pulls off his T-shirt, rubs his shoulder and scratches his crotch. The gravestones around him are like tiled stoves with heat pouring out of them. 'Jesus H. Christ! It's bloody hot!' He never knows how loud something like that's going to come out, but at least he doesn't have any trouble saying it.

'Keep it down a bit,' says Jan.

'Shut your trap.' Johan walks on. He has no idea how late it is. If he wanted, he could look on the mobile phone clipped to his belt. If he wanted. There's a bucket on the path near Hanne's grave. A bucket that reminds him of the car that passed him about an hour ago. Or two hours ago. The bucket's empty. He sits down on a gravestone and pulls off his shoes and socks. He doesn't stuff the socks into the shoes, but drops them on the ground under his feet. His brother comes up too, with the bag of gravel. 'B-eautiful,' says Johan. 'V-ery nice. Well done. And al-most finished.' He waves at the headstone and sees something strange on top of it. 'What's that?'

'An envelope.'

'Y-es, I can see that.'

His brother picks up the envelope. 'The baker gave it to me.'

That's such a mystery to Johan he just ignores it.

'How did you get here anyway?' Jan asks, sticking the envelope into the waistband of his shorts, at the back.

'Walked.'

'You walked? With that bag?'

'Y-es.'

'From Schagen?'

'Yes. Where else?' He lies down very carefully, letting each bit of skin get used to the heat first. Then he brushes his long hair out of his face and waggles his feet in the air.

'Sore?' Jan asks.

'And hot.'

'Should I fill up the bucket?'

'Yes.'

Jan walks off.

Johan stares up at the milky sky. When did the sun disappear? Before he's able to come up with an answer, Jan's back. He puts the bucket down on the path. Johan gets up and leans over it with his hands on the rim and drinks. When he's finished drinking, he plunges his head into the water. And after he's slowly lowered himself back down onto the stone he sticks his feet into the bucket. They don't fit: he can't put his feet flat. Instead he lets them dangle as loosely as possible, toes on the bottom.

'Why didn't you get someone to pick you up?'

'D-unno.'

'Did you even try?'

'Forgot.'

'Jesus, that bag weighs at least ten kilos.'

'No, not ten. M-ore.' He sits up and prises the packet of cigarettes out of his back pocket. It would have been easier if he was still lying down. Jan is standing opposite him; he doesn't smoke. Klaas does smoke and Klaas's wife smokes too. He lights a cigarette and looks at his brother. Does he look like me or not? No, I've got a lot more hair. But he's better at thinking. Now he blinks and rubs his stomach. Oh, yeah, I'm not supposed to stare at him. That's what he told me once. Or was that somebody else? And should I listen to them anyway?

'Is "Piccaninny black as black" a he or a she?'

Johan keeps his eyes on Jan. He draws on his cigarette and lets the smoke billow back out of his nostrils. Something is floating up to the surface, something from the old days. A cloth on the wall in Hanne's bedroom. 'Pic-aninny? Cooking pot? The sun?' Yes, a big cloth, with bits of material sewn onto it. With palm trees too. Jan turns around and sits down in front of the small headstone. He takes a brush from a small tin of paint. 'I'll w-ait till you're ready, then we'll tip in the stones.' And little black kids. There were little black kids sewn onto the cloth too. Something else comes floating up, which is weird: there's all kinds of stuff in your head, but it only comes to the surface when somebody else says something. Like a fish hook with a worm on it. 'Once I pulled a ring off that c-loth. I wanted to give it to Han-ne. And . . . But that r-ing was too big, way too big.' From the bedroom, long ago, Johan sees himself going into the kitchen. To the windowsill, where there were some scrawny pot plants. 'Then I s-tuck it in a pot. I pushed down on it until it made a hole in the dirt and then I c-losed it up.'

'How can you remember that?' Jan says. 'You were only four or five.'

'I r-emember.' Johan stubs his cigarette out on the stone, next to his knee. 'I d-ream a lot about the old days.' He pulls his T-shirt out from where he's tucked it in under his belt, folds it and lays it down on the grave-stone where his head will be if he lies down. Then he lies down. He turns his head slightly and sees a big tree, and when he turns his head a little further he sees a small bench under the tree. He hadn't noticed that at all. 'When things were s-till good.'

'Yeah,' his brother says. It sounds faint, as if he's not just a few metres away, but a lot more than a few metres away.

Johan lights another cigarette after having scooped some more water out of the bucket and slurped it down. He tears off the filter; next time he'll have to buy cigarettes without filters. Or tobacco. Klaas and Klaas's wife smoke roll-ups. It's hard though, rolling those fiddly little things. That's true too. 'Then I d-ream things like I'm lug-ging Hanne down the hall, but she's a wo-man and r-eally heavy and I don't know where I'm sup-posed to take her. So I keep lugging her up and down.' Jan keeps his back stubbornly turned and doesn't answer. But of course that's because he hasn't asked him anything. 'H-ave you put on some sun block?'

'Yes,' Jan says, running his free hand over his neck. 'Why?'

'N-o reason.' His brother's neck is bright red. He must feel that? Wait a second: now he also sees three bare bottoms in front of him. Or rather: two bare bottoms. Seeing who's got the best tan after a day on the beach. Although all three of them are so burnt they won't sleep well tonight, and maybe longer. Red hair, freckles, sunburn. There's something else, from around that time. Johan sucks hard on his cigarette. In a foreign language. '*One small step for man*,' he says. That's English!

'What?'

'Around Han-ne. Some body on the m-oon!'

'Was that in the summer of nineteen sixty-nine?'

'D-on't you remember? I can see it in f-ront of me!'

'We didn't even have a TV.'

'We d-id have a TV.'

'I don't think so. I can't remember that at all. Wasn't it in the middle of the night?'

'Y-es.'

'There you go.'

'I s-till saw it.'

'Fine. Whatever you say.'

Yes, thinks Johan Kaan. I say. I saw, I remember. He scratches his crotch. I remember! Being burnt, red, itchy, not just from the sun, something else too. He sucks hard on the cigarette again; the harder he sucks, the more he remembers, at least it was like that just now, but the cigarette is almost finished, so he burns his finger. 'Ow! Jesus!'

'What?' Jan has turned around.

'Nothing. Christ.' He sticks his hand in the bucket of water.

'Why are you swearing like that? Now I've gone over the edge.'

Johan stands up, walks over to Jan and shoves him out of the way. There's a white smudge next to a number. There's all kinds of things lying next to the grave's raised border. Screwdriver, pieces of worn-down . . . pieces of worn-down . . . well, stuff, sandpaper. And a rag. He twists the corner of the rag into a tight point and pushes the paint carefully but firmly back into the curve of the 6. 'There,' he says. 'No problem.' He throws the rag down onto the ground and has a good stretch, with his mouth wide open. Then he picks at his belly button. 'I'm going to sit down on that bench o-ver there.' He goes over to the bench. 'Jesus H. Christ, it's bloody hot!' As he sits down, he adds something, quietly, as if he doesn't want Jan to hear. 'It's g-oing to r-ain soon.' He likes the feel of the sharp edges of the shells on his feet, but still brushes them off. Then he picks the remaining pieces of shell out from between his toes. When he's finished, he casually knocks a dead bird off the bench. He'd already seen it lying there, but needed to get his feet clean first. He looks up into the tree. Sitting on a low branch is a second bird. 'Oh dear-oh-dear,' he says quietly. 'H-ang in there, you.' He looks back down at the dead bird on the shell path and then his phone rings. He pulls it out of the clip on his belt, looks at the screen and presses the green telephone. 'Y-es?' he says.

'. . .'

'N-o, Toon, I'm with my little sister.'

'. . .'

'I don't. This one is dead, al-most f-orty years now.'

'. . .'

'Jan is here too.'

'. . .'

'Texel, y-ep.'

'. . .'

'It's Saturday. Every body's gone! Why do I need per-mission?'

'. . .'

'Y-es, ye-es.'

'. . .'

'I dunno. I'll see.'

'. . .'

'Six o'clock? C-an't make that.'

'. . .'

'I will.'

'. . .'

'Fuck off!' He presses the red telephone, checks the time and puts the telephone back in the clip. 'Toon says hel-lo,' he calls out to his brother.

Jan stands up and uses the screwdriver to tap the lid back onto the paint tin. 'Does he know I live on Texel?'

'Yes.'

Jan gathers up everything and carries it to the path. He takes the bucket, tips out the water and dries it with the rag. Then he puts all the painting gear into it and finally takes the envelope out from under the band of his shorts and puts that in there too. 'How's he know that?'

'I t-alk to him some times, don't I? He really does have a v-ery big dick.'

'You told me. Anyway how do you know?'

'I'm not b-lind! How many times do I have to tell you?'

'Keep it down, will you?' Jan comes over to the bench. 'You have to visit some time.'

'And what makes you think I like big dicks?'

'You're a poofter, aren't you? They like them.'

'Oh.'

'You have to visit me some time.'

'Hey, what happened here?' Jan picks the dead bird up from the path.

'That s-parrow's dead. It was lying on the bench here.'

'It's not a sparrow, it's a blue tit.'

'It's s-till dead.'

Jan looks at the dead bird, takes a couple of steps towards the tall hedge and hurls it over. They hear a splash. 'Apple cores, banana peels, a dead bird,' he says.

'What?'

'Nothing.'

Sometimes Johan thinks his big brother isn't altogether right in the head. Banana peels? Where? Jan sits down next to him and he looks at him. Jan doesn't look back. First he looks up at the bird that's still alive, then he looks at a hole in the hedge opposite the hedge the dead bird disappeared behind.

'What did this Toon guy want?'

'He said I'm not al-lowed to be here.'

'And now?'

'N-othing.' Johan worms the packet of cigarettes up out of his back pocket again. 'He says he knows you. Toon.' He lights a de-filtered cigarette.

'I don't know any Toons.'

'How come you don't have a b-oy friend?'

'I don't know.'

'If you ask me, you m-ust be about f-orty five.'

'Yep, about that.'

'It's b-eautiful weather, you should be sunbathing on the n-udist beach with a nice b-loke. But, no, his lord ship is sitting in a b-oiling church yard.'

'Cemetery.'

'What?'

'Never mind. You don't have a girlfriend either.'

'No, but . . .' If Jan is about forty-five, then I'm, then I'm . . . a couple of years younger, thinks Johan. He sucks on his cigarette and blows out a cloud of smoke that only slowly rises. He sees himself standing next to his mother in a flower shop. Grandfather Kaan was dead and they needed to order a bunch of flowers from the grandchildren. The girl in the flower shop had gulped, he'd noticed that. His mother had asked him what to write on the ribbon. Something like, 'Thanks, Grandpa, see you later,' he'd said, but he wasn't thinking about it and he wasn't looking at the flowers either. He was looking at the girl. He sucked hard on his cigarette again. 'Nice,' his mother had said, but he'd scratched his dick – now, here, he sees it clear as day in front of him – and the girl turned red. He didn't want to do it, but it happened, his hand did something, as if it had a mind of its own. What a beautiful girl she was. And her gulping and turning red, that must have had something to do with him. He must have been the reason. But they placed the order and his mother left the shop and he followed her. Jan coughs and slides back and forth on the bench. Oh yeah, he was saying something, something about . . . 'But it's r-ight, isn't it? You coming here to p-aint the head stone. There's no n-eed.'

His big brother stands up and pulls off his T-shirt. He hangs it over the back of the bench and walks back to the bag of gravel.

'Jan?'

'Yeah?'

'Am I u-gly?'

Jan turns around. 'No, Johan. You're not ugly. Far from it.'

'Far from it,' says Johan. That girl should have . . . No, *he* should have gone back to pick up the flowers. But when had his mother done that? How was he supposed to know? Couldn't she have rung him up? But I can do it myself, he thinks. I can go back to the flower shop myself, can't I? But it's already . . . 'How long's G-randpa been dead?' he asks.

'About ten years.'

'Ten.' That's a long time, thinks Johan. Is that shop even there any more? He throws the butt away, jumps up and strides over to the bag of gravel, pushes his brother aside, tears the bag open in a single movement, picks it up and walks over to the grave.

'Slowly!' Jan cries. 'That paint's still wet, don't make too much dust.'

There's something else he wants to say, from before the girl in the flower shop butted in. He has to retrace his steps: Grandfather Kaan, the flower-shop girl, banana peels. 'A-ny way, I knew it was a blue tit. I know a lot a-bout birds.'

'I know that, Johan. You were just joking.'

'Yes, j-oking.' He empties the bag within the upright border of the grave. While smoothing out the pebbles with one hand he feels Jan's arm against his. 'Do you feel better?' he asks. Now he feels Jan's hand too, bumping into his own while brushing over the gravel.

'How so?'

'N-ow you've done this for her?'

'Somebody had to do it. We agreed on it at the get-together.'

'Oh, the zoo. When was that a-gain?'

'A fortnight ago.' Jan takes the empty bag from his hands and stuffs it into the bucket. 'What did you tell Mum?'

'What?'

'Yesterday. On the phone.'

Yesterday, on the phone. Johan stands still and thinks back to the hall of the house in Schagen, where the phone is. 'Oh, y-eah. I asked if you were already there.'

'How did you know I'd be here?'

'Well . . . D-ad told me.'

'And nothing else?'

'Nothing else.'

'You must have. She's up on the straw. You must have said something.'

Did I say anything else? The hall, the sound of the TV that's always on in the communal living room, the telephone, his mother's voice. Johan looks around. What did I say?

Then he sees the blue gravel at his feet. 'Y-es! I w-anted to know where to buy these s-tones!'

'What did she say?'

'She h-ung up.'

Nature Reserve

Klaas obeys his mother, but takes his time. After he's finished breathing in the smell of the inflatable pool, he gets out and pulls his clothes on over his wet underpants. He looks in through the side window. There are still cactuses, just not woolly ones any more. He sends Dieke inside. She doesn't want to go. 'You can watch TV,' he says.

'Can I close the curtains?' she asks.

'Of course you can. You have to close the curtains, otherwise you won't see anything except the reflection of the windows.'

'But what are you going to do?'

'I'm going to pick Uncle Jan up from the cemetery. And if all's well, Uncle Johan will be there too.'

'Uncle Johan!'

'Yep.'

Dieke disappears inside. Normally he'd take the car like he did earlier in the day, but it was parked in the sun and the shadows have only just crept over it, so he grabs the bike. At his most leisurely, like a little boy sabotaging his mother's orders, he pedals into the village, greeting people along the way.

*

Bloody hell, Johan *is* there. How could she have known that? His brothers are standing right in front of the grave. Jan with a bucket in his hand, white as white can be. Johan is bare-chested too, but nice and brown, which is quite an achievement for someone with such red hair. What's the point of that? Klaas wonders. Johan's hair is thick, long and gleaming. His body is broad and muscular. His teeth are white and his lips are full. Who decided that someone like him should be so good-looking? His youngest brother who, after crashing down from a pile of tree trunks on his KTM, became both uninhibited and slow. They look up when they hear him coming, and all at once he sees what his mother said to him yesterday. 'You're all in league with each other. You and your father and Jan. And Johan too.' He doesn't understand exactly what she meant, but he sees it, in those two faces turned towards him.

'You p-iss your pants?' Johan shouts.

Before looking down at his crotch, Klaas sees familiar names on an old headstone to his left.

Zeeger Kaan 1858–1917
Griet Kaan-van Zandwijk 1862–1957

Why doesn't Jan paint that stone sometime? Does he even know that this is his great-grandparents' grave? He walks on and looks down. The shape of his underpants is visible as a wet mark on his jeans. 'Yes, Johan, I pissed my pants.'

'Ha ha ha,' goes Johan.

'You back again?' Jan asks.

'I've come to pick you up. Orders from your mother. And Johan has to leave here too.'

'You M-ummy's little boy again?' Johan asks.

Klaas stares at Johan calmly and pulls a crumpled tobacco pouch out of his back pocket.

His youngest brother looks back equally impassively, if not more, and pulls out his pack of Marlboros. 'S-moke first,' he says.

'Sure,' says Klaas. 'Always smoke first.'

'You h-ave to take your s-hirt off too.'

'Fine.' He unbuttons his shirt and drapes it over a grave before rolling a cigarette.

Johan still has his lighter out and offers him a light.

'Why aren't you wearing shoes?'

'H-ot. And I've got b-listers on my b-loody feet!'

'Did you get the gravel?'

'Y-es.'

'All finished?'

'Y-es.'

'So we're not going yet?' asks Jan, who feels excluded because he doesn't smoke.

'Nope,' Klaas says. 'Relax, we've got all the time in the world. I do, anyway.'

The three of them stand there like that for a while: Klaas and Johan smoking, Jan still holding the green bucket. Klaas has another good look at the grave that's brought them here. The fourth Kaan, his little sister, Dieke's aunt, his parents' daughter, lying here under a thin layer of sky-blue gravel with a headstone that should actually have a sign hanging from it, a sign saying *WET PAINT*.

'M-e too,' says Johan.

'And you?' Klaas asks Jan.

'Are you bored?'

'Quite.' Let it go. Don't take the bait, he thinks. It's true anyway.

'You're n-ot going to sell the farm, are you?' Johan asks.

'Why not?'

'You bastard! We were b-orn there!'

'Don't shout. I can't take all that into account.'

'Of course he's not going to sell it,' Jan tells Johan. 'He can't, anyway.'

'Oh?' says Johan.

'No. He'd have to buy us out first.'

'Huh?'

'Oh yeah?' says Klaas.

'Yeah,' says Jan, who then tells Johan, 'We have a say in it too.'

'Wh-at do you mean?'

'Klaas owes money to Dad, who didn't just give it all to him. And probably to the bank too?' Jan studies him.

Klaas gives a curt nod. He shouldn't have said he was at a loose end. And now Jan is stirring up Johan. Still, he thinks, it's all true.

'R-eally?' says Johan. 'Were you a-llowed to g-et rid of the cows?'

'Yes,' says Klaas.

'It's fine by me,' says Jan. 'I'm not stopping you.'

Enough's enough. 'No, you're on Texel. You're not here.

Why don't you just mind your own business? Isn't it really busy over there now? Do you even have time to be here?'

'I –'

'All that land!' shouts Johan out of nowhere, a sudden spark in his drowsy eyes. He sends the filter of his cigarette flying with a flick of a finger.

'Not that I even have a clue what you do over there on Texel.'

His brother looks at him and raises his chin a little, probably to say something that's not true.

'That l-and!' Johan cries again.

'I don't do anything there at all,' Jan says.

'How's that?'

'They sacked me.'

'When?'

'A while ago.'

'Hey!' Johan shouts. 'Are you l-istening to me?'

'What is it?' Klaas asks.

'That l-and, I said!'

'What about it?'

'Y-ou can do other things with it, too!'

'Like what?'

'A tree nursery,' says Jan, relieved.

'Y-es!'

'A Center Parcs holiday village,' says Jan. 'With a sub-tropical swimming paradise.'

'Y-es!'

'You're mad,' Klaas says. 'Both of you. You've been out in the sun too long.'

'Some thing with f-lowers!' Johan screams. 'And then we sell them!'

'Something with flowers? And who's going to do that?'

'Us! An-d a girl. For in the shop!'

'Or give the land back to nature,' says Jan.

'F-lowers are better, but n-ature's good too. With el-der shrubs and those b-ulls and c-ows with big horns.' Johan scratches his crotch in excitement. 'And p-aths!'

'Highland cattle,' Jan says. 'That bit of land on the other side of the road already borders the wood that guy planted there, what's-his-name, and if you plant trees and shrubs as well, you can turn it into a nature reserve.'

'Y-es!' Johan screams. 'They always have those cows! Tons of them!'

Klaas looks at his brothers. Paths? Highland cattle? A nature reserve? They don't have a clue. They're taking the piss. He stubs out his roll-up on the top of Hanne's headstone.

'Hey!' Jan finally puts down his bucket. He brushes the ash off the stone, but can't get rid of the black spot.

'It'll be gone the first time it rains.'

'Why'd you do that?'

'Because you two keep nagging.'

Johan takes a step forward and stubs his cigarette out on the stone as well.

'We're not n-agging, we've got plans!'

'For something that's no concern of yours.'

'T-oon says I have to do some thing. Work.'

Jan picks up the bucket. 'I'm going.'

'Me too,' says Johan. 'G-et Mum down off the straw!'

'That's your job,' Jan tells Klaas.

'Why me?'

'You're the oldest.'

'Piss off.'

'Then *you* have to do it,' Jan tells Johan.

'Wh-y?'

'It's your fault she's up there.' Jan walks off.

Johan follows him. He picks his T-shirt up off the stone Dieke cleaned so thoroughly earlier in the day. 'W-ait!' he yells. 'I s-till have to put on my shoes!'

Jan waits under the linden, taking his T-shirt off the back of the bench and putting it in the bucket.

Klaas picks up his shirt but doesn't put it on yet. The idea of wrapping his body in checked flannel is unbearable. He looks up. The sun really has gone now, the sky is filthy, but not so you can tell what's going to happen. A thunderstorm? Rain? It doesn't feel like it, although it's muggy and still. He waits until Johan has his shoes and socks on and has reached Jan. Jan who already has a slight stoop; Johan, straight, broad-shouldered, an unruly gait. He quickly bends down to the grave and runs a hand over the blue gravel, although it's already as smooth as they're going to get it. They're beautiful, he thinks, the small, brightly coloured stones. Over time, the gravel had grown scruffier and sparser until it was almost all gone. Then he stands up to follow his brothers. Passing the bench he looks up into the linden. A solitary blue tit is sitting on a branch, panting its way through the hot day. Odd, Klaas thinks, you don't usually see a blue tit by itself.

Shit

Now he's busted. He can't turn back. Well, he could, but they'd still see him. He heard shouting in the distance but thought it was somewhere off in the village. There's never anyone here, especially not when it's hot like today. 'Wait!' they shouted, so he'll just have to stand here, there's nothing else he *can* do. What should he do with the bucket? Hold it, hold it tight, it's his bucket. Can I keep that up? he wonders. He has to. Putting it down would show him up.

He's six. Black hair, a fairly sharp, slightly freckled nose and sullen grey eyes that look bright in his dark face. His bike is lying on the ground behind him; there were already two bikes leaning against the trunk of the tree closest to the gate. He is wearing a light-blue T-shirt, shorts and wellies. Plasters on both knees.

They stand opposite each other: him and three bare-chested men.

'Hello,' says one of the men after a while.

'Yes,' he says.

'What have you got there?'

'Shit.' There's no point lying, it's plain to see. He could have said 'nothing' or 'none of your business', but that wouldn't get him very far either.

'What's your name?' This time it's another man who's

asking the question. They're quite hard to tell apart. Only one of them, the biggest, with the longest hair, is different.

'Leslie.'

'L-eslie? Wh-at kind of name is th-at? Are you from Africa?'

'Africa?' he says. 'Why would I be from Africa?' This guy talks really weird. He looks at the man who said hello to him and gestures at the long-haired one with his thumb. 'What's wrong with him?'

'What makes you think there's something wrong with him?'

'He looks a bit slow and talks funny.'

'I never noticed,' the first one says to the second one.

'Me neither,' the second one replies.

The third one takes a step forward. 'D'you w-ant me to grab you?'

'No.'

'O-K.'

It's kind of scary, having three big ginger men in front of him. But he's not going to let it show. He doesn't care about any of it. It just makes him wish he'd gone to the swimming pool instead. It's not as if they can do anything to him anyway.

'If you ask me, Leslie's a friend of Dieke's,' says the first one.

'How do you know that?' he asks.

'And Dieke thought Leslie was at the swimming pool. But it turns out he's not.'

'No.' He keeps looking from one to the other. Actually, he thinks they look a bit weird like this. Without tops on. Old men. And one of them is apparently Dieke's dad. But which one? 'The pool's boring,' he says, for the sake of saying something.

'What are you doing here?' the second one asks.

'I wanted to make things dirty,' he says.

'Why?'

'I'm bored.' That's true, but it's not the whole truth. He started because he wanted to see what would happen. No matter what it was. And there was an article in the paper. About him. Without his name, of course, because nobody knows he's the one who's doing it. But still. In the newspaper. His father read it out loud. They called him 'unknown vandal or vandals'. None of his classmates got called that.

'Where'd you get the cow shit?'

'A field.'

'With your hands?'

'Yes.'

'How come your hands aren't dirty then?'

'I washed them in a ditch.' The bucket's starting to cause problems. He feels a tendon in his arm start to vibrate. But he doesn't want to put it down. If he does that, he might just as well turn around and walk away. 'Are you brothers?'

'Yep,' says the first one. 'I'm Jan.'

'And I'm Klaas,' says the second.

'J-ohan,' says the third.

'Do you live in the village?' asks the man called Jan.

'Yes.'

'Do you know him?' Jan asks the man called Klaas.

'I've heard the name now and then.'

'I haven't lived here very long,' he says.

'Aren't you scared someone will catch you at it?' the man called Klaas asks.

'No. Why? There's never anyone here.'

'Yeah? It's p-retty busy here today. Are you really called Les-lie?'

'Yes. Is that such a strange name?' Now it really is time for these questions to stop; more tendons are starting to quiver. He moves the bucket to his other hand – why didn't he think of that before? 'Is there something wrong with your head or something?'

'Y-es, there's some thing wrong with my h-ead.'

Klaas and Jan look at each other. It's the same kind of look his father and mother give each other before deciding on something he's not going to like. What were they going to do with him?

'You see that headstone there?' Jan says.

He looks in the direction Jan's pointing. It doesn't help, the place is full of headstones. 'No,' he says.

'Come with us a minute,' says Klaas.

They lead the way. The man called Johan stays put. A few yards into the cemetery they point again.

'The tall one, see? With the weeping willow on top of it,' says Jan.

'Is that her husband's grave?' Klaas asks.

'Yep,' Jan says. 'Can you see it now?'

'I see it,' he says.

'Go ahead,' Klaas says. 'And if we find out that you smeared shit on any other stones at all, we know your name's Leslie and it won't be hard to find you.'

Now they're threatening him too. He hesitates.

'Go on.'

He stares at the men. 'Don't think I'm going to do something just cause you want me to.'

'Of course we don't think that,' Klaas says.

'No, OK then.' Now he has to get away. They're letting him go. He moves the bucket back again and walks over to the headstone the men have pointed out and puts the bucket of cow shit down on the ground. He looks at the writing on the headstone. There aren't that many letters and he can read it, if slowly. *K-e-e-s-G-r-i-n-t. B-a-c-k-H-o-m-e*, it says. What's that supposed to mean? Home? In the ground? As long as they don't think he's going to start with them still standing there. Maybe he'll just go away or choose another stone. No, he'll wait till they're gone and then make a run for it through the back gate. Get rid of the bucket somewhere, circle around on the road, pick up his bike and ride home. Or somewhere else. He sees the three men pulling on their tops. He hears them laughing. Are they laughing at him? 'What a f-unny little kid,' the man called Johan says loudly. Then he yells 'Pic-ca-nin-ny!' at the top of his voice. 'Will you stop shouting for once?' says Klaas. Funny little kid? He'll show them. Piccaninny, is that a swear word? When they turn their backs and disappear through the gate, he plunges his hands deep into the bucket.

Barn

Standing on the big boulder next to the green letter box, Dieke can hardly wait. She's got her yellow boots back on. 'Hey, Uncle Johan!' she cries.

Uncle Johan jumps off the pannier rack. Uncle Jan's given him a ride from the cemetery on the back of his bike. He rubs his bum, picks her up and gives her a loud slobbery kiss full on the lips.

'Yuck!' she says, but doesn't care. 'You should see what Grandpa's done!'

'You're not swimming?' Uncle Jan asks.

She doesn't have time for pointless questions like that now, there are much more important things happening. Uncle Johan still hasn't put her back down on the ground. 'He's cut down all the trees! And Grandma's up on the straw!' she bawls in his ear.

Her father lifts the lid of the letter box, but doesn't take anything out of it. When he lets the lid fall back down again, the wooden post the box is attached to cracks and the whole thing lurches to one side. He kicks the post, and then it breaks completely and the letter box falls into the grass.

'Hey, Re-kel!' shouts Uncle Johan.

Rekel comes running up and Uncle Johan puts Dieke down so he can lie flat in the yard and let the dog jump on top of him and lick him. He doesn't even put his hands over his face.

'That's dirty,' she says.

'N-o, it's nice.'

'Has Uncle Jan finished painting, Dad?'

'Yes, Dieke,' her father says.

'Does it look pretty again?'

'Perfect.'

'And my stone? Is that still pretty too?'

'It is.'

'And the little birds?'

'Which little birds?'

'In the tree next to the bench.'

'I only saw one bird.'

'But there were two, and they had to breathe really hard because it's so hot.'

'Oh. One must have flown away for a moment to get something to eat.'

'That's right,' says Uncle Jan. 'Birds get hungry too some-times.'

As if she doesn't know that. Her father and Uncle Jan walk into the yard, both pushing their bikes. The bucket hanging off Uncle Jan's handlebars taps against the frame. Uncle Johan is still lying on the ground. Rekel is getting wilder and wilder. Nobody's said anything about the trees or Grandma. Is it all normal to them, or what? Not to her. Grandpa's front garden is an enormous mess, a big jumble of branches and leaves, and one of the trees is lying on Grandma's vegetable garden. She's going to be cross later. Uncle Johan has stood up. He's picked Rekel up and is carrying him over to the ditch. 'What are you doing?' she asks.

'Re-kel's hot. He needs to s-wim.' With the dog in his arms, Uncle Johan walks down the bank of the ditch.

'Are you going to throw him in the water?'

'Y-es.' Uncle Johan lets go of Rekel, who falls into the ditch with a big splash and disappears underwater. When he comes up, he splutters furiously. He swims to the other side, climbs out, creeps under a chestnut branch like an enormous wet rat and goes around to the back of the house, where he lies down under the rear willow, not looking back once.

'Now he's cross with you,' she says.

'N-o he's not! He loves me. I'm his f-avourite h-uman!'

It's as if everyone's gone crazy today. Her mother's grumpy and she doesn't know why. Just because of the pot? It wasn't that bad. Uncle Johan throwing Rekel in the ditch for no reason, but yeah, Uncle Johan does lots of strange things because he had that accident, of course. Grandpa cutting down three trees and leaving them in the garden. Grandma up on the straw and not even answering when she asks her a question. And her father breaking everything.

Uncle Johan comes up from the ditch and follows her father and Uncle Jan into the barn. Now she's alone in the yard again. What a strange day. If she'd just gone to the swimming pool this morning, maybe none of this would have happened. Or else it would have happened, but without her being there! She looks in through the kitchen window. Her mother is standing at the sink holding a tea towel. She doesn't look out. Dieke looks in the other direction, at Grandpa's house. Grandpa is just coming out of the side door. He pulls on his clogs and comes over the bridge. He doesn't seem to notice her and then he too disappears into the barn. She runs over quickly, the tops of her yellow boots slapping against her shins.

Straw

How am I going to get down? she thinks. How the hell am I going to get down? The heat has got under her skin. The water's finished, she's eaten her way through a whole packet of Viennese biscuits, drained a bottle of advocaat, and now – it must already be six or so? – the heat, which until recently was just surrounding her, has crept into her body. She's lying on her back and rubs her breastbone with two fingers to suppress a persistent nausea. She has a slight nagging headache and notices that her hands still feel cold to the touch. When she rubs them together, it's like she has chilblains on her fingers. What am I trying to prove? Why am I lying here making a fool of myself? The rectangle of sky she can see through the hole in the roof hasn't grown any paler. She can forget about that drop of rain.

Her sons are down below. And Zeeger. With Dieke blaring away in between. 'Horrible boys,' Anna mumbles, but even that's half-hearted. Everything's half-hearted here. Don't they hear the creaking? It actually sounds more like groaning now, as if the beams and timbers and even the tile laths are worn out and defeated, as if they're crawling with an army of woodworms and borers. They're talking loudly, of course; they want her to hear that they're talking about her.

'It's over there, next to the hay cart.'

'You think she doesn't know that herself?'

'I'd say she does.'

'M-ay be.'

'She's not mad.'

'Grandma!'

'Leave it, Diek. She won't answer anyway.'

'Why not?'

'Do you always answer when I ask you something?'

She's quiet for a moment. 'No.'

'Well, then.'

'I'll d-o it.'

'Wait, that thing's heavier than you think. Klaas, give him a hand.'

'I'm starting to get hungry.'

It's so hard for her to just keep lying there. She's desperate to see what's going on. I'm tipsy, she thinks. A bit drunk. Of course I know that this rickety thing lying here next to me isn't the only ladder. Of course Jan's hungry, he's spent the whole day at the cemetery, but that's his own fault and I don't have an ounce of pity for him, and you can bet your life Zeeger didn't give him anything to take or remind him to make some sandwiches. Maybe Klaas's wife gave Dieke something to eat. She grabs the empty one-and-a-half-litre bottle and throws it over the edge of the straw.

'Look!'

'Yes, Diek, Grandma's thrown down a bottle. Fortunately empty. And fortunately, it's made of plastic.'

'Where's Rekel?'

'Outside. He's too scared to come in here.'

'She's got the parade sword up there too.'

'Huh? What for?'

'Boy, if I knew that . . .'

'She b-etter n-ot throw that.'

'Of course she won't, Johan. Now walk the ladder up carefully, don't slide it out until it's vertical. Make sure it's on the right side of the rafters.'

Slowly, Anna Kaan sits up. She grabs her ankles and pulls her stiff legs towards her until she's sitting almost cross-legged. She straightens her dress at the shoulders and puts her hands on her knees. The straw rustles when they lean the aluminium ladder against it, momentarily drowning out the hordes of borers and woodworms. Her tummy rumbles, her back is itchy, it's as if the creepy-crawlies are all over her and inside her at the same time. The top of the ladder appears and then sits back down a little. Each step that's taken vibrates in the bales of straw; she keeps count and around the time she's expecting a head, Johan's thick red hair appears. They look at each other for a moment.

'M-um?' says Johan.

'Johan,' she says, as quietly as possible. 'Will you be careful?'

'Y-es.'

'Don't shout.'

'N-o.'

Why Johan? She forces herself to look at him. Her Johan, her big, strong, handsome youngest son. Slowness and rage in a single body, dull eyes and gleaming hair. A boy to look after, but not really.

'You coming?' he asks.

'No.'

'W-hy not?'

'Go back down. Carefully.'

'N-o.'

'Please, Johan.'

'J-an made it really p-retty.'

'I'm sure he did.'

'He only s-lipped once with the p-aint.'

'That's fine, Johan.'

'I got l-ittle s-tones.'

Is Johan the raindrop she's been waiting for? He rang her yesterday. With the absurd question as to where was the best place to buy little stones. She didn't understand at first, then it gradually dawned on her. They hadn't listened to her. They'd pressed ahead with the job they'd talked about at the dinner. Jan had arrived. No doubt Klaas and Zeeger spent quite a while hanging around the cemetery too, despite her being dead set against it. 'No question of it,' she'd said. And how did Johan get to the cemetery from Schagen? Surely he hadn't come all the way on foot? Zeeger must have told him Jan was coming, but she'd missed that. She'll stay up here a little longer after all, so they don't start to think she's come round. All those men, doing things, organising things. Who's the boss around here anyway? Me, surely? And I expressly told them not to do up that headstone.

'Johan?'

Zeeger.

'Y-es?' Johan says, without looking down.

'What's she doing?'

'S-itting.'

Anna Kaan raises a finger to her lips.

'What else?'

'N-othing.'

'Johan,' she says quietly. 'Go back down. I'll come soon.'

'N-o, now.'

'I'll come soon, really. Take that ladder away. Look, I've got my own ladder.'

Johan looks at her. 'M-um,' he whispers.

She'd like to pull him up over the edge of the straw, hugging him tight, stroking his forehead and his back, rubbing his feet, especially if he really has walked all the way from Schagen. She'd like to go back in time to drag him off that bloody motorbike, or tip sand and salt into the petrol tank. If she could, she'd put him back on the breast. But more than anything, she can't bear looking at him. He has to go away. 'Don't. Don't say anything. Go back down.'

'N-o.' He climbs another rung.

'I'm coming. Really. Soon.'

'Anna!'

'Keep out of it!' No, don't shout. Don't shout at Zeeger.

'Come back, Johan,' Zeeger calls. 'Come back down. Don't climb any higher.'

'Y-ou h-ave to come w-ith me,' Johan whispers.

'Grandma!' Dieke shouts. Why does that child keep shouting at me? Does she *really* want me to come down? You'd expect her to dislike me.

Anna Kaan reaches for the parade sword, but it's too far away. She flops over onto her side, getting her legs tangled in the process. All fours then, it's only Johan. If anyone else had been standing on the ladder she might have thought twice. She groans, everything's a strain. First she finds the empty advocaat bottle, which she picks up and flings back over her shoulder without thinking. It lands where the aluminium ladder was lying just a few minutes ago.

'Daddy! Glass!'

'Yes, Diek, now she's throwing real bottles. Fortunately we're not standing over there.'

'I'm going inside.' Jan. He doesn't want any part of it.

As far as she's concerned he can go, but at the same time she wants to scream that he has to stay there. Everyone has to stay. They have to do their very best to get her down. All of them, no exceptions. Why isn't Klaas's wife here anyway? But they have to go too, and the sooner the better. And that bull? What's that bull doing now? Is he looking out through his bars and enjoying the company? She can't hear him. Why is Rekel too scared to come in? Where's that bad-tempered Barbary duck? She's got her hands on the sword now and struggles over to the edge of the straw. To her youngest son. 'Johan,' she whispers. 'Here.' The edge of the straw, but she makes sure to stay out of sight of the others.

'W-hat do I do with this?' He looks at her. She sees the muscles of his shoulders and chest quivering. The white of his shirt is a very stark contrast to his skin. What do they do in that home, go to the beach all day?

'Give it to your father. I want you to go now. I'll come soon.'

'All right,' he says, holding out one hand.

'Give it to your father, then he can hang it back up under the bookshelf.' God, as long as the boy doesn't fall. 'Here, hang it over your shoulder and push it round to your back, otherwise you might get it caught between you and the ladder.'

Johan follows her instructions. Excruciatingly slowly. It's excruciating to see him holding on first with one hand and then the other.

'Anna!' Zeeger again.

She doesn't answer, swearing under her breath. Next thing all that shouting will frighten the boy and he'll let go with both hands at the same time. Johan has stopped looking at her, he's concentrating on the trip back down and the sword over his shoulder. He's already gone. Like

a child, that's how fast his attention fades and turns to
something else.

'Yeah? What's the idea?'

'I have to give it to you. H-ang it up. On the bookshelf.'

'Is she coming down?'

'No.'

'What did she say?'

'I've for-gotten.'

Zeeger sighs.

Dirk answers by finally butting in.

'Teatime, Diek.'

'But what about Grandma?'

'Grandma will come down. She can't stay up there forever.'

'I don't understand.'

'S-teak!' yells Johan. 'With chips!'

Dirk keeps snorting, and by the sound of it he's banging
his head against the iron bars every now and then too. The
straw trembles, the wood groans. The swallows have stopped
flying in and out. Anna Kaan tries not to think. She can't
stay up here forever. That bull, won't he ever stop? They've
walked off and nobody thought to remove the ladder.

A little longer. Steak. Cold water. Don't think about the
wedding anniversary, or earlier celebrations, the granddaughter, don't think about quinces or Notaris apples, grey
Volkswagen vans, the Saturday evening to come. No, just a
little longer, the day she was too late, she doesn't even
remember why, but *that* was why the old Queen pulled off
her leather glove. She puffs warm air on her cold hands
then rubs her knees, which have now grown cold as well.

Fish

Zeeger Kaan turned on the deep fryer and fried up some chips and croquettes. The steaks were still in the freezer, there wasn't enough time to thaw them out. He considered cooking some French beans, but a single glance at the felled chestnuts was enough to dissuade him. This is the time of year to eat outside at the table near the side door, but Johan and Jan sat down at the kitchen table.

Besides things like 'Wh-ere's the k-etchup?' and 'You going to leave the trees lying there like that?' they hardly speak during the meal. (Yes, he thinks, maybe I will leave them lying there a while.) Jan drinks two bottles of beer, Johan and he drink water. Johan asks for beer too, but Zeeger doesn't think he's allowed to have it. All three have sweat running down their faces. When everything's finished, Dieke rushes in. 'Fishing!' she says. 'Dad's ready!'

'Yeah!' says Johan. 'Ang-ling!' Johan has been crazy about fishing his whole life, that's why he calls it angling.

'But not too long,' Jan says. 'The ferry doesn't run all night.'

They're biting surprisingly well. All the floats are pointing straight up. There's a bucket in the middle of the bridge for everyone to slip their fish into. When Dieke catches one,

Klaas takes the hook out of its mouth. Every now and then they hear the sound of a very hard head banging against iron bars in the barn.

'Don't know what's got into Dirk,' Zeeger says.

'It was a bit busy for him today, I think,' says his oldest son, who then shouts 'Two!' and raises his rod. A small catfish is wriggling on the hook.

'We should take size into account too,' says his second son.

'N-o!' yells his youngest son, who's up to four. Four tiddlers.

'Or what kind of fish,' says Jan.

'What's worth the most then? A catfish or a bream?' Klaas asks.

'Rekel! Here, boy!' Zeeger calls. The dog is lying under the back willow. It's not the first time he's called him, but he stays put, lying stubbornly with his head turned away.

'Re-kel doesn't like f-ishing.'

'No, he's cross because you threw him in the ditch,' says Dieke.

'Did you throw Rekel in the ditch?'

'Y-es.'

'Me too.'

'Me too.'

'Oh,' says Zeeger Kaan. 'That explains it.'

'Diek, how many fish are in the bucket now?' Klaas asks.

Dieke sticks her rod through the railing of the bridge and bends over the bucket. 'I can't count them, they won't stay still.'

Klaas looks in the bucket too and starts to count out loud.

Zeeger Kaan has stopped listening. He looks at the sky. He can see a lot more of it now: looking west towards the village, at least half of the horizon is open again. A strange sky. It's like a sea mist hanging over the land, which is something you almost never see in June. You get that kind of thing in August and usually it cools off immediately, unlike now. There doesn't look to be any rain on the way, no rumbling in the distance either. He thinks of Anna. Soon everyone will leave again. He doesn't want to be alone in the house, to have to go to bed alone. Just before dumping the chips in the fryer he'd hung the parade sword back up on the two hooks under the bookshelf. An ugly thing, really, but what can you do: an heirloom from some uncle or other who'd stood guard in front of an important building. He can't imagine why Anna took it up with her.

'Thirteen,' says Klaas. 'I've got two.'

'F-our,' says Johan.

He's caught one himself. 'You, Jan?'

'Just the one. But a very big one.'

'Then you've got five, Diek,' says Klaas.

'Does that make me the winner?'

'If we stop now it does.'

'N-o!' cries Johan.

'Why isn't Mum fishing?' Dieke asks.

'Your mother thinks fish are slimy,' Klaas says.

Zeeger looks at the farmhouse. Klaas's wife is standing at the kitchen window with a tea towel in one hand. Isn't that the second time he's seen that today? A little further along, the old Barbary duck comes out through the side doors of the barn. Halfway across the yard it takes flight.

That surprises Zeeger, who thought it was well past flying. The duck lands awkwardly in the ditch near Rekel, who finally looks up and barks.

'Hey!' Johan yells. 'You're s-caring the fish!'

Jan raises his rod, fiddles the worm off the hook and winds the line around a spool.

'Had enough?' Zeeger asks.

'I want to go home.'

'Home?' Klaas asks. 'But you've –'

'Shut your trap,' says Jan.

Rekel barks again. The Barbary duck swims in circles and hisses. It doesn't mean anything. Zeeger once saw them in the yard with Rekel lying stretched out while the duck put on a courtship display for him. Rekel probably thinks the duck's a dog and the duck probably thinks Rekel is a duck. By the sound of it, Dirk has banged his head against the bars of the bullpen again.

'I want to go home,' his second son says again. He looks at Klaas and rubs his forehead, back and forth over the mosquito bite Zeeger saw this morning. He's still only wearing shorts and a T-shirt.

'N-ow it's no fun any more,' Johan says.

'Then I'm the winner!' Dieke cries.

Jan walks over to the barn, goes inside and comes back out a little later with the green bucket. He stayed inside longer than necessary. He rummages through the bucket on the way back and pulls out something. Is that an envelope?

'D'you get a letter?' Zeeger asks.

'Y-es,' says Johan. 'From the baker.'

'The baker? Blom?'

'Yeah,' says Jan. 'I'll put all this away and then get changed.' He walks over to the side door with Johan behind him.

'Well done, Dieke,' says Klaas, who leaves too.

Dieke has already forgotten her victory. She leans on the middle rail of the bridge and stares big-eyed at the gas well.

'Something interesting down there?' he asks.

'I can see the bogeyman,' she says. 'He's breathing.'

Straw

She really cannot remember why she was running so late. It doesn't matter. Jan and Johan had already left for school, and would go to the Polder House from there. Klaas was already gone too. She'd been left behind with Hanne. Zeeger was working. Was that the day Hanne put her little hand in the empty apple-sauce tin with the razor-sharp lid still attached? When she'd had to hunt for iodine and plasters and scissors? When she'd had to comfort her? No, that was earlier. Why was I so late? But if I'd been on time, the Queen wouldn't have touched Hanne or spoken to me.

It's getting more and more difficult to think straight. The creaking and groaning, the sliding in the silo, the marching borers and woodworms, and the restless crashing of that superfluous lump of meat make it almost impossible. And the cold. She can't understand where that's coming from, she doesn't have the impression the weather's suddenly turned. If she'd known, thinks Anna Kaan. If she'd known that the child whose cheek she'd stroked after lunch would be dead that afternoon. But she was already in Anna Paulowna by then, and the next day she was on Texel. Noises make their way in from outside, where they are now fishing. She's lying on her back with her arms by her sides, the straw has moulded itself completely to her body, not a single snapped stalk is poking her in the back. I want to go to the beach tomorrow, she thinks. Go to the beach again after all this time, and Zeeger's coming with me, whether he wants to or not. Maybe Rie and Jenneke will be there too. Zeeger in the blue swimming trunks that are so old they're almost disintegrating. Floating in the sea on my back with my toes sticking up out of the water. Just like I'm lying here now, but flapping my hands. I'll try to lure Rekel into the water. It's strange, Rekel doesn't like salt water. I want to clean the old toilet bowl in the cowshed too, she thinks, and tear off the old calendar pages while I'm at it, so it's today there too. 'Rekel, here, boy!' she hears Zeeger call. But Rekel won't come. Besides disliking salt water he also hates fishing.

Only the empty biscuit packet is lying next to her now. And the ladder, of course. I can go down now, she thinks. Without a word – or maybe just a 'See?' to Johan and a quick dirty look at Jan – then cross the bridge and make some coffee. Slice some gingerbread cake. Coffee and ginger-bread cake to round off the fishing. Then everyone can go home. Turn on the telly. Feed Rekel, hoping that Zeeger won't ask or say too much.

When she tries to sit up, she can't manage it. The cold has crept up through her arms and legs, numbing her limbs. She no longer feels like steak, cold water or crispy-fresh

French beans. 'N-o!' she hears Johan shout. No? No, what? Then she doesn't seem to hear anything at all for a while, until Rekel suddenly starts barking. I was too late, my bike fell down. Back home, I carried a basket full of washing out into the yard from the milking parlour. Clothes and sheets, washed in the Miele. It was quiet on the other side of the ditch: the labourer, his wife and two children were on holiday. I hung up Zeeger's underpants with the pegs and thought, he buys a new radio and a new camera, he gets a new bulk tank and a new pipeline installed, but new underpants never occur to him. He was hammering away upstairs. Jan and Johan were at the swimming pool. Klaas might have been at home. Hanne was playing in the living room. I called out to her when I went into the kitchen. 'Ah,' I heard from the living room, so I went to check on her after all. She was kneeling down at the glass-topped table, scribbling on the back of a piece of wallpaper with two felt tips at once. She'd already forgotten about the Queen, she didn't even know who the Queen was. Tinus was lying next to her, all four legs stretched out. I almost said, 'Don't lean too hard,' because we'd already replaced the glass four times. A big mistake, that table – how are kids supposed to know how fragile a sheet of glass is? I walked back to the kitchen, got a mixing bowl out of a cupboard, shook a packet of flour into it, poured in some milk, broke a few eggs into the mix and added a couple of pinches of salt. A Saturday dinner. Because it felt like a Saturday.

The packet of butter on the sink, the frying pan on the stove, all much too early, but I couldn't sit still. The Queen spoke to me, I thought, covering the pancake batter with a

tea towel. I wanted to keep it to myself. For me and Hanne.
I thought I'd seen the baker scuttling around. With a camera?
It was high time he came, we were almost out of bread. An
hour later, or two, he finally showed up. And left again, and
how on earth did Hanne and Tinus get out? I heard it. I heard
a car, a bang and then the brakes. I had to go out to see
what it was. Zeeger was busy hammering and sawing, he
didn't hear a thing. The baker. Everywhere that whole day
long, the baker. I'd planned to tell them about the Queen
later, maybe that evening over the pancakes. But then it
was already too late.

The creaking and groaning has grown duller, the cobwebs
woollier, Dirk's thudding muffled. It's inside of me after all,
she thinks, that creaking and groaning. I'll . . . Shall I call
out? She tries to open her mouth but her lips feel stiff. She
wants to run her fingers over her mouth to rub them and
manages to lift one arm. The elbow bends, the hand flops
down onto her stomach. She's able to stroke herself lightly
with her fingers; scratching is beyond her, let alone lifting
her arm up again. The rectangle – the hole directly overhead
with however many tiles to the right of it and a few more
to the left, she counted them not long ago – no longer gives
her a view of the outside world. Yellow, she thinks. Rain,
after all? A real drop, after all?

Someone comes into the barn, she hears them despite the
muffling of her ears. 'Mum?' she hears, even though she
needs to summon all her strength to make out the word.
Jan. No, wait, she thinks as the cold reaches her shoulders
and pelvis, there's something I have to tell him. I don't want
to let him go like this. She pricks up her ears, ignoring all

the other noises. 'I'm off.' He leaves. Then all of the dead appear. Griet Kaan first, in her three-quarter bed, the fire cold, the paraffin lamp empty, the Frisian clock that won't stop ticking, Zeeger who's ignoring her; her parents and parents-in-law, she sees their eyes, sees them walking and riding their bicycles, eating cake on birthdays, hospital beds, flowers; she sees time too, racing by, the unbearable duration of a human life, but also the little things, seemingly insignificant, and through it all everyone's eyes; then someone must have turned on the radio because she hears 'Oh Happy Day' and instead of Hanne, who should appear too, Anna Kaan sees the hanging, the enormous wall hanging her mother-in-law made – it hung in the children's room for years, with palm trees made of green felt, cooking pots, Piccaninnies with real rings in their ears – and, although the cold has now reached her midriff, her lethargic brain starts wondering where on earth that hanging's got to; the old Queen's empty study, her legs suddenly buckling when the tour guide said 'Juliana lay in state here'; and now she adds something to those images she saw earlier of girls making preserves and the boys from nearby farms: all dead – grandparents, parents, girls, farmhands – now she feels that this barn, this place once smelled of fresh wood, of resin, that countless people who can no longer walk have walked here, and that she is a part of that countlessness; and then back to the borers and the woodworms, seething and teeming without a sound. It gets quiet, very quiet, no dog, no Barbary duck, no husband and no children, beyond the dead, the light coming in through the three round windows at the front of the barn, very vague thoughts like

Did I really just knock back a whole bottle of advocaat?
and *Gravel? You buy that at a garden centre, where else?*;
the rectangle in the tile roof – she can no longer move her
head – changes from yellow to white, the cold that has crept
from her toes and fingertips into her core seems to be trying
to get out again through her nose, slowly, more and more
slowly, and changes from cold to smell, as if that's ultimately
the most important thing, overshadowing everything else,
and now it turns sweet.

As sweet as autumn.

Stewed pears.

Is that it?

The smell of stewed pears, in June?

Toasting

'Dinie,' he says simply.

'Herm,' says the cemetery caretaker. 'Come in.'

He steps into the hall, puts his stick in the umbrella stand
and walks through to the living room. The dog doesn't look
up, but thumps the rug once with its bushy tail. The beast
pants and drools. As usual the place is spotless. He glances
at the photo of Dinie's late husband as if asking his
permission to come in and sit down at his wife's dinner table
and, later, possibly – it's something he can never count on
– kiss her and lie down next to her in bed. Dinie follows
him into the living room and closes the lace curtains. She
does it every time and the baker's never mentioned it, though
he wonders why she doesn't do it before he arrives. The

table is already set, as tastefully as ever, with a runner, silver cutlery, crystal wine glasses. Wine. He thinks of the three glasses of lemon brandy he's already knocked back. It will probably be white wine, lightly sparkling, he likes that and so does Dinie. He's put on a clean shirt, but the armpits already feel damp. The window behind the lace curtains is a single large pane, without any small windows above it or to the side to let in some fresh air. Not that there's much difference today, inside or out, it might even be cooler inside.

'I'll serve dinner straight away,' Dinie says. 'It's all ready.'

He sits down on the chair that gives him a partial view out onto the street through the lace curtains.

'Take your jacket off, for goodness' sake. It's stifling in here.' She sets the dish of potatoes down on the table and walks back to the kitchen.

He half rises and worms his arms out of the jacket before hanging it over the back of his chair. He was right: now that the shirt has been strangely twisted by his contortions, a wet spot has appeared over his breastbone.

Dinie brings in a dish of runner beans and two plates with two beef olives on each. 'God, I've forgotten the wine.' And she's gone again. The dog doesn't seem interested in the food. The baker sucks up the smell of the beef olives. It's been the kind of day he forgets to eat. Not counting breakfast, but that seems a lifetime ago. Dinie returns with a bottle of wine – white, because it's in a cooler.

'Delicious,' he says.

'You can't say that yet.'

'Knowing you.'

'*Bon appétit.*' She fills the two wine glasses

Before starting on his meal, he raises his glass and looks at her. 'To?'

'You tell me.'

'To today.'

'Has it been a good day?'

'I'm not sure yet. I think so.' The shell grit hurt, but that was superficial. Now the pain is deeper, in his knee-caps, which feel numb and hard. Less stiff now after the short walk from his house to Dinie's, but he'd needed to use his walking stick again.

She doesn't ask for details. Or what's happened. She drinks her wine almost grimly. 'I'm glad it's over.'

'Whoa, not so fast, there's a lot to go yet.'

Dinner

Soon he'll ask why, that's the kind of man he is. Herm Blom. Retired baker. A baker with a past. She studies him over the rim of her wine glass. An old man with a dry neck. Dry from shaving day in, day out. She never looked at Herm Blom the way she looked at Albert Waiboer almost forty years and a few hours ago. Herm Blom was always delivering bread, and if he wasn't delivering it, he was baking it. She never saw him in his trunks at the swimming pool with a firm young body. Sometimes when he's lying next to her in the double bed in the dark and she's in the mood she can guide her hands with thoughts of someone else. She coughs, glugs down the last mouthful of wine and refills their glasses, although Herm's was only half empty. 'Don't you like it?' she asks.

'What, the wine? It's fine. Refreshing.'

The beans are fine too, fresh, and the potatoes are just right, but she can't enjoy it. Her visits to the cemetery have left a bitter taste in her mouth that even the juicy beef olives can't displace. And this morning she had that bitter taste too of course, after the Negro . . . She hacks off a piece of beef olive, shoves it into her mouth and chews fiercely. In a while, after dinner, she wants to suggest a stroll to the baker, a stroll that will include the cemetery. She wants to see what's happened there, she doesn't trust those redheads. She definitely wants to be the last person to visit the cemetery today.

'What's happened?'

'Huh?'

'To make you wish the day was already over?'

'Ah, nothing special. You get days like that.'

'Yes.'

They eat their meal in silence. After clearing the table and rinsing the plates and cutlery, she returns to the living room with two apples and two oranges. While she peels the first apple, Herm drains his glass. She quarters the apple, removes the core and hands him a piece. He should stay the night, she thinks.

'I'm thinking of getting a dog,' he says.

'A dog? You? I've never seen you so much as touch Benno.'

'Benno's not the kind of dog I'm thinking of.'

'No?'

'No.'

Ridiculous. Herm with a dog. It'll be the death of him. A broken hip first and then downhill from there. She pops the last quarter in her mouth and starts to peel the second apple.

'That son of yours,' he says.

The continuous strip of apple peel breaks. 'Yes?' she asks warily.

'Where's he live?'

'What makes you think of my son all of a sudden?'

'This afternoon I was looking at the photos I took on the day of the Queen's visit.'

'Oh, yes. When was that again?'

'The seventeenth of June, nineteen sixty-nine.'

'Almost forty years ago.'

'Your son was in them too. Teun, isn't it?'

'Yes. I don't have any photos of that at all. I know she was here, but I had to work. The swimming pool didn't close just because the Queen was coming. Some people wanted to enjoy a quiet swim for a change. Maybe my husband took Teun.'

My husband. That's what she always says, never Kees.

'But, where does he live now?'

'Schagen.'

'Married?'

'Divorced.'

'Kids?'

'Two daughters.'

'Does he still see them?'

'I believe so. I see them regularly, they live in Den Helder. I still see my daughter-in-law, you see.'

'You believe so?'

'Herm, I don't have much contact with him. I don't even like him any more . . .'

'What?'

She hands him a last piece of apple and then starts to elaborately peel and pith an orange. She doesn't want to talk about Teun, she doesn't want to start crying again. 'Nothing,' she says.

'What's he do?'

Now she's had enough of the interrogation. 'Social worker,' she snaps, popping a segment of orange into her mouth and plonking the rest in the baker's hand. 'There. Cup of coffee and then a stroll?'

'Fine. I could use a walk, my knees are a little stiff.'

'Lovely.' She clears away the peel and puts on some coffee. Benno has followed her into the kitchen. He yawns loudly. 'Yes,' she whispers. 'You can come too.' The coffee machine bubbles. She puts her hands on the worktop and looks out through the kitchen window at the hole in the hedge. 'With your mistress.' It's actually much too hot for coffee.

Shit

'See, until sunset.' Dinie points at the green sign with white lettering that's screwed to the gate.

'I've learned something new,' he says. He'd been counting on a walk along the Molenlaan, maybe even popping into The Arms for a second cup of coffee, or something stronger. He should have known better. If Dinie closes the lace curtains when he's in the house, he can't expect her to sit down at an outdoor cafe with him. The dog seemed happy about being taken out for a walk, but the moment they were out on the street it started to drag its feet as if something terrible was about to happen. Dinie suggested walking through the cemetery and he said it would be closed by now. 'Not at all,' she said.

They're now walking through the section that's still empty, with dry grass on either side of the path. After coming in through the gate, she'd taken his arm, making his walking stick superfluous.

'And the sun won't be going down for quite a while yet,' she says.

'Not that we'll see it.' He sneaks a look at her from the side and tries to imagine what she'd look like if she stopped dyeing her hair. The dog pads ahead slowly, dragging its tail over the shell grit. Dinie is big and buxom, he likes having her next to him in bed. As far as he's concerned, that's as far as it needs to go. Just lying alongside each other, touching. He is determined not to go back home tonight. He'll also have a look at the headstone Jan Kaan was painting this afternoon. Dinie is holding him tight.

He hears a vague rumbling in the distance. A thunderstorm after all? 'Did you hear that?' he asks.

'What am I supposed to have heard?'

'Thunder, I think.'

She looks at the sky. 'No,' she says.

They pass between the two low hedges and into the populated section.

'Look,' she says, when they've more or less reached the stone. 'Freshly painted.' It's as if she's led him straight to it.

'Hey,' he says, not even feigning surprise because he's

looking at the gravel. Blue gravel that he doesn't remember seeing earlier in the afternoon.

'It's something we've never talked about.'

'No.' As far as he's concerned, there's no need either. Not any more. Yesterday, there might have been.

It's as if Dinie senses that. 'Maybe it's not necessary either.'

'No.' He suddenly feels the wine. He hadn't wanted to drink more than one glass but she'd kept pouring until the bottle was empty.

She guides him towards the bench under the linden. There's a dead bird lying on the ground in front of the bench. He looks up. The branch is empty. That can mean several things, but it *is* strange. This afternoon two birds, and now one dead one. He can't imagine the other one just flying off. But if it hasn't, wouldn't it be lying there too? Dinie spots the blue tit and silently slides it under the bench with the tip of her shoe. Now he feels the lemon brandy as well. He flops down on the bench. The dog follows his example by slumping on the ground.

'Are you two tired?' she asks, turning and sitting down herself.

'Yes,' he says.

The dog doesn't react.

Dinie grabs his arm. At first he thinks she wants to support him even now, seated, but when she keeps squeezing he realises it's something else. She stands up and, as she doesn't let go, he's forced to stand up too. And now she starts walking, pulling him along behind her, he has to watch carefully where to put his stick. Swinging it and putting it down, swinging it and putting it down again. Then suddenly she stops, clapping one hand over her mouth. Without a single word of encouragement the dog has followed them and now rushes on past and up to the tall and narrow but, above all, filthy headstone, which it starts to lick with abandon.

Bedtime

Dieke looks out through one of the living-room windows. The window with the crack. The blades of grass are still completely motionless, but the colour is a lot different from this morning. It's around eight o'clock, she should have been in bed ages ago. Standing behind her is her mother. Her father is in the kitchen, sitting at the table that still has to be cleared. He rustles the newspaper.

Everybody's gone. Uncle Jan and Uncle Johan got into Grandpa's car and drove off. Grandpa's not back yet. Dieke is waiting to see the car turn into the yard of the house next door and she'll only manage *that* if she keeps her nose pressed to the glass. She's expecting a lot more to happen today and sleep is the last thing on her mind. With all the things that have broken so far, there's a chance the whole barn might collapse – and what if she was in bed and missed it? 'Who broke this window?' she asks.

'I don't know, Diek.'

'Not you?'

'No, not me.'

'Is it going to fall out?'

'Don't be silly.'

Dieke sighs deeply.

'Ask Grandpa who did it. He's sure to know.'

'When he comes home? Can I ask him then?'

'No, give him some peace and quiet first. Tomorrow. You're going to bed now.'

'I don't want to.'

'It's already gone eight.'

'But it's holidays!'

'You're five.'

'Why is Grandma up on the straw?'

'I don't know.'

'You never know anything.'

'More than you. Maybe for Grandma, being up on the straw is like drawing for you.'

'Huh?'

'The way you start drawing when something's bothering you.'

'I draw all the time.'

'Yes, but when you're angry you use different colours and your tongue's poking out of your mouth.'

'Grandma's mean.'

'Why do you say that?'

'She pinched me, when we went to the zoo.'

'You must have done something to deserve it.'

'No, I didn't. Was that a real sword?'

'Yes, with a sharp edge.'

'Did people fight with it?'

'I don't think so. Brush your teeth.'

Dieke sees her grandfather's car drive past and slow down. She pulls her nose back from the glass and turns, walks to the kitchen and slides the plastic step over in front of the sink. She takes off everything except her knickers, dropping her clothes on the floor. A big blob of toothpaste on her Jip and Janneke toothbrush. 'Cn ywu tuck mwe in, D-ddy?' she asks.

Her father lays the newspaper on the table. 'Sure,' he says.

'I'll tidy your clothes up,' says her mother, who doesn't sound nearly as nice as her father.

Digging

Dieke skips ahead of him up the stairs as if it's early in the morning. It will take her a while to fall asleep. Upstairs, she doesn't go straight into her bedroom, but looks up at the door first. 'Somebody changed my letters!' she bawls.

'Gosh,' he says. 'How could that have happened?'

'Yeah! Who did it?'

'Me.'

'You? When?'

'This afternoon. It said Dekie. I didn't know who that was.'

'Me. That's me!'

'I know. But now it's written properly, now it says Dieke.'

'Hmm,' she says. She goes into her bedroom and looks around carefully. 'The window's broken!' she screeches.

'Yep,' he says.

'How'd that happen?'

'It was the heat, I think.'

'It's scary!'

'Why?'

'It might fall out.'

'No, it won't. It's the outside window.' Klaas draws the curtains. 'There. Now you can't see it any more.'

'I don't like it.' Before lying down, she goes down on all fours to peer under the bed.

'Did you look in my bag?'

'Of course not. It's your bag, not mine.'

'That's OK then.' She crawls under the bed and re-emerges with the bag.

'Pyjamas?'

'Too hot.' Before lying down, she opens the treasure bag and, after rummaging around a little, pulls out the ring she found this morning. Then she pushes her legs in under the duvet. 'It was fun, wasn't it? Uncle Johan coming. Uncle Johan's nice.'

'Yes, he is. And Jan?'

'Mm, him too. But Uncle Johan's nicer. Can I go to Leslie's tomorrow?'

'Leslie?' He chuckles.

'What? What are laughing about?'

'Have you ever been to Leslie's?'

'No. Just at the swimming pool.'

'Then we'll have to ring up his dad.'

'We can do that, can't we?'

'It's fine by me. Ask your mother tomorrow morning.'

Despite the heat, Dieke pulls the Sesame Street duvet up to her chin. 'Nighty-night,' she says.

'Goodnight, Diek.' He straightens up and walks out of the bedroom. 'Open or closed?' he asks in the doorway.

'A little bit open.' She's almost forgotten him already, holding the golden ring between thumb and index finger in front of her face, peering through it with one eye closed.

He leaves the door ajar. And looks once again at the letters his father made. *NAHNE*, he reads. *ENNAH, HANEN*, and finally *HANNE*. Before going back downstairs, he studies the painting on the landing. A painting his father and mother left behind when they moved out of the farmhouse and into the house next door. Long ago Jan and Johan thought it was a portrait of Great-grandmother Kaan, although they never knew her, of course. He used to make fun of them about it, but looking closely now he does see a resemblance between this woman and his father. Griet Kaan as a young, carefree girl. Halfway down the stairs, he suddenly remembers where he's seen that golden ring before: the Piccaninnies on the wall hanging in the bedroom. How on earth did one of those rings end up in a flowerpot?

'This place is a madhouse,' his wife says as he re-enters the kitchen.

'Yep,' he says, still thinking about the wall hanging and where it's got to.

Dieke's clothes are still on the floor, the plastic step hasn't been moved out of the way. His wife is smoking a cigarette. Between the plates and cutlery on the table in front of her there is a mug of coffee. There are pans on the stove.

'Dieke just told me that your mother pinched her.'

'Really? When?'

'At the party.'

'Why?'

'I don't know.' She sucks hard on her cigarette. 'But actually your father's even worse than your mother.' She gestures outside, over the lopsided cactus. Zeeger Kaan is wriggling between the branches of the chestnut. It looks like he's picking beans.

'Yes,' he says, sliding a chair out from the table to sit down. He rolls a cigarette very calmly, lights it and stares at the drinking trough full of dry grass for a couple of minutes. 'What do you think of Highland cattle?' he asks.

'What do you mean? As meat?'

'No, on the land. On paths. Between elderberries.'

She fixes her eyes on him. 'I want to get away from here, Klaas.'

He lets the smoke drift out of his nostrils. 'Maybe,' he says. 'Maybe.'

Entering the barn, Klaas is surprised by the silence. Dirk is no longer restless and doesn't even look up when he goes over in front of the bullpen. He breaks a chunk of hay off a bale lying against the wall and tosses it into his feed trough. Some linseed cake goes on top. There's already enough water in the big black trough. The bull sticks his head through the bars and starts feeding. There are no swallows flying in and out. Klaas steps up onto the bottom rung of the ladder, though he doesn't know what he's going to do. About halfway up he stops, pushes the extendable section up a little, then climbs back down. The upper part of the ladder rustles down past the bales of straw as he descends. After locking the hooks of the extendable section onto the bottom rung, he tilts the ladder back, lowers it and lays it flat on the floor. Then he takes an old broom, sweeps the shards from the advocaat bottle together and pushes them into an old cardboard box that is lying around. 'Mum?' he asks. No reaction. He calls again, louder this time. Silence, not even a crackle of straw. She must have fallen asleep. What do you expect after a whole bottle of advocaat, when she usually limits herself to a single glass on birthdays? Leaving the barn through the big doors, he sees that she's switched on the light. He smiles.

He has the idea that the light is already fading as he, bare-chested, starts to dig a hole just to the side of the gate he, Dieke and Jan were sitting and leaning on yesterday evening. It's heavy work: the ground is dry and hard. He runs a hand across his forehead a couple of times. When the hole is deep enough, he fetches the wheelbarrow with the dead sheep and pushes it to the edge. Rekel, apparently no longer offended, is doing a circuit of the yard and comes over to see what he's up to, stopping at the open gate and sitting. He's learned not to go onto the road or into the fields. He holds his head at an angle, finding it difficult not to approach the dead animal. Klaas tips the sheep into the hole and shovels earth on top of it. The burial mound will sink in time. When he's finished he leans on the spade, looking out over the fields. They're empty. He sees grass and grey sky. He only notices how very quiet it is when he hears quacking from the broad ditch a bit further to the right. Rekel wanders over to the ditch. He doesn't bark, he already did that earlier this evening. He knows the Barbary duck, he knows how old it is.

Empty fields, and he sees all kinds of things.

Calling

Johan watches the car drive off. Jan is sitting in the back, staring at the headrest of the front passenger seat where he, Johan, was just sitting. Behind him a door opens. TV noise fills the wide hall. 'Y-es, Toon,' he says. 'N-o, Toon. O-K, Toon.'

'I didn't say a word,' Toon says. 'Leave the door open for a bit. Why are you walking so funny?'

'I w-alked ten kilo metres with a bag of s-tones on my back. I've got b-listers!'

'Shall I look at them? With a needle and some iodine?'

'N-o, leave it. I'd have to t-ake my socks off and I don't f-eel like taking my socks off. They'll be fine.' He goes into the communal living room, where three of the other guys are slumped on an old brown sofa. They're staring at some game show or other and don't look up when he comes in. Two of them have taken off their T-shirts. When Toon comes in, one of them shouts, 'Door!' Toon leaves it open and sits down at the dining table with Johan, in the short section of the L-shaped room. There is big cane lampshade over the table. Johan rests his forearms on the tabletop and intertwines his fingers. 'I just c-aught four fish,' he says.

'Did you wash your hands?'

'Yes.'

Toon looks at the clock on the wall. 'You're more than two hours late home.'

Home, thinks Johan. Is this my home? 'I've h-ad a busy day.'

'You were with your little sister.'

'Y-es. Shall I tell you about it?'

'That's OK. I already know.'

'Oh, y-eah?'

'Yep.'

'Shhhhh!' shouts one of the guys on the sofa.

'And Jan was there too.'

'Y-es. He's g-oing bald.'

'That doesn't matter, does it?'

'Y-ou'd like him, Toon.'

'I do like him.'

'Oh, y-eah?' Johan stares at his support worker. That doesn't bother Toon. Someone like Jan can't bear it, he noticed that again this afternoon. People get nervous around him. Even his own brother.

'Yeah,' says Toon, staring right back.

'He was just in the car. My f-ather d-ropped me off, but you didn't see the car.'

'Pity.'

'Shut up!' someone else shouts from the sofa.

'Y-ou're a p-retty nice guy,' Johan says, watching his fingers wriggle. 'And I th-ink Jan's p-retty nice too, though I'm n-ot sure.'

'I think he is.'

'He's th-inking about Hanne and that's why he for-got to get out of the car and see who you are.' Johan screws up his eyes, making a deep frown appear in his forehead. 'I s-aid, come in for a s-econd, see who T-oon is.'

'And?'

'And n-ow he's on the t-rain and thinking, sh-it.'

Toon smiles and looks over at the sofa where the three other guys are still slumped in front of the TV, feet up on the coffee table.

Johan pulls the pack of Marlboros out of his back pocket and lights one. 'He'll c-ome some time. He has to come v-isit me some time, doesn't he?'

'We'll wait till he does.'

'Cut the crap, will you?' shouts the third guy.

Crap? Johan sucks in a lungful of smoke and then thinks of something, something from the afternoon. 'A t-ree nursery,' he whispers, leaning over the table. 'Is that a lot of work?'

'Not at all,' Toon whispers, looking like he knows what he's talking about. 'You plant trees, let them grow, weed them occasionally, and then you sell them at a profit.'

'Th-at's all?'

'Sure. Do you want to work at a tree nursery? It's time you did something, Johan. You can't spend your whole life sitting in the courtyard in your undies.'

'Y-ou don't m-ind that,' he whispers.

'Of course not. Beer? You've earned a beer.' Toon stands up and gets two cold beers out of the fridge. He flicks off the tops and sits down again.

Johan holds the bottle against his cheek before taking the first mouthful. 'Toon,' he whispers, 'I'm not ug-ly, am I?'

*

'Telephone!' shouts one of the guys. 'Toon! Telephone!'

Toon looks up from the papers he was reading with a pen in his hand. 'Johan, can you get that?'

He stands up, puts his empty bottle on the table, takes the first steps with one hand on the tabletop. The hall door is still open and so is the outside door. The old-fashioned phone is on a rectangular side table. He picks it up.

'Y-es?'

'. . .'

'Jo-han.'

'. . .'

'Who?'

'. . .'

'Oh, Toon. Y-es, I'll call him. Toon!'

Toon is already in the doorway. 'You have to say, "Good evening, this is the Link,"' he says, taking the receiver from Johan.

Johan's legs feel very heavy. Although both doors are open, there's not a breath of air in the hall. He sits down on the chair next to the table – the phone chair – and rubs his nose dry. 'Do it y-our self then,' he says quietly. On the wall opposite is a poster of a sunny island. With a beach, palm trees and a green sea. Next to the poster is a big pot plant. Judging by the sound of the TV, a police series has started.

'Yes?' Toon says. 'Toon speaking.'

'. . .'

'Calm down. Take a deep breath.'

'. . .'

'Just say Toon for once. It can't be that difficult.'

[233]

'. . .'

'What? What's happened?'

'. . .'

'Cow shit?'

'Who's that?' Johan asks.

Toon waves for him to be quiet.

'Y-es, b-ut . . .'

'Johan, not now. Mother . . . calm down a little . . . Who are you talking to?'

'. . .'

'The baker? Which baker?'

'. . .'

'Clean it off.'

'. . .'

'No, you don't have to go straight to the police. Talk to someone from the council first.'

'. . .'

'I know it's Saturday night. You can still –'

'. . .'

'The Kaan boys? Which ones?'

Johan has long since stopped looking at the sea, the beach and the palm trees. He's looking at Toon, who's talking a little impatiently and tracing circles in the air with one hand. That means hurry up, at least Johan thinks it does. He's a Kaan boy himself and the woman he just spoke to wanted to talk to Teun but there's nobody called Teun here at all. Now Toon's looking at him with a relieved expression and his hand has stopped going round in circles and started twisting back and forth instead. As if to say 'that was a close one' or 'we got out of that by the skin of our teeth'.

Or something else, he can't think straight. Besides giving him heavy legs, the cold beer has also made him light-headed.

'Mother. Wait. Did you see them at it?'

'. . .'

'So how do you know –'

'. . .'

'What's the baker say?'

'. . .'

'He's absolutely right about that. Tomorrow.'

Johan can't stay where he is any longer. His legs are itching, he can't stop wracking his brain about which women he's seen today except for his mother and Klaas's wife, and he also saw the Piccaninny with the bucket full of cow shit, and although he remembers climbing up a ladder and talking to his mother, he now thinks about his mother properly for the first time today, that she's up on the straw, and the bucket full of thrashing fish. Did somebody remember to tip them back in the ditch? He stands up and walks outside, where it's still refusing to rain. But it does feel a little cooler than the hall. 'Jesus H. Christ!' he screams into the silent street. 'It's hot!' He limps over to the other side of the road, sits down in the gutter and stares back at the building he lives in. The sign over the door says *THE LINK*; the neon light above it has already flicked on. He takes off his T-shirt. He's tired, very tired.

A little later Toon comes out too. He crosses without looking left or right and sits down next to him.

'Do you think Jan will e-ver come to v-isit me?' Johan asks.

'Ah, Johan.' Toon wraps an arm around his shoulders. 'Sh-all we go to the s-tation?'

'Later. Maybe.'

A woman comes past with a dog. She frowns at them, or so Johan thinks. 'What you looking at?' he says. 'Bitch.'

Sitting

Strange perhaps, but he can't stop thinking about those French beans. After getting home and parking in front of the garage, he walks into the kitchen for a glass of water, then immediately heads back out to crawl through the branches of the first chestnut he cut down. It's not easy, sometimes he has to hang almost upside down to pick a few beans. It's not very solid, chestnut wood, and a few branches crack under his weight. When he thinks he's picked himself a decent meal, plenty for two people, he calls it a day. He wipes the sweat from his face and puts the colander of beans in the scullery. Rekel is sitting on the tiles by the side door, making a show of yawning while doing his best not to look at his master. 'You want to eat!' Zeeger says. 'I completely forgot.' He scoops two mugs of dry feed into the bowl and moves into the kitchen to let the dog eat in peace.

He turns on the TV and goes over to stand at the sliding doors. 'Why doesn't it rain?' he asks himself out loud. He turns the TV off again. As he makes his way through the scullery on his way out, the dog growls quietly. In the garage he's welcomed by the same guy who was reporting from the beach this morning, saying exactly the same things.

When they hand over to Jan Visser, the weatherman, he realises that it's a repeat. '*Tomorrow, listeners, we'll have a completely different take on the world.*' Good, thinks Zeeger. He picks up a couple of Christmas trees off the pile in the corner and inspects them. They're still unpainted. He puts them on his workbench and picks up the tin of green paint. When he's about to flick off the lid, he changes his mind and hangs the screwdriver back up on the tool wall. Tomorrow's better, when Anna's back and will call him in for coffee around ten. Maybe she'll feel like going to the car boot sale in Sint Maartenszee next week; she can sell something herself too. The fishing rods are standing in another corner, he's already tidied them away after everyone left them lying on and near the bridge. He emptied the bucket as well; there were already two fish floating belly up. Rekel comes into the garage slowly, his head hanging. 'Come on, boy,' says Zeeger. 'We'll go and sit by the ditch for a while.'

The dog sits obediently next to the deckchair he's set down between two willows. Zeeger thinks about the grave and decides that tomorrow – no, Monday – he'll buy a sack of gravel to really finish it off. Light-coloured gravel. And maybe a new shrub? There was a conifer once, a conifer that was supposed to stay small, but after about four years it had already plunged a few of the neighbouring graves into shadow. He removed it just in time, before the roots went too deep. No, no shrub. But fresh gravel, definitely. I have to ask Klaas if he'll strip the chestnuts. I'm not up to that any more. Not three big trees in one go. 'Come down, woman!' he shouts. 'It's light! Your kitchen isn't dark any more!' He's startled the dog, which stands up and crosses the bridge, then wavers in the barn doorway at the border of light and dark. Something's moving behind the tilting window in the farmhouse roof. The curtain slides aside a little and Dieke's face appears. She waves to him. Zeeger waves back. She can't sleep, of course, after a day like today. He wonders whether he'll be able to sleep himself later: another night alone. Maybe she'll come down off the straw. Everyone's gone, the job's been taken care of. She must get hungry and thirsty sooner or later? Dieke slides the curtains shut again. When he looks back at the barn, Rekel's gone. Has it got something to do with Soestdijk too? he wonders.

Soon after the party, Anna wanted to go to Soestdijk. She was irritable. 'While we still can,' she said. 'Soon they'll turn it into a hotel.' One morning, ten or so days ago, they'd climbed into the car, although he actually found driving increasingly difficult and didn't want to make long journeys any more. The drive went smoothly, but at the entrance they ran into a hitch. The woman at the counter asked them for their tickets. 'Tickets?' said Anna. 'That's what we want to buy.' It turned out that wasn't possible, you needed to order and pay for the tickets on the internet. 'Internet?' said Anna. 'Do you know how old we are?' They had to wait and, just before the first tour was due to start, they were allowed in after all, as a few people hadn't showed up. It was quite a walk from the entrance to the palace and Anna had linked arms with him. He noticed that the guide annoyed her: she spoke with a German accent, as if she was entering into her role just a little too much. Anna was indifferent to the old rooms and grew a little nervous on their way to Bernhard's study. There was nothing there. The room was empty. 'But, why?' she asked the guide. 'Well,' the answer went, 'just as in ordinary families, things are shared out among the next of kin after a bereavement.' 'Terrible,' Anna said quietly, so quietly only he could hear. A tear appeared in her eye at the sight of how run-down it was, how drab and decrepit, even the dining room, where furniture *had* been left in place, original and simple. 'They sat in here,' Anna said, running her fingers over a damaged sideboard. 'No touching!' the guide exclaimed. 'Zeeger, they sat in here,' Anna repeated, 'back then too.' Finally, Juliana's study, also empty. But with new carpet on the floor. It was good that Anna was standing close to him because when the guide told them that this was where the old Queen had been laid out, her knees went weak and she leant heavily on him. 'Terrible,' she said again. 'Did that poor old woman spend her last years in these run-down rooms?' After that they did a circuit of the garden. 'There's nothing left,' Anna said when they reached the greenhouses. 'All empty.' There were sweet peas growing in front of the greenhouses. It was a brisk day, drizzling. The next day it warmed up and it hasn't cooled off since.

Rekel comes out of the barn yowling, and when he lies down next to the deckchair the yowling gives way to whimpering. 'What's the matter?' Zeeger asks. 'Has she chased you off?' A slight ripple passes through the dead-still ditchwater, the top of the ancient pear tree rustles. Zeeger turns his head. He can't see if it's already formed minuscule little pears, but in four or five months they'll be ripe, even if it's not always easy to tell with stewing pears: they're that hard.

And green. It's only after hours of simmering at the lowest setting that they change colour. It's a Gieser Wildeman, the tastiest stewing pear there is. If only it was October already.

Flirting

The young guy in the light-blue T-shirt is the last to board the 8.38 to Den Helder. It's a double-decker, the kind that sings, something you hear best in the vestibule. It's not very busy, but there are at least two people in each of the four-seat sections. He puts his bag in the baggage rack and chooses the spot next to a girl reading a newspaper. Opposite her is a man with ginger hair. He has his bag on the seat next to him and is staring out the window. His forehead is burnt. The young guy feels that the T-shirt he put on just before leaving for the train station is already wet. The air conditioning doesn't seem to be working properly. He's jealous of the girl next to him, not a trace of sweat on her nose. The ginger-haired guy seems to be feeling the heat too, though. He runs a hand over the back of his neck and looks at him. A little too long. Then he moves his lips as if he's saying 'fucking hot', but in that very same moment the conductor announces 'Anna Paulowna' over the PA. When the doors open, a very brief draught passes through the carriage. Nobody gets on. The young guy slumps down on his seat, making sure to end up with his legs spread. He pushes his long blond hair back behind one ear. He can smell himself: fresh sweat and deodorant. Nice. Maybe the man can smell him too.

'Ticket?' He opens his eyes. The conductor is looking at him impatiently. He pulls his wallet out of his back pocket, gets his ticket out and hands it to the conductor. The girl next to him shows a monthly pass. The man looks through his wallet, starts to blush and looks up apologetically. 'I don't have a ticket,' he says. 'I completely forgot.'

'No problem,' says the conductor. 'Off-peak discount?'

He shows her his card.

She writes out a ticket and charges him two forty. Apparently she's in a good mood this evening. Then she gives his card a closer appraisal. 'This is almost expired,' she says.

'I know,' the man says. 'Thanks.'

As the conductor strolls off, the young guy gives the man a conspiratorial glance. The man turns away and puts his wallet back in the front pocket of his rucksack. Evidently he really had forgotten. The girl has to get off at Den Helder South. He flops his legs to one side to let her pass, then slides over to the window so that he's directly opposite the man. He spreads his legs again and slides back and forth a little until he's happy with the bulge of his crotch. He looks out: wiry grass, small horses in the dunes, grey sky over the bunkers. He feels that the man is looking at him, waits, then turns his head to look straight ahead. And keeps staring until he's forced the man to look away.

'*Den Helder, this train terminates here. Please remember to take all of your belongings with you when you get off the train.*'

He stands up, bumping his knee against the man's. 'Sorry,' he says.

'No problem,' says the man.

He stretches to get his bag out of the rack and feels his T-shirt creeping up. He's also aware of the sweat patches. The man can't go anywhere until he's got his bag down. The young guy gets off in front of him and saunters along the platform. There's no harm in having a bit of fun. He knows the man is just behind him, he can feel his eyes on his blond hair, moving down to his bum, his legs.

Walking through the train station building, he sees her waiting. She comes towards him. He puts his bag down on the ground, wraps a hand around the back of her neck and pulls her face towards his. She closes her eyes and opens her mouth. He kisses her long and hard without closing his eyes. Looking past her ear, he sees the man cut across the Middenweg and walk onto the deserted Julianaplein on his way to the Spoorstraat. He's not in any kind of hurry. He turns back once. The young man smiles and pulls the girl closer. 'I want you,' he says, but sees himself: his six-pack, his damp neck, his hands on her breasts and belly.

Swearing

'Oh, fucking hell.' The Dutch Navy Museum employee is standing with his hands on his hips and his head tilted back to look up at the side of the *Tonijn*. Someone had noticed something strange and called the museum and, since it was after closing time, a message had ended up on the answering machine. He's in the habit of checking the answering machine on Saturday evenings; people often ring up enquiring about opening hours on Sundays or requesting other information. Plus he doesn't mind having something to do. In the summer he likes to take an evening walk around the grounds, which have been open to the public since the opening of Cape Holland. His wife often comes with him. This is something new, something that's never happened before. How did they get that writing up there anyway? They must have done it from the top, it's at least six metres from the ground to the bottom of the black submarine. They must have used ropes, but the letters are so neat he can't imagine anyone daubing them on while hanging upside down. It must have been a right performance, with all kinds of climbing gear, done after the five o'clock closing.

OH, YEAH? YEAH! No obscenities fortunately, but the lettering is enormous. Someone is approaching from behind, from the direction of town. He looks over his shoulder. A man with a small rucksack, striking red hair. He looks a bit sad. Sad and pissed off. The man stops and looks up.

'"Oh, yeah? Yeah!"?' asks the man.

'Makes a change from "Fuck you" or "Eat shit",' says the employee.

'How'd they manage that?'

'I haven't got the foggiest. Maybe the fire brigade did it, with a ladder truck, because they were bored.'

'No.'

'No, of course not.'

'It's encouragement,' the man says. 'But who for? Us? The museum?'

'Pink. That's a strange colour.'

'It stands out, on the black background like that.'

He looks to the side. The man is no longer staring up at the graffiti, but looking through under the *Tonijn* and into the distance, a serious expression on his face. 'Headed for the ferry?'

'Yeah.'

The employee checks his watch. 'You better keep moving then, the last one's about to sail.'

'Yep.' Once again, the man looks up at the submarine's black hull, then turns and starts walking back into town.

'Hey,' he calls. 'You're going the wrong way.'

The man doesn't react.

He wonders if he should call someone. 'Oh, fucking hell,' he says again, but his heart's not really in it. It's not that bad. Tomorrow's visitors will have an extra attraction at no extra cost. And maybe it will change their view of things, just like this guy's right now.

Jumping

The man who's bought two bottles of cola from the vending machine rubs his thighs cautiously and uses one bottle to cool the back of his neck. I would too, she thinks, if my neck was that burnt. She checks her watch. Almost ten. The train leaves at four minutes past and has been at the platform for a while, but almost no one has got on yet. It's much too hot to sit on a stationary train. The man gulps down the first bottle in one go. Gosh, he's thirsty. Has he just arrived from Texel? The fluorescent lights on the platform have flicked on. It's not dark yet, but with the sky overcast like this, it's gloomy under the platform roof. Today the sun will set at this train's exact departure time. She knows that because she's a fan of Jan Visser, the Radio North-Holland weatherman. She keeps precise daily records of everything – wind velocity, rainfall, hours of sunlight – and checks Jan's predictions. If he's wrong, which doesn't happen often, she sends him an email. Occasionally she gets a reply. Today, whether it's visible or not, the sun will shine exactly sixteen hours and forty-one minutes. In her back garden she even has an amateur wind meter. She's on her way to her sister's in Schagen; it's her birthday tomorrow and she's promised to be there all day to help.

When people start to board the train, she gets on too and sits facing the direction of travel. The man with the bottle of cola gets on after her and sits down opposite her. He puts his rucksack on the seat next to him and crosses his arms. He jiggles his feet restlessly. She gets a book out of her small overnight bag and lays it on her lap. First leave the station, then open it. When the train starts to slow down for Den Helder South, she looks at the sky. There'll be light rain before it gets dark – she heard Jan Visser say that this afternoon. The man is still sitting with his arms crossed, staring out the window. Maybe he doesn't have a book. It's so hot in the train that she can't imagine sitting there with crossed arms like that for long. He has reddish hair, she finds him attractive. There is a group of raucous youths across the aisle, some drinking beer out of cans. Saturday night. She tries to concentrate on her book.

In Anna Paulowna she checks her watch: 10.14, right on time. The red-headed man drinks the second cola and stuffs the bottle into the rubbish bin under the small table. The train shudders as it pulls out of the station, the whistling noise rises and then falls in pitch, then rises and falls again. The jerking doesn't decrease as the train gains speed, it gets worse. After a few minutes the train stops. 'Not again!' shouts one of the youths. 'Turn on the boosters!' shouts another.

After the train has stood still for about five minutes, the youths stop talking. There haven't been any announcements. She reads, and checks her watch every now and then. A slight delay is not a problem, she's not being picked up in Schagen, her sister lives near the station. Suddenly the man bursts into action. He takes his rucksack, puts it on his lap, unzips it and, after rummaging around in it, pulls out a white envelope. She pretends to carry on reading, but watches through her eyelashes as he tears it open. A piece of cardboard emerges, which the man lays on the table in front of the window. He's sitting there with a photograph in one hand, a very slight shadow of the image showing through the back. The raucous boys stand up and walk to the vestibule. She hears banging and yelling, as if they're trying to force the doors. Then the sound of feet landing on gravel. She looks out the window – nothing. They must be walking in the direction of Schagen. The man is staring at the photograph, sniffing a little. Then he lays it on the piece of cardboard, stands up and walks out to the vestibule as well. Two girls follow him and stop in the carriage doorway.

'Did some people just jump down from the train?' one of the girls asks.

'Yep,' she hears the man say. From where she's sitting, she can't see him any more.

'Is that allowed?'

No answer. A little later the girls walk past the window on their way back to Anna Paulowna. She didn't hear them jump down from the train. Someone could make an announcement now, she thinks. Where's the guard? She's never experienced anything like it; a slight rebelliousness bubbles up inside her. She checks her watch again. It's 10.30 already, and they were supposed to arrive in Schagen at 10.20. It is still quite light on her side of the train, towards the sea; in the east the twilight has already set in. The man comes back just as an announcement is finally made. '*H.C., door lock, carriage thirteen-eight.*' That's all, nothing about why the train's stopped, nothing about the rest of their journey. The man hesitates, then picks up his rucksack.

'Wait,' she says.

He's not listening. To her surprise she sees him a little later jumping over the narrow ditch that separates the tracks from the adjacent field. He lands on all fours, the rucksack rides up, covering the back of his head. The photograph, he's forgotten his photo. Finally a guard comes by, no cap, his tie pulled loose. He goes into the vestibule. It's strangely quiet on the train, a couple with large suitcases are the only other people left in the carriage. They're silent, the woman fanning herself with a magazine. The guard comes back and asks the couple if people have left the train. When the man says yes, the guard swears softly and starts walking to the front of the train. She lays her book aside and picks up the photograph; she can't help herself. There are three people in it, one of whom she recognises instantly. The former Queen. Otherwise a fairly young woman and a child, a girl who is pressing her head against the woman's shoulder and clearly doesn't want to have anything to do with the Queen. The Queen's hand is extended towards the child's cheek, as if she's just touched it or is just about to touch it. In the background, on the other side of a canal by the looks of it, there's an old-fashioned van, grey. She has to hold the photo a bit further away to read the writing on the side of the van. *Blom's Breadery*. The Queen is wearing a hat, a round hat made of fabric with a zigzag pattern that doesn't actually go with her dress. She remembers thinking the same thing almost forty years ago. Where is this? She's never heard of Blom's Breadery, and doesn't recognise the houses behind the van. She looks up. The man has wandered off into the field. She stands up and walks to the vestibule.

'You've forgotten your photograph!' she calls.

'No,' he calls back.

'Yes, you have,' she calls, waving it at him.

'I'm coming back,' he says. 'There are people on the tracks, the train's not going anywhere.'

'What are you doing?'

'Nothing,' the man says.

She sticks out an arm. It has started to rain, very lightly. Visser was right yet again. She goes back to her seat and gets her mobile out of her overnight bag. After informing her sister of the delay, she looks at the photo once again. I feel like some rain, she thinks. She stands up and swings the bag over her shoulder, and is soon lowering herself carefully down from the train's footboard. Can I make that? she asks herself, looking at the narrow ditch. No, she thinks, getting ready to jump. No, don't delude yourself, Brecht. You're just consumed with curiosity and you couldn't care less that you're betraying the fact you've already looked at the photo. She tosses her bag over the ditch.

She surprises herself. She calculates how long it's been since she jumped a ditch. At least forty-five years, but it went quite smoothly; fortunately she's wearing her comfortable shoes. She didn't even need to use her hands, and that's just as well, because she's holding the man's photo in her right hand, along with the envelope and the piece of cardboard. When she reaches him, she looks back. The lights inside the train are on, the door is still open. It reminds her of the TV images of the train-hijacking in the seventies, only then the windows were blacked out with newspaper. It's a beautiful sight, a yellow train up on a railway embankment in the middle of the landscape like this. 'Here,' she says.

'Thank you.' He takes the photo and looks at it again.

'June, nineteen sixty-nine.'

'The seventeenth of June. How do you know that?'

'I had dinner with her that evening at the Bellevue. The Den Helder council had invited an average cross-section of the city's professionals. I'm not making that up, they called it that themselves. I was apparently average enough: district nurse.'

'Did you talk to her?'

'I shook hands with her and spent the rest of the evening sitting quite far away. The meal wasn't anything special.'

'I didn't have a clue about this,' the man says. He's

standing beside her, and also facing the train. The hand with the photo is down next to his leg.

'She went to Texel the next day. It was a two-day working visit.'

'My mother never said a word about it. She must have talked to the Queen.'

'You'd think so, yes. In any case she would have asked the child's name. Is that you? The child?'

'No. That's my little sister.'

'And she never mentioned it either?'

'She died.'

'Oh.'

'That same day.'

'No!'

'And it was the fault of the person who took this photo.'

'What?' She's curious, that's why she got off the train and jumped the ditch. She runs her fingers through her hair. The rain is still very light. There are two girls standing at the train door. They stick their heads out. One looks in the direction of Anna Paulowna, the other in the direction of Schagen.

'My grandfather was at our place just before. He came to see the new bulk tank. He probably looked at it too, but mainly he stood there staring at the sign the milk-tank people had screwed on the outside wall. A yellow sign. *We cool our milk with a Mueller bulk milk cooler. Beentjes Bros. Assen.* That's what it said. It was like he thought the sign was more beautiful or more important than the tank itself. And then my father pressed a new camera into his hands and we all had to stand in front of the house. Stand or sit on the step in front of the blind door. My father and mother, my brothers, me, my sister and Tinus, the dog. He was an Irish setter and wouldn't sit still. In the two photos my grandfather took he's more a brown smudge than an Irish setter. My father bought him for hunting, but that was over the first time he fired the gun. He never pointed once and he was always scared to death of loud noises. We didn't look happy enough, I guess, because after a while Grandpa called out, "It's not a funeral, you know!" It was beautiful weather, the sun was shining and the photos turned out well, they're in my parents' album.'

'But how old were you then?'

'Seven.'

'And you still remember all that?'

'Memories, huh? Who can say? You make something of it.'

Brecht Koomen can sympathise with that. Sometimes she makes Jan Visser's emails that little bit more interesting when she tells her friends and acquaintances about them.

The girls have disappeared. The train looks like it could leave at any moment, going either left or right. The light inside it has grown brighter, as the sky behind now really has turned dark grey. The rain is getting a little heavier too. The man takes his rucksack off and unzips it. She hands him the envelope, which has already grown quite damp, and the piece of cardboard. He sticks the photo and the cardboard in the envelope and puts it in the rucksack. 'I'm getting a bit nervous now,' she says, running her fingers through her hair again.

'The train's stuck here until they're sure nobody's left on the tracks.'

'But how long will that take? We don't know. Where are you going?'

'Schagen. My youngest brother lives there.'

'I'm going to my eldest sister's. She lives there too. It's her birthday tomorrow.'

'What's your name?'

'Brecht Koomen.'

'I'm Jan Kaan.'

They shake hands.

'When you get to your brother's, you should rub some cream on your neck.'

'Why?'

'It's badly burnt. Can't you feel that?' She's so anxious to get back on the train she can hardly stand still. Knowing her luck it will drive off and leave her standing in the middle of the field with this man. In the dark and the rain. But her curiosity is stronger. Now she's come this far, she stays there, with him.

June

Tuesday 17 June, but no school. Jan and Johan had their checked swimming bags on their backs, ready to leave. Assembling at school, going to the Polder House together, eating at school (something else neither of them had done before) and school swimming lessons in the afternoon. From the moment the new radio had been placed on the wide windowsill, there had hardly been a second's silence in the kitchen. Only at night, really. They heard 'Oh Happy Day' coming out of the radio. Hanne was sitting with her back to the cold oil heater. There were plasters on two fingers on her right hand. A few days earlier she had stuck her hand in an empty apple-sauce tin. That went fine, but pulling it out again was less successful because the sharp-edged lid that had pushed down so easily came back up with her fingers between it and the side of the tin. Tinus was asleep in his basket, under the windowsill and the radio. Klaas had already left.

'Get going,' said Anna Kaan.

Sawing noises coming from upstairs.

'Promise you'll keep an eye on Johan.'

'I promise.' He did his very best to get the 'r' right, but nobody noticed.

Jan was seven and had a bike. Johan was five and already knew how to ride, but still had to make do with a blue scooter.

'Slow down!' Johan kept shouting. 'Wait for me!'

Jan wasn't listening to his little brother, he was busy saying all kinds of words with an 'r' in them. He found it difficult and because Zeeger had promised him a Dinky Toy if he could say it properly, he was desperate to get it right. The day before he'd suddenly figured it out and now he couldn't stop.

The baker's grey van was parked in front of the notary's house. He swerved round it and suddenly had to swerve even further, because the baker had opened the door. 'Hey!' he shouted. The baker quickly pulled the door shut again. When Jan turned to glare at him, he saw the baker raising a hand and holding his head to one side. He guessed that meant he was sorry. The baker had a strange red face, a face that didn't go with custard buns and almond cakes. Johan scooted around the van as fast as he could, not even noticing the baker. 'Wait for me!' he shouted again. Jan didn't wait. He said a few more words with an 'r' in them and thought about the Queen. He decided to scowl as hard as he could and make a point of looking in the other direction. It was almost too much to bear that the butcher's son and the baker's daughter had been chosen to present the flowers instead of him.

Half an hour later the children were standing in neat lines along the Polder House drive. Class by class. Johan was standing right at the front, near the gate; he was still in the baby class. Klaas should have been somewhere near the door, but wasn't. Everyone was really nervous. The year-four teacher squeaked once that they had to hold up their flags, but that was as far as their instructions went. The West Frisian folk-dancing group did a run-through without any music. An ancient man holding a violin down next to his knees stood and watched. He was wearing new clogs. A few children from year six burst out laughing when a farmer came walking up leading two pygmy goats and wearing overalls that were so new they still had creases in them. Everywhere there were photographers taking up position or walking around. Jan was in the front row. Next to him was his best friend, Peter Breebaart, who nudged him a few times without saying anything. They had to stand hand in hand, but of course you can't do that and wave a flag at the same time. He did his best to stare down at the ground and got crosser and crosser and more and more indignant, especially after he saw the two flower-presenters standing there in their smart clothes, not lined up with the others, but at the gate. He thought his Norwegian cardigan, knitted for the occasion by Grandma Kaan, was stupid.

And then Teun Grint suddenly appeared. Even though year six were further along, under the linden espaliers at the front of the building. Just then the Queen's car pulled up. Teun wormed his way into the line and took hold of Jan's hand. He looked sideways at Jan. The Queen got out of the car and approached them. Jan suddenly remembered that he was angry, bowed his head and looked down at his feet. His mother had polished his sandals. He didn't want to witness the presentation of the flowers at all. That hand around his. It was very quiet. Nobody cheered, nobody spoke. It was only when the ancient man began to play his violin that people started making noise and he heard the rustling of the traditional skirts. All at once Jan wanted to see the Queen after all, pulled his hand out of Teun's and discovered that the lines of children had dissolved and all the mothers and teachers were standing in the way. He didn't get to see her. A little later they lined up again, class by class, and walked back to the school building.

After eating at long tables in the gym, they rode bikes, ran or rode scooters in a disorderly rush to the swimming pool. Not a single teacher called out 'let your food settle first'. Johan went looking for Jan, shouted, 'Wait for me!' a couple of times, and was relieved to find that his big brother really was waiting for him at the entrance, together with Peter

Breebaart. Jan still looked miserable, his anger was still eating away at him. Silently they held up their season tickets at the ticket office. 'Ah, if it's not the Kaan boys again,' said the ticket lady with the black hair. She was smoking a cigarette. That made Jan even crosser. It wasn't his fault that there were three boys and one girl in his family and that they were all called Kaan. There wasn't anything he could do about it. He gave the woman a dirty look. 'Now, now,' she said, stubbing out her cigarette. 'The Kaan boys are moody today.'

Johan wanted to go into a cubicle with Jan. Jan pushed him out of the way and went into one with Peter. Inside they quickly turned the lock.

'Dickheads,' said Johan, two cubicles down.

They changed and came out of their cubicles at exactly the same time, hanging their swimming bags, clothes and sandals up in the big changing room with the hooks. Then Jan and Peter crossed the imaginary line that divided the swimming pool grounds in half, indicated by a white sign with the words *Experienced swimmers only past this point*. Now they'd got rid of Johan, who had swimming lessons in zone two and wasn't allowed to cross the line. Music was coming out of the funnel-shaped speakers on the ticket booth. The ticket lady had turned on the radio.

They hadn't even bothered writing numbers on the temperature sign next to the sweet counter, just a drawing of the sun with a Dutch flag to mark the special occasion. The swimming instructor was already holding the long white pole with the hook on the end. Backstroke. Jan preferred swimming on his back to swimming face down. At least then you didn't feel all that water pressing against your chest – in zone three it was at least a couple of metres deep. Deep water that, as he'd found out recently, could also turn inside out. And ever since Johan had asked the pool attendant if there was a bogeyman in the swimming pool and the pool attendant had just laughed, Jan couldn't help thinking about that sometimes too.

'Diving!' shouted the swimming instructor.

They climbed out of the pool and lined up in position. Jan turned his head slightly. The ticket lady had turned the radio up and the song he'd heard earlier in the morning was playing. He sang along under his breath. Johan screamed something at him from zone two and he looked up and saw him waving. He didn't wave back, of course. Peter nudged him. 'See who can go furthest?'

Underwater, Jan realised that he hadn't had enough to eat. He wondered if there'd be pancakes or French toast when he got home. He thought it was Saturday. Normally they had swimming lessons on Saturday mornings. Klaas isn't here either, it suddenly occurred to him. No, he thought afterwards, it's Tuesday today. And it's not morning, it's afternoon. Because he wasn't thinking about the competition at all, he surfaced at least half a length past Peter.

He swam to the duckboards that separated zone three from zone four and pulled himself up to get his elbows on the wood, resting his chin on one arm and looking up at the diving board. Teun, the year-six boy with the yellow swimming trunks, bounced up higher than he was tall. Jan didn't know what he'd done to deserve that hand earlier in the day. It was as if Teun wanted to protect him.

But who from? The photographers? The Queen herself? It seemed like he was doing his best to bounce in time with the music until he pulled up his knees, wrapped his arms around them, did a somersault and plunged into the water with his body almost perfectly straight, not pressing his arms against his sides, but holding them out a little and bent slightly at the elbows. Did he already have his C? Jan stayed dangling there for a while, though it was quite tiring as the duckboards were fairly high up. He stared at Teun, who climbed up out of the pool and waited for a few other kids, mostly older than him, to finish their clumsy jumps. Again he got up to an incredible height and even from this distance Jan could see his hamstrings appearing and disappearing again, and that one knee pulled up in front of the other, and then both feet landing together again on the end of the diving board. This jump wasn't as beautiful. Teun hit the water a bit crooked and sent thousands of orange water fleas flying up into the air. Jan shook the water out of his hair and lowered himself back down into the water. He wanted a pair of yellow swimming trunks too.

'Come on, we're not finished yet,' the swimming instructor shouted.

Jan swam calmly over to the side of the pool. Peter was already up on dry land. He looked up at the big clock. Time was passing fast enough. Soon he'd buy a liquorice shoelace or a marshmallow. The ticket lady was nodding her head in time to the music. She was the mother of the boy with the yellow swimming trunks. They lined up again and waited for the swimming instructor's signal. Behind the windbreak that separated the swimming pool from the fields beyond, a few lambs started bleating.

Jan had left Johan behind in one of the changing cubicles. A little later he left Peter behind, halfway through the village where he lived. By then they'd finished the liquorice shoelace he'd bought with the ten-cent coin in the front pocket of his checked swimming bag. 'It'll turn your teeth black,' the ticket lady had said. The look he gave her in reply was just as dirty as when he'd arrived at the swimming pool. He rode through the village, making up words with as many 'r's in them as possible. Here and there, flags and pennants were still flapping in the wind; at the garage a man was standing on a ladder to take the flag out of the flag holder. It reminded him of that big bunch of flowers and he remembered that he was cross and sulking.

'Jan!'

Who was calling him, now that he was almost home? Without realising it, he had almost reached the Braks' big white house, which was just before his own. Only now did he really look around and ahead. What was the baker's grey van doing there?

'Jan!'

He braked, put one foot on the ground and looked back. Uncle Aris, Peter Breebaart's father, was following him on his bike. I wasn't supposed to eat at Auntie Tinie's, was I? he thought. Wait, the baker's van is parked right across the road, in front of the labourer's cottage. But they were away. The baker was sitting at the wheel. Not properly, his legs were dangling down to the side, Jan could see that from the feet poking out under the door, which was wide open. The baker looked up: maybe he'd heard Uncle Aris calling too. First Jan felt like he was looking straight through him, but then he raised a hand very slowly and held his head a little crooked. Just like earlier that day. Then it had meant, I'm sorry. Except now the hand had gone up differently and his face, definitely from this distance, seemed even redder than usual. The wind was blowing on the right side of Jan's face, the roadside elms were rustling. The sun was shining down on the road at an angle, but not now, because a cloud had drifted over. Jan kept his eyes fixed on the baker, mainly because he had no idea what he was going to do next, or what he was doing there in the first place. Since the baker had seemed to be waving to him, he too stuck his hand up in the air. They were both holding up a hand and Jan felt that this situation could go on for quite a long time, maybe the whole afternoon.

'Come with me,' said Uncle Aris.

'Where?' asked Jan.

'To see Auntie Tinie.'

'Why?'

'You'll find out later.'

'But I'm almost home.'

'I know.'

'What's the baker doing there?'

'Come on.' Uncle Aris laid a hand on his shoulder.

He turned his bike around. The checked swimming bag slipped down off his shoulders. He looked back one last time. The van door was closed. Uncle Aris didn't say anything.

'I can say "r",' said Jan.

'That's clever of you. Say it then.'

'I just did.'

'Do it again.'

'Rrrrrrr,' said Jan.

'Excellent,' said Uncle Aris, staring straight ahead. 'That's a real "r".'

Jan couldn't be bothered any more. He felt like his 'r' had become completely meaningless. They turned left to ride back towards the village. Into a headwind.

'Hi,' he said to Auntie Tinie and Peter. But mainly to Johan. 'What are you doing here?' he asked.

'I don't know,' Johan said. 'Eating.' He had his right elbow on the round kitchen table and was holding a spoon that was way too big in his right hand. His other arm was resting next to his body. He was sitting crooked and staring at Uncle Aris with big eyes. Jan looked away, ashamed that he had left Johan behind at the swimming pool and realising now, from the size of the spoon and how crookedly he was sitting, that he was still little. He was also ashamed of his sulking and his 'r'. Auntie Tinie hugged him and kissed him as if it was the last chance she would ever have to hug or kiss him. She ruffled his swimming-pool hair. Then, after putting a bowl of Bambix on the table in front of him, she absent-mindedly smoothed it down again. She didn't sit down. Uncle Aris did, but didn't eat anything.

Peter was eating. The corners of his mouth were still black from the liquorice shoelace and he stared at the Kaan brothers. 'Why don't you sit down?' he asked his mother.

'Shh,' said Auntie Tinie. 'Be quiet.'

Jan looked at the bowl of cereal in front of him. Whenever he ate at Auntie Tinie's, he always got something yummy. He loved Bambix. He knew it was baby cereal, but he didn't care, it tasted a lot better than the Brinta they had at home. Auntie Tinie's fried rice was a lot better than his mother's too, with lots of tomato paste and meat out of a tin you had to open by turning a key. He didn't feel like Bambix now. It wasn't even teatime yet. Uncle Aris and Auntie Tinie looked at each other. Johan was still sitting slumped on his chair. Peter had emptied his bowl and was about to say something. He opened his mouth, but thought better of it and leant back. Jan stared at his lukewarm cereal. It was quiet in the kitchen, the orange clock was ticking.

Then there was a sound. Auntie Tinie turned to face the window, both hands pressed to her chest. An ambulance drove past. Uncle Aris brushed something off the plastic tablecloth with a large hand. The sound faded quickly.

Peter couldn't resist any longer. 'What is it?'

Johan started crying. 'I want to go home!' he bawled.

Jan stuck a finger in the cereal. Almost cold and way too thick by now, anyway.

That evening Peter, Jan and Johan sat in a brand-new bath in a brand-new bathroom. There was something wrong with the tub: it didn't seem to have been finished properly. The enamel was rough, very finely rough, but they didn't realise until they got out again. Auntie Tinie rubbed them with a soapy flannel as if she was scrubbing potatoes, and washed their hair twice. Jan and Johan didn't say a word; they liked Auntie Tinie. Peter whinged and moaned, and kept on shouting 'Ow!' After that it started to burn, sting and itch.

They had to stay the night. They wanted to know why, but got no answer. Nobody mentioned the Queen, it was as if she hadn't even been to visit. They went to bed. Jan and Peter in one bed together and Johan in the other bed crossways at the foot of theirs. Peter soon fell asleep and Jan pushed him out onto the floor. He did that often, especially when Peter stayed at their house. He found it annoying, having someone next to him in bed like that, snoring contentedly or smacking their lips, while he couldn't get to sleep because someone was next to him. Peter didn't even wake up. Jan sat up straight and scratched his arms and legs. They kept on burning. He tore off the blanket and threw it on top of Peter. He pulled the sheet up to his chin, it was light and thin.

'Jan?'

'Yeah?'

'What's wrong?'

'I'm itchy.'

'Me too.'

It was almost completely dark in the bedroom. Outside, it was still light. There were even birds singing. The curtains were thick and heavy. Johan started to cry softly. Jan's head started to get itchy too; his hair was way too clean, his scalp rubbed dry by Auntie Tinie's strong fingers. The phone rang, four times.

'Johan?'

No sound from the other bed.

'Come here.' Jan heard Johan climb out of bed and,

because his eyes were already used to the darkness, he saw him step carefully over Peter. He held the sheet up. Johan slid in next to him and sniffed loudly two or three times.

'Something terrible's happened,' he said.

'Yeah,' said Jan. 'Maybe with Hanne.'

'Where's Klaas?'

'I don't know. Home, I guess.'

Johan scratched his neck.

'The baker,' said Jan.

'What about him?'

'He's got something to do with it.'

'With what?'

'He didn't look right.'

When they woke up the next morning, Peter was in the other bed. Jan and Johan stared at him until he woke up. He rubbed his eyes with the back of his hand and looked around with surprise. 'How'd I get *here*?' he asked. An hour later he had to go to school while Jan and Johan were allowed to stay at Auntie Tinie's. Peter shouted that it wasn't fair. His mother gave him a whack.

Wednesday evening they went home. Klaas was already there. Or still there. They gathered in the hall, in front of Hanne's bedroom. Anna opened the door and they went in one by one. There was a small coffin under the cracked window, as if the coffin had been positioned there deliberately to catch the light for as long as possible. Tinus sauntered in through the open door as well. He sniffed at the coffin and was about to jump up against it. 'Get,' said Zeeger, pushing the dog aside with one foot.

Hanging on the wall opposite the windows was a cloth of coarse material attached by rings to two bamboo rods, one at the top and one at the bottom. Grandma Kaan had made it. There were three Piccaninnies black as black on it, a fire with a pot, a few palm trees, a straw hut. The Piccaninnies were made of pieces of material and two of them had rings in their ears. The third Piccaninny only had one ring. The fire was made of pointy bits of yellow material, the trees from strips of green cloth. The roof of the straw hut was real straw and the poles holding up the cooking pot were satay sticks. There was a big orangey-red sun in one of the top corners, exactly the same kind of sun as the one shining in through the bedroom window at just that moment. The wall hanging had been there for a very long time. Klaas, Jan and Johan had reached the age of two in a bed under the three Piccaninnies black as black. No matter what happened outside, whether it was stormy or hailing, still or misty, nothing in the bedroom, nothing in the whole house was safer than Grandmother Kaan's home-made wall hanging.

'Go on,' said Anna. She pushed her three sons towards the coffin. Jan mainly kept his eyes on Klaas and Johan because he was frightened by the strange yellow dress Hanne was wearing. Bought by the district nurse who, when she got to the children's clothing shop in Schagen, didn't know what exactly Anna Kaan had meant by 'something smart'. Klaas and Johan couldn't keep it up long either. Klaas stared out the window. Johan cleared his throat and looked up at Zeeger.

'Was it the bogeyman?' he asked.

'No, Johan,' said Anna, 'it wasn't the bogeyman.'

Tinus started whimpering. Zeeger grabbed him by the scruff of the neck and dragged him out of the room. They stayed standing there for a while longer. Jan didn't want to, but he couldn't help looking at Hanne's fingers: no plasters, not even any cuts or scratches. The real sun was going down. Behind them the sun was fixed in the same spot and the leaves of the palm trees were still blowing in the same direction.

Later, Klaas, Jan and Johan went to the kitchen, where their four grandparents were sitting round the table. It was quiet; someone had finally turned off the radio. That must have been Grandma Kaan: she didn't like radio, TV or anything that wasn't calm and quiet. They were addressing each other by their first names and to the boys that sounded very strange. Grandpa Kooijman saying 'Neeltje' to Grandma Kaan and Grandpa Kaan calling Grandma Kooijman 'Hannie'. Hannie and Neeltje. Hanne. The first girl and both grandmothers' names covered. Even stranger was the baker coming to visit later that evening, when Jan and Johan were about to go upstairs to bed. The baker, on Wednesday evening, without any bread.

It wasn't until the following Monday, two days after the funeral, that they went back to school. In no time Jan's hand was up in the air.

'Do you have to go to the toilet?' the teacher asked.

'No, sir. I want to tell you something.'

'Yes?'

'No, sir, just you.'

'Come to the front.'

Jan stood up and set out for the blackboard. He felt important; everyone was staring at him. He looked at the butcher's son and the baker's daughter to make sure they'd noticed him walking up to tell the teacher something very important. The baker's daughter looked down, which Jan misinterpreted, because even after six days he still didn't know what exactly had happened. Hanne was playing with Tinus, that was about all they'd been told. He'd show them. Presenting flowers to the Queen, so what! When he got to the front, the teacher looked at him expectantly. Jan gestured for him to come closer. The teacher bent down towards him.

'My little sister's dead.' He whispered conspiratorially, almost proudly. Loudly as well, so the whole class, and especially the two flower-presenters could hear. 'Did you know that?'

'Yes, Jan,' said the teacher. 'I knew that.' He laid a hand on top of Jan's head. 'And it's a terrible thing. Go back and sit down again now.'

Jan walked back to his seat, in the last row by the window. Next to an enormous pot plant that hung partly over his desk. It was still quiet in the classroom. On the way, he looked at his classmates and tried to work out what they were thinking. Did he see a gleam in the butcher's son's eyes? Was he smiling without raising the corners of his mouth? At least the baker's daughter was still staring down at the exercise book in front of her. The conspiratorial feeling he'd just had was gone completely. Slipping in behind Peter to sit down again he felt, there's something wrong here. Peter nudged him. He didn't feel it.

In the schoolyard the marble craze was already over again. It was almost the summer holidays. Jan and Peter were standing near Klaas, who was telling tall stories about barges making waves in the canal. Peter was talking at him. If only Klaas would say something to him, but no, he blabbed away to his own classmates and made a point of looking in the other direction. Teun was leaning against the wall of the school building. Alone. Staring down at the paving stones under his feet. He glanced up, then looked back down at the grey paving stones, as if there was a lot to see there. It was dry, the drizzle of the previous weekend had blown over. Peter was talking; Jan heard the schoolchildren yelling and running and screeching around him, the clicking of a skipping rope, the wind in the hedge around the schoolyard, and the quivering thumps of the diving board.

On the third day after the funeral, Tuesday again, Jan and Johan did their sixth funeral drawings. Jan finished first and watched Johan add the finishing touches to his. 'The coffin wasn't black.'

'Yes it was.'

'Grandma Kaan didn't stand there.'

'Yes, she did.'

'Why isn't Klaas crying? Klaas was crying!'

'I can't do tears.'

'The sun is yellow, not red. Why have you put in the sun? It was raining!'

'Hey, you can do the "r"!'

Jan didn't say anything.

'The sun is red, anyway.'

'Why don't you use green? There's a new green felt tip right here.'

'What do I need green for?'

'Are you stupid?'

'What? What's green?'

'Trees are green. Dad's coat's green.'

'Can you do the hands?'

'OK.' Jan drew hands on the stick figures that represented people according to Johan. He slid the drawing back over to Johan, who made a futile attempt to change the red sun to yellow by colouring it in again with a yellow felt tip.

In Jan's drawing there were dripping trees. Big trees with fat drops. And Uncle Piet. Instead of simply standing on the ground, he was on the black ledge that stuck out at the bottom of the Polder House wall. It was a very narrow ledge and Uncle Piet had big feet. Jan had noticed it when they came around the corner behind Hanne's coffin, which was being carried by four men wearing light-grey hats. A group of wet people were clustered together and Uncle Piet towered over everyone because he was standing on that black ledge. It was impossible. That was why he drew it. The brown shoes stuck out ridiculously far, and to leave no doubt about who it was, he had written *UNCLE PIET* next to him in big letters.

Both grandmothers had spoken. Grandma Kooijman recited something from the Bible by heart. That went in one ear and out the other for almost everyone. Grandma Kaan read something from a piece of paper that got so wet it fell apart before she'd finished. She paused, then did the rest from memory. She was wearing a light-grey jacket and her dark-grey hair drooped like the paper she was holding. She looked like a heron that could fall over at any minute.

It was a short funeral. The undertaker in charge of proceedings didn't seem very sure of himself. After Grandma Kaan had rounded off her reading, there was brief, calm confusion. The rain was so light it didn't make any sound. The undertaker asked if anyone else wanted to speak. He looked around. 'May I then re –' he said, and then Aris Breebaart started to cry. Tinie Breebaart took him by the arm and led him away. Grandparents followed, Uncle Piet, the baker. Klaas, Jan and Johan walked off too. Anna and Zeeger stayed behind.

In the evening they ate rice pudding with brown sugar. Something they usually only ate on Saturdays. During tea, a few flies flew into the sticky strip that hung from the fluorescent light over the table. They buzzed and buzzed and beat their wings furiously until their wings were stuck to the strip too. Then they just buzzed. Nobody thought of turning the radio back on.

After Johan discovered that yellow over red doesn't work, his sixth funeral drawing was finished and the boys went looking for their mother. They couldn't find her anywhere. Along the way they picked up Tinus, who was whimpering on the other side of the kitchen door. Finally they ended up in the bedroom that was no longer a bedroom, and sat down together on the floor under the cracked window. Tinus jumped up on Hanne's bed. They stared at the wall hanging with the three Piccaninnies.

'The sun *is* red,' said Johan.

Jan didn't say anything.

Tinus turned around on the spot a couple of times and, sighing, lay down on the pillow.

That evening Grandma Kooijman came.

Anna Kaan came down off the straw after one and a half days. 'So,' she said, nudging her mother, who was standing at the stove, over to one side.

Hannie Kooijman stared at her daughter as if she was Lazarus emerging from the grave.

'I wish it would stop blowing,' said Anna. 'I hate it when it's windy.'

Silently, her mother handed her the wooden spoon she had been using to stir the contents of a saucepan.

'You can go back home now,' said Anna.

The baker simply continued to deliver the bread, although he no longer whistled while he was at it and stopped doing his flourish with the one and a half loaves too. They milked the cows and did the second round of haymaking. Tinus grew quickly and the swimming lessons carried on as normal. Jan had no trouble at all getting his A, even if treading water took forever and he had cramp in his neck when he climbed up out of the pool. Anna sewed the badge on the front of his swimming trunks by hand. 'The B goes here,' she said, pointing to the other side.

'Where's C go?' he asked.

'On your bum!' shouted Johan.

Johan can shout all he likes, thought Jan. Now he was allowed to cross all of the imaginary lines in the swimming pool whenever he liked, not just for swimming lessons. He was an 'experienced swimmer' too now, but not Johan. After long afternoons at the swimming pool, he cycled to the Breebaarts' with Peter and, before he rode on, Auntie Tinie made him crackers with cheese he didn't get at home, delicious cheese. She never said anything about Hanne. Neither did Peter. Nobody said anything.

The boy with the yellow swimming trunks was the only one who could jump higher than he could. Older boys tried too, without success. Jan, Peter and the others spread their towels out near the diving board. After all, that was where you hung out when you had the run of the whole swimming pool. A narrow strip of grass, wedged in between the pool and a ditch that formed a hairpin curve. At the bend in the ditch there was a pumping station that buzzed. Johan never got that far, he was right over on the other side of the pool, sometimes in zone three now, having his lessons.

They closed their eyes and listened to the poplars that bordered the pool like a rustling wall. Like that – with their eyes closed, the sun red through their eyelids, hearing the trees, the voices of boisterous children and worried mothers, the splashing, the buzzing of the pump and the sound of the big lambs in the fields behind the windbreak, still bleating like babies – it was as if the summer could last forever.

Jan learned to listen really closely, and after a while he

was somehow able to tell when it was Teun up on the diving board, he didn't even need to open his eyes. Teun touched the board less often before disappearing into the deep water of zone four with an upright jump, a somersault or a swallow dive. Sometimes Jan would sit up after all, the only one in the group of boys to put his hands on the grass behind him and watch. The Edwin Hawkins Singers stayed at the top of the charts, the summer days remained happy days. After a while the ticket lady stopped turning up the radio. The boy in the yellow trunks jumped, Jan watched and gradually started to think he was doing it all just for him.

Almost every day, no matter how delicious Auntie Tinie's jam, cheese or homemade cake was, there came a moment when Jan was on his way back home and reached the spot where the baker's grey van had stood, where Uncle Aris had caught up to him on his bike. Besides Johan, nobody had noticed that he could do a real 'r'. Zeeger forgot to give him a Dinky Toy. Jan didn't remind him.

Uncle Aris, the baker, the yellow dress, the diving board. June, July, August. A summer at the swimming pool, no bogeyman but plenty of water fleas. Johan, shivering sometimes at the edge of zone two. 'Hey, Jan!' he called, when his brother was on his way to the shop to buy liquorice shoelaces. Lips quivering, feet turned inward. Klaas, who only came to the swimming pool for lessons for his C, and otherwise swam in the canal. Or jumped off the bridge with his friends just as a barge sailed past.

*

The attic with the half-finished bedroom, the doorjamb without a door. Long, light nights. The painting at the top of the stairs, a grey painting. Of a woman with pursed lips holding a dandelion. Jan and Johan thought that it was Great-grandmother Kaan when she was young. Zeeger told them so. In Grandma and Grandpa Kaan's house there was a similar painting but slightly later, the dandelion parachutes were blowing around and the young woman had a mysterious smile. Klaas made fun of them when they told him. Klaas slept alone in the small bedroom; Jan and Johan shared the big one with the balcony doors.

Behind the green curtains it refused to get dark and Johan had started snoring almost immediately.

'Johan,' Jan whispered.

Nothing happened.

'Johan!'

'What?'

'Nothing.' Now he was awake at least.

But not for long. Soon Johan was breathing deeply again.

Every evening Jan waited for Klaas. When he heard his big brother come upstairs and close the door of his bedroom behind him, his night could begin. He pulled the blankets up over his head and thought he was asleep. He also imagined himself waking up the next morning – when it had been dark for a little while after all – and saw people tumbling through a kind of infinity.

Auntie Tinie, the baker, the yellow swimming trunks, the hand around his, the invisible Queen, the swimming pool, June, July, August, September. The bedroom downstairs, with the strange crack in the window. Hanne's bed, which was taken away at the end of summer. The bedless bedroom that was no longer a real bedroom, where the cloth with the Piccaninnies was left hanging on the wall. Johan, who, when he was awake, didn't put any green in his funeral drawings. One morning, while fishing in front of Grandma and Grandpa Kaan's house, he fell into the wide canal. Grandpa Kaan pulled him up out of the water, but he would probably have managed to climb up the side himself. He didn't die and held on tight to his fishing rod, so that didn't get lost either. Teeth chattering, he muttered something about 'the bogeyman'; Grandma Kaan couldn't make head nor tail of it. Jan, who thought he hardly slept but still dreamt much more than he suspected. One afternoon, his hands slid off the rung of the ladder he was climbing up to the hayloft and he fell backwards onto the concrete. It didn't really hurt, the stinging white whack blocked out most of the pain, and a wet flannel eased the lump. He didn't die. Klaas, alone in his small room with the soles of his feet hurting after jumping from too high up off the rail of the bridge. One evening after it had been raining, he slipped on the bridge's wet boards, grazed his thigh so badly it bled and ended up almost upside down in the water. But he didn't die. Anna, who was away for one and a half days, though no one even mentioned her absence. Zeeger, who mostly milked, made hay, shore sheep and cleared the banks of the ditches in silence. And started planting trees. That was something new.

Five summers later, anyone at the swimming pool who wanted to make out the lyrics of the song that had been number one for almost two months had to listen very carefully. The ticket lady didn't like it. If she wasn't busy checking a season ticket and there weren't any children standing at the sweet counter, she'd turn the radio down when it came on, and by early August she'd begun turning the volume dial all the way to the left. '*Sugar baby love, sugar baby love. I didn't mean to hurt you. People, take my advice, if you love someone, don't think twice.*'

They all had at least two certificates and seemed to have established a permanent claim to the narrow strip of lawn between the diving board and the hairpin ditch. Jan had already begged for a new pair of swimming trunks a couple of times: the A and B badges sewn on the front were for kids. What's more, the rubber cut into the tops of his legs, especially when his trunks were dry. Johan had two certificates too; he sat a bit further along with his own friends. He'd learnt to stop saying 'Hey, Jan'. The moment Klaas had got his C, he stopped coming to the swimming pool at all.

As hot as the days got, the water wasn't appealing. Lying around, talking and looking, that was appealing. Looking at the girls lying by the corner of zone four. Talking about dicks. Jan listened, but kept getting distracted by the diving board.

'He did. He pissed spunk!'

'You can't piss spunk.'

'Yes you can!'

'Who told you *that*?'

'*He* did.'

'Who?'

'Bram.'

'His brother, you know who that is, don't you?'

'Oh, him. How old is he anyway?'

'Eighteen.'

'So your brother pisses spunk?'

'Yep.'

'I don't believe it.'

'It's true.'

'What's it look like then?'

'Well, kind of bit whitish. And thick.'

'Thick?'

'If you've got a hard-on then your, what's-it-called, the tube your piss comes through. It doesn't work any more.'

'So you always piss spunk if you piss with a hard-on?'

'Um . . .'

Jan only saw Teun in summer now. He still wore his yellow swimming trunks, although they were getting more and more faded. His jumps were still high, the water still swallowed him like a transparent plastic bag after a somersault. He climbed out of the pool and sat down, directly behind the diving board, without drying himself off. Alone. He always sat alone. With his knees up and his hands on the ground behind him. His black hair was like a helmet on his head, one wisp over his ear. Jan looked at the grass behind his back, at the hands supporting his weight. The pump started to buzz louder and burst into action, water gushing into the ditch. A girl walked up.

'Here,' she said, handing Jan a note that was folded up as small as possible.

It took him a moment to smooth out the paper. It said: *Do you want to go out with me? Yvonne.* He looked diagonally across the pool at the girls' group and then at the messenger, who was staring down at him quizzically and a little impatiently.

'OK,' he said.

The girl walked back. It was that easy, the other boys didn't even mention it. Because the messenger walked back past Teun with Jan watching her, he saw that Teun was staring at him. Then Teun stood up. He pushed a few boys waiting their turn at the diving board out of the way and walked out to the end of the board, raised one leg, jumped and dived.

'I'm off,' Jan said to Peter.

'Already?'

'Yep.'

'To the girls?'

'No, home.'

'Same tomorrow?'

'I'll pick you up on the way.'

Teun surfaced at the end of zone four, pulled himself up onto the duckboards and slid back into the water on the other side. Then swam leisurely to the side. Jan walked alongside the ditch to the paddling pool. Johan was lying on his towel on his stomach and didn't see him passing. Cutting through between screeching children and hushing mothers, he reached the changing cubicles, avoiding Yvonne. Tomorrow, he thought. Starting tomorrow I'll go out with her. In the changing cubicle the rustling of the poplars sounded much louder than outside. He deliberately took his time getting changed. Teun's mother was sitting behind the counter smoking. He was pretty sure that wasn't even allowed. Her pitch-black hair stood out against the white planks. 'Bye-bye, Kaan!' she called as he walked towards the exit. Unbearable woman. Teun was waiting outside.

He lived near school. There were fields behind the house all the way to the north dyke. Jan never went to the north dyke; his dyke was the east dyke. It was a small house with a narrow kitchen and big furniture in front of a television set. 'It's boring,' Teun said, 'being an only child.' And, 'Tech's OK, but all the way to Schagen on a bike, do you know how far that is? Especially when you've got a head-wind. Soon,' he said, 'I'll have a moped.' He asked where Jan was going at the end of August (the state comprehensive) and whether he was hungry (no, Jan wasn't hungry). It was muggy in the house, or did Jan think it was OK? 'Come on, let's go for a walk to the dyke. Leave the bag here, you can pick it up later,' Teun said.

Jan let Teun lead the way. He didn't know these fields, every now and then he turned and saw things he'd never seen before. The village houses from the back, with unex-pected sheds, extensions and shrubs. The playing fields behind the school, the grass green and summer-holiday empty. The swimming pool through the windbreak (Yvonne on the other side of the trees, invisible from here), the yelling audible even at this distance. Past the swimming pool, a piece of land with a low embankment around it: for now a sheep field with lamp posts; in winter, the ice-skating rink.

To the right, a strip of wheat, already changing colour. The north dyke itself, on the other side of a wide ditch, accessible across a narrow board that sagged badly. When they were standing up on the top, Teun pointed east. There, where the canal curved and three polders came together, there was a triangle of water, a small lake. The Pishoek. 'You know it?' Yes, Jan had heard of it. Klaas went swimming there sometimes; he'd never been himself. Strange name. Yeah, maybe people used to come here to piss. Jan tried to laugh, but it didn't come out right. 'Later, at home, I can show you on a map. It's really called that,' Teun said. 'OK,' said Jan. 'Towels?' Ah, no need, it was hot.

Jan followed in Teun's footsteps, climbing over fences and walking past sheep that turned their heads away, but kept chewing their cud and didn't run off down the dyke. As the crow flies, he was at most three kilometres from home, but it felt like a foreign country. After walking for some time they reached the lake but Teun kept going, along the top of the dyke.

'How do we get into the water?' Jan asked.

'A bit further along there's a place without reeds.'

Jan was scared that he wouldn't be able to swim any more, that his certificates weren't valid here. There weren't any duckboards to climb up on in the Pishoek. And his swimming trunks were rolled up in the damp towel in his swimming bag, and the swimming bag was on a big armchair at Teun's house.

Teun took off his clothes and threw them down in a heap. 'Come on,' he said.

Jan waited until Teun was in the water before taking off his own clothes.

It wasn't deep and the bottom was like zone three in the swimming pool, a thin layer of gunk oozing up between his toes like custard. Teun swam to a red post that stuck up above the surface to mark the waterway for boats coming from the canal.

'Can you stand there?'

'No. But you can hold on to the post.'

Together they hung on to the waterway marker and gently trod water, their knees bumping against the post and each other's. Jan did his best to look around. It was quiet, no barges sailing past and no waterbirds nearby. Lots of water in all directions, bordered by reeds everywhere. Deep water, as Jan imagined it, especially in the channel whose edge was invisible because of the lake all around it. Teun let his hand slide down the post until it was touching Jan's hand.

'I want to go back now,' Jan said.

'OK.'

A brace of ducks coming in to land were startled by the swimming boys and flew up again. Teun swam faster than Jan, spitting out mouthfuls of water the whole time. Sometimes he waited briefly, floating on his back. Jan took his time, following. He didn't have much to say and let Teun do the talking. He hardly knew Teun's voice. It had all started during the Queen's visit, with that hand taking hold of his. Jan still felt its pressure, now that he was pushing the water of the Pishoek to the side and back and making such slow progress. He remembered how he had stood there that day. Grandpa Kaan had taken photos, even though he hadn't seen him there at all. Tummy pushed forward, a scowl on his face. 'I hope the Queen didn't look in your direction right then,' Grandpa Kaan said later. 'Otherwise she would have said something. She's like that.' Sulking and angry, because of the baker's daughter and the butcher's son. And he was still sulking later when Hanne was run over and killed.

When Jan climbed up onto land through the gap in the reeds, Teun was lying on the slope of the dyke with his head resting on his hands. 'There you are,' he said.

June, July, August. Yellow dress, the baker, a doorjamb without a door. Flowers for the Queen. Foreign country, here. Uncle Aris, the fly strip over the kitchen table, Auntie Tinie, Grandmother Kaan as a toppling heron, the window with the crack in it in the bedroom that wasn't a bedroom any more. Teun in his yellow swimming trunks, the raised knee. Sulking and cross, while Hanne was run over and killed.

Jan reached Teun and started to cry.

Teun sat up and grabbed him by his calf. 'Jan,' he said.

Jan started crying even louder, he couldn't understand where it was coming from. He didn't mind. Jan, Teun had said. That was him. Jan. He wasn't ashamed of crying, he wasn't ashamed when he grabbed Teun's hand. A big hand, with strong fingers, short nails that even long afternoons of soaking in the swimming pool hadn't cleaned of the remnants of dirt from the technical-college practical week.

Half an hour later the brace of ducks landed after all, or maybe they were different ducks. The birds weren't bothered by the boys, who were apparently less frightening lying on the dyke than they had been swimming near the post.

'What were you crying about?' Teun asked.

'Nothing,' Jan said. The back of his throat was itching, it was a feeling he knew from the days he sometimes lay down next to a calf and let it lick him with its rough tongue.

The next day Jan lay down in a different part of the swimming pool for the first time. There were two other year-six boys there. Peter wasn't there, he didn't have a girlfriend. Jan tried not to look over to the narrow strip of grass where he'd lain before. Things were very different here with the girls. When Yvonne got out of the water, using the ladder, she gave him a little kiss. He gave her a little kiss back, while keeping his eye on the diving board over her shoulder. Maybe he'd go back to the dyke later in the afternoon. Or tomorrow, or next week. He stretched out on his back and closed his eyes. He listened to the noise around him, which sounded just that little bit different from here. Strange, those girl kisses: so light, so easy. So girly. Teun's mother was busy and didn't have time to turn the volume dial to the left. '*All lovers make, make the same mistakes, yes they do. Yes, all lovers make, make the same mistakes as me and you.*' A whiny bloody song.

Some days Jan took a detour on his bike. Never in the morning, because in the mornings he was always standing on the Kruisweg corner waiting for the large group heading from the village to Schagen. Like birds or cows, they sought cover and safety in numbers, cycling the ten kilometres to Schagen in a long column. In the afternoon he sometimes took a detour; there wasn't a big group then because not everyone went to the same school. It was at least two kilometres further to go through the village, but he didn't care. It led him past Teun's.

There, in the cramped attic above the garage, was a pile of burlap bags. The smell was faintly reminiscent of the big barn where the Wool Federation collected the wool once a year. On a day that was usually warm, all the farmers who kept sheep would come with trailers full of wool to be pressed into bales by a big machine. It wasn't warm now. September, October. The garage attic couldn't possibly smell of sheep's wool, Jan knew that too, but the smell still hung there. If Teun could smell like fresh hay, which he sometimes did, the attic could also smell of wool. Now and then it smelled like wet dog instead, when it was damp from rain or mist or sweat.

Sometime that autumn Teun's mother's head popped up through the trapdoor opening. There was nothing he could do about it. Just lie there calmly, acting as if he wasn't there, hoping nobody would say anything, while inside his head he couldn't avoid hearing an annoying 'Ah, if it's not the Kaan boys'. Somehow she had looked at him as if that was what she was thinking and, for the first time, the ticket lady and Teun's mother really were one and the same person. Her face turned red, all at once, and slowly retreated back down again, until he had a more or less free view of the open trapdoor. It seemed to take minutes, but that was an illusion. He didn't have the impression Teun had noticed anything at all.

It happened over a weekend. One Friday in winter he came by and pretended not to be looking in, as if he couldn't see the little attic window above the garage. It was easy enough, he knew when he and Teun would be seeing each other again. The Monday that followed he was able to look straight through the house at the sheep in the fields behind it; he could even see the north dyke in the distance, despite the drizzle. There were no curtains up, the windowsill was bare, the lightshades had disappeared. Big holes in the front garden – they'd even dug up the perennials. The swing-up door to the garage was open, it was horribly empty. The window above it looked as if it had been cleaned, but that must have been his imagination.

'Now I'm going to run,' Brecht Koomen says. The train still looks like it's been hijacked, the door is still open. She starts to hurry over to it. 'Are you coming?' she asks, without looking back.

'Yes,' the man says.

Just before jumping the ditch, she sees the woman who was fanning herself with the magazine standing at a window with both hands up against the sides of her face to block out the light. 'I'm coming,' Brecht calls, as if the woman has beckoned her, as if she could somehow hold back the train if it started to move right now. She tosses her bag over the ditch. The Rubettes pops into her mind. She reserves judgement on whether or not it was a whiny bloody song.

Either way, she never liked it. She jumps, lands well and walks across the gravel to the door with her arms stretched out in front of her. When she puts her hands on the floor of the vestibule the PA starts to hiss.

Waiting

'I'm t-aking off my T-shirt,' says Johan.

'Then I will too,' says Toon.

They're sitting on the last bench on Platform 1, a good distance from a group of passengers on the opposite platform. The train the other people got out of has been stopped for a long time; every few minutes there's an announcement about an obstruction further up ahead. It's been raining for a while. Not hard, but fat drops have started to fall from the crown of the elm behind the bench. On their shoulders. The platform lights are on.

'N-ice,' says Johan.

'Yes,' says Toon.

'Ob-struction?'

'I don't know what's going on either. They never say.'

'But this way too?'

'It's a single track between here and Anna Paulowna.'

'He's s-till coming though.'

'Of course he is. And if he doesn't come now, he'll come some other time.'

'*Attention all passengers, because of an obstruction between Schagen and Anna Paulowna, trains are not currently running. It could take some time for this to be rectified. Please keep listening to these announcements, we will provide more information as soon as possible.*'

Yells and swearing from across the track. 'Bring in a bus, then!' someone shouts. There are other people who are almost undressed too, mostly young.

'You really don't know, do you?' Toon asks, looking at Johan. Long wet hair, gleaming shoulders, big hands resting on his thighs.

'T-eun?'

'That's right. From the swimming pool.'

'But why are you called Toon now?'

'Yeah . . . There was a time I thought that if you changed your name you automatically became someone else. My mother thinks names are very important.'

'Some one else?'

'I used to know you Kaans very well. And then we moved. I know *you* from the old days too.'

'Yeah? I don't know you. I d-idn't know you.'

'That's because of your accident, I think.'

'But J-an knows you?'

'Be funny if he didn't. But what he doesn't know is that I'm me.'

'Huh?'

'Never mind.'

Across the track a group of young people have started chanting, 'Bus, bus, bus. Now, now, now.'

'Do you remember the Queen's visit?'

'Wh-ere?'

'To the village.'

'N-o.'

'The Queen came in . . . June nineteen sixty-nine . . .'

'Just before the man on the moon!'

'Yep. How come you remember that? I helped Jan then. I held his hand.'

'Wh-y? Was he s-cared?'

'No. He was angry. Your mother wasn't there. He was all alone.'

'J-ust like that?'

'Yes. Don't you ever have that? A sudden urge to grab hold of someone?'

'All the time,' Johan says. 'F-lower girl.'

'What?'

'Once I w-anted to g-rab a flower girl.'

'But you didn't?'

'No.' Johan looks down at his hands.

It's getting busier and busier on Platform 1. The red letters indicating the length of the delay disappear. Then all the place names and the departure time rattle out of sight and exactly the same place names reappear with a new departure time. 'They've just cancelled a whole fucking train!' a girl swears.

Teun wraps an arm around Johan Kaan's shoulders and pulls him closer. 'And that same day your little sister died.'

'Yes,' says Johan. 'But n-ow she's got pretty s-tones. B-lue. And Jan made the letters white.'

Teun licks the rainwater off his upper lip and thinks about his yellow swimming trunks, and then about his mother, who couldn't understand why he didn't want a new pair. Because of his mother, he thinks of his father's grave, wondering if he should go there tomorrow morning to clean it himself. The diving board. His diving board. Johan stares across the track, a deep groove over his nose.

'Poofters!' someone shouts from the other side.

'Shut your trap!' Johan screams.

'Easy,' says Teun.

'I'm no p-oofter,' says Johan.

'I am.'

'D-irty bastard.'

'Shall I let go of you then?'

'N-o.'

'OK.'

'*Attention all passengers, the obstruction between Anna Paulowna and Schagen has been resolved. The delayed train to Amsterdam and Arnhem will enter the station in several minutes. The delayed train in the direction of Den Helder will depart after the arrival of the previously mentioned train.*'

'Phew,' says Johan. 'F-inally.'

Headlines

'If it were up to me, Brouwer, we wouldn't be mooring just yet.'

The captain shrugs and looks back. 'Unfortunately, it's not up to you.'

'No,' the Queen says. 'You are absolutely right there.'

It's a little colder than yesterday. There was a passing shower during the short crossing of the Marsdiep, but the sun is shining again now. The *Piet Hein* will arrive at 't Horntje in plenty of time, wisps of brass-band music are already reaching them over the waves. Not a moment's peace. Röell and Jezuolda Kwanten are sitting in the saloon, two deckhands are already standing on the fo'c'sle. Ten minutes ago, Röell was already huffing with today's documentation on her knees. The others crossed on the ferry. Pappie didn't come and Van der Hoeven spent the night somewhere else. If everything goes according to plan, he'll be standing on the Ministry dock with Beelaerts van Blokland. Dierx will be joining them today too. She had a restless night, as she often does after eating in restaurants; she has the impression it's caused by the butter or oil they use. She hadn't had much of an appetite anyway, after visiting the fish market. Tossing and turning, she'd kept thinking about the square that bore her name, the one with the theatre on it. Rarely had she seen such an ugly, impersonal square, and lying awake in her bunk she couldn't help but be annoyed about it. Surely it's almost a snub, naming something like *that* after her?

The Queen excused herself from the greater part of the fireworks that followed the dinner at the Bellevue Hotel. Röell and Kwanten did the honours and only people with binoculars would have seen that she was no longer on deck.

The island looks like a photograph in a travel brochure, but those photographs never smell of fish. She turns and goes down into the saloon. One more day and things will be quiet again for a while. Rather than these work visits, she much prefers receiving people herself at Soestdijk.

'Programme?' Röell asks.

'Go ahead,' she says.

'Arrival nine forty a.m.'

The Queen looks at the brass clock. 'We have a little time then.'

'Shall we go through the details now?'

'What's he called?'

'Sprenger. Flowers will be presented by Janneke Harting, ten-year-old daughter of the district head of the Ministry of Waterways and Public Works.'

'Yesterday I received flowers from the baker's daughter and the butcher's son.'

'And?'

'No, nothing.'

Röell starts huffing again.

No, thinks the Queen, this is the last time I'm putting myself through this. Next time, Van der Hoeven.

'After that, we'll drive to the mussel-seed farm.'

'God Almighty,' she mumbles. 'On an almost empty stomach. With a whole day to go.' She sees a few newspapers on the gleaming tabletop, sits down and pulls them over.

'Are you going to read the paper?'

'Yes.'

'And the programme?'

'We'll be in the car the whole time. You can fill me in as we go.' Ignoring Röell, who is angrily stuffing the papers into her handbag, she unfolds the newspaper.

Although the *Piet Hein* has a sharp bow, the swell is very noticeable. Jezuolda Kwanten holds the edge of the table tightly. The *Schagen Courier* and the *North Holland Daily*. Before she has a chance to study the pictures on the front pages, the headlines leap out at her. *Spontaneous character plays havoc with schedule. Great enthusiasm in the Head of North Holland.* And, as expected: *Queen cuddles pygmy goats.* Almost all of the photographs show her walking, one foot in front of the other. She races through column after column of newspaper prose. 'Look,' she tells the sister, 'here's a long piece about you.'

'Oh,' says Jezuolda Kwanten. 'A journalist did ask me a few questions.'

'"*The high-spirited sister began as an art teacher, but retrained and now uses her creative talents as a sculptress. Proudly, she showed me a sketchbook in which she has already immortalised our monarch in pencil. Mr Samson of the Government Information Service commented, 'With spec-*

tacles on, Her Majesty will be a sure hit. They add contrast to her face."'" The Queen sighs. 'A bronze bust,' she says. 'A sure hit.'

'Ah,' says the sister. 'Newspapers.'

'Your name, by the way, is completely misspelled. It says Jeseualda.'

'Humph.'

'What was yesterday's highlight as far as you were concerned?'

'The barefoot skiing. I didn't know that was even possible. I did some sketches of it.' The sister reaches for the sketch-book, possibly to show her drawings of the waterskiing.

The demonstration itself made little impression on the Queen, she doesn't need to see the drawings too. She was constantly distracted by unruly schoolboys, who were being held back from the dais by policemen. She's finished with the *North Holland Daily* and picks up the *Schagen Courier*. Once again, the whole front page, as if nothing more import-ant has happened in the world. One of the photographs shows her sitting on a wooden chair and leaning over a small fence to look into a plastic box full of fish. 'Ugh,' she says quietly, telling herself firmly that she must remember to think of her legs today. She searches the article for a comment about the elderly violinist. *Merrily moving his bow up and down over the taut and slender strings, Van der Goes kept his old eyes open wide so as not miss one iota of the regal apparition.* The editors have let their hair down in Schagen. She turns to the next page to find out what the real news was yesterday. Next to an article with the headline *From 87 cents down to 40, bread war in Harderwijk,* a small article stands out because of its brevity. *Child run over*, it says. She hears Jezuolda's pencil softly scratching away, sees the jerking movement of her right arm out of the corner of her eye. Of course, she thinks, a bust of the Queen in a relaxed state. *A fatal accident yesterday afternoon claimed the life of the two-year-old daughter of the Kaan family. While playing with the dog, the girl apparently found her way onto the road where she was hit by a delivery van. The child died on the spot.* The muted scratching is suddenly no longer quiet; the snatches of brass-band music have merged into a cheerful march, dominated by the trumpets. The *Piet Hein* bumps against the dock; Röell slides along the leather bench. 'Stop drawing,' the Queen says, 'now.' She takes the packet of cigarettes out of her bag and lights one.

Jezuolda Kwanten looks shocked.

'What's got into you all of a sudden?' asks Röell, who has slid back to her original position and is looking down her nose at her.

The Queen stares at her hands, feels an itching on the knuckles of her index finger. That child, she thinks. That mother and child. The beams of light shining in through the portholes disappear one after the other; it must be another passing shower. The mother's smile breaking through, the story taking shape in that instant from all the little things that come together to form a greater whole – the kind of story that lasts a person's whole life, that *should* last a person's whole life. The falling bike, the photograph taken so close by it almost hurt her ear, her hat, her gloves.

[295]

'We have to go,' says Röell.

The Queen looks up. Just like yesterday, Jezuolda Kwanten is very close by; the woman who belongs to the Order of the Sisters of Charity has her eyes trained on her. For a moment she's distracted and wonders what exactly the sister thinks of the description 'high-spirited'. The brass band is irrepressible, they've probably been instructed to play as loudly as they can during disembarkation. Kwanten stares shamelessly, studying closely, counting the crow's feet, registering lines, while out of nowhere 'Blom's Breadery' pops into her head. She draws on her cigarette.

'Have you read something unpleasant?' Jezuolda Kwanten asks.

'You must stay very close to me today,' she says.

'It would be my pleasure, ma'am,' says Jezuolda Kwanten.

There's a knocking on the saloon door and Van der Hoeven enters. 'They're waiting for you,' he says in his warm young voice. 'Dierx is very enthusiastic.'

'Van der Hoeven,' the Queen says, 'could you take Röell's place today?'

'But . . .' says Röell.

'Of course, ma'am.'

'Röell has the programme.'

'I have it too,' says Van der Hoeven.

'And, Röell, could you please use the formal "you" when speaking to me from now on, and most definitely in company? Then I'll use it when speaking to you too.' She stubs out her cigarette and pulls on her leather gloves, trying to suppress thoughts of the little girl's cheek. She is the first to leave the saloon. The island air is fresh; she takes a deep breath and braces herself for a whole day of music, pensioners, schoolchildren, the handicapped, fluttering tricolours and, above all, the stench of fish. Van der Hoeven puts up an umbrella and the Queen notices that he has beautiful hands, hands that match his voice. She feels like touching those hands. Not now, later perhaps, in the car. Jezuolda Kwanten hums softly. Did Röell stay behind in the saloon? The Queen thinks of the pygmy goats, and the mayor of Texel approaches her, glowing with delight. When he welcomes her warmly by taking her hand in both of his, the new day has officially begun.

Wednesday 18 June.

penguin.co.uk/vintage